POPULAR PUBLICATIONS   FACSIMILE EDITIONS

Dime Detective Magazine #8 (June 1932)

Dime Detective magazine was the flagship detective pulp in the Popular Publications stable, running for almost 300 issues over twenty years. The June 1932 issue contains stories by Edgar Wallace, T.T. Flynn, Fred MacIsaac, Frederick Nebel, and Maxwell Hawkins, and includes an installment in Nebel's Sgt. Brinkhaus series.

Authors:

Edgar Wallace, T.T. Flynn, Fred MacIsaac, Frederick Nebel, Maxwell Hawkins

Illustrators:

William Reusswig, John Fleming Gould

YOU
can be one of these Men!

Aircraft Draftsmen
Salary $50 to $100 a week

Airport Managers
At $100 to $150 a week

Airplane Salesmen
Make $50 to $100 a week and UP

Pilots
Earn $3000 to $6000 a year

Aircraft Mechanics
Make $50 to $100 a week

I'll show You how..
to earn $50 to $100 a week in Aviation!

YOU MEN who are sick of small pay and hard, grinding work—here's your chance! Edward Dick took my course and received an immediate offer of a fine job as Chief Mechanic and Assistant Manager. Paul Boehn connected with a big airplane manufacturer. Ira Bergen left his old job to become Chief Draftsman with an aeronautical concern in Brooklyn—And many more have turned their backs on low-paid drudgery to take *real* jobs in *Aviation*.

All You Need Is Ambition

If you've got red blood and an ounce of grit in your make-up, then you'll like the fascinating, active, adventuresome life that Aviation offers. I'll train you for it —right in your own home. Don't give up your job! Don't go to a strange city! Stay right where you are: I'll bring the whole Aviation Industry to *you*. My course is written in easy, simple language—hundreds of photos and charts make everything clear. You don't need a high-school education; many of my most successful students never finished the grades—in Aviation you need *practical* knowledge only! I teach you practical facts

Walter Hinton

Former Navy flier, first to pilot a plane across the Atlantic The NC-4), first to use an airplane in exploration work, instructor of war-time fliers at Pensacola, Florida. His proven home study Course, endorsed by prominent fliers and aircraft manufacturers, prepares you for a real future in Aviation—as a Field Superintendent, Airport Manager, Plane Mechanic, Engine Mechanic, Air Traffic Manager, Pilot, Engine Expert, Airplane Assemblyman — or in any one of forty other highly paid jobs on the ground or in the air.

about airplanes, engines, airports, mechanical details and shop kinks that you can use right on the job.

Employment Service FREE of Extra Cost

Just as soon as you are trained, my Nationwide Employment Department will help you find the job you want. This service comes to you absolutely FREE of any extra cost. It's getting results, getting real jobs, for other ambitious men, and can for YOU.

Save $50 to $450 on Your Flying Time

I've arranged with flying schools all over the country to give special discounts to graduates of my ground school. Often these discounts save you much more than the whole cost of my course! You get a discount check worth actual CASH as soon as you graduate.

Get the Facts — FREE

Send for my big book of facts about YOUR OPPORTUNITY in Aviation TODAY. It's free—you don't obligate yourself in any way. This book has been the turning point to success for many other fellows—it will show YOU, too, the way to *big success* and *big pay* in Aviation. Just mail that coupon NOW!

10¢ DIME DETECTIVE MAGAZINE

EVERY STORY COMPLETE   VERY STORY NEW

Vol. 2   CONTENTS for JUNE, 1932   No. 4

COMPLETE MASTER-MYSTERY NOVELETTE

Follow the trail of

PAGE

The Shadow Man..Edgar Wallace   6

As England's greatest detective-story writer unravels the threads which tangle Scotland Yard.

GRIPPING BOOK-LENGTH DETECTIVE NOVEL

Pass along that row of withered dead until

The Fourteenth Mummy..T. T. Flynn   38

Stares you in the face with sightless eyes—confounds you with its dread secret.

TENSE NOVELETTE OF MURDER AND THE LAW

Cut carefully along the danger line for a

Tailormade Clue..Frederick Nebel   90

Won't always fit the crime—even when stitched together by a master hand.

THRILLING SHORT CRIME STORIES

Dig for ghostly gold—unearth

The Phantom Nugget..Fred MacIsaac   74

From its mystery mine—then follow on its double danger trail.

Gasp with horror at the

Monkey Murder..Maxwell Hawkins   111

As Angelo from Nicaragua's jungleland chatters his accusation.

Now turn to

Master of Mysteries..Editor   123

And learn of the amazing career of the greatest detective-story writer of them all.

Cover—*"Rigid and Stiff He Stood"*..William Reusswig

Watch for the July Issue   On the Newsstands June 20th

Published every month by Popular Publications, Inc., 2256 Grove Street, Chicago, Illinois. Editorial and executive offices 205 East Forty-second Street, New York City. Harry Steeger, President and Secretary, Harold S. Goldsmith, Vice President and Treasurer. Entered as second class matter Feb. 26, 1932, at the Post Office at Chicago, Ill., under the Act of March 3, 1879. Title registration pending at U. S. Patent Office. Copyrighted 1932 by Popular Publications, Inc. Single copy price 10c. Yearly subscriptions in U. S. A. $1.00. For advertising rates address H. D. Cushing, 67 West 44th Street, New York, N. Y. When submitting manuscripts, kindly enclose sufficient postage for their return if found unavailable. The publishers cannot accept responsibility for return of unsolicited manuscripts, although all care will be exercised in handling them.

BETTER CHECK UP

on yourself

You hear a lot about pay-cuts these days—economic readjustments sometimes require drastic steps. The subject is broad — and *personal!*

If your pay has been cut or your income otherwise reduced, talking about it won't help the situation any. Of course you already know this — but has this thought occurred to you: *The only way to restore your old pay and then increase it is to make your services more valuable!*

Here's how you can make your services more valuable—and there is no substitute.

Training is an asset today without comparison in value. Training makes men more secure on their jobs, puts them in line for *better* jobs and *more* pay. Are you interested?

Men who a few years ago believed nothing could stop their progress have been forced to face an undeniable fact—they lack the training to go ahead. Many of them — wisely — are enrolling with International Correspondence Schools to acquire this training. Are you satisfied? Are you *sure* you are secure with the present training you have? The coupon will bring the information you need—free. *Mail it today!*

INTERNATIONAL CORRESPONDENCE SCHOOLS

Half a Million People
have learned music this easy way

**You, too, Can Learn to Play
Your Favorite Instrument
Without a Teacher**

Easy as A-B-C

YES, over half a million delighted men and women all over the world have learned music this quick, easy way.

Half a million—what a gigantic orchestra they would make! Some are playing on the stage, others in orchestras, and many thousands are daily enjoying the pleasure and popularity of being able to play some instrument.

Surely this is convincing proof of the success of the new, **modern method** perfected by the U. S. School of Music! And what these people have done, YOU, too, can do!

Many of this half million didn't know one note from another—others had never touched an instrument—yet in half the usual time they learned to play their favorite instrument. Best of all, they found learning music **amazingly easy**. No monotonous hours of exercises—no tedious scales—no expensive teachers. This simplified method made learning music as easy as A-B-C!

It is like a fascinating game. From the very start you are playing **real** tunes, perfectly, by note. You simply can't go wrong, for every step, from beginning to end, is right before your eyes in print and picture. First you are told how to do a thing, then a picture **shows** you how, then you do it yourself and **hear** it. And almost before you know it, you are playing your favorite pieces—jazz, ballads, classics. No private teacher could make it clearer. Little theory—plenty of accomplishment. That's why students of the U. S. School of Music get ahead twice as fast—**three times as fast** as those who study old-fashioned, plodding methods.

You don't need any special "talent." Many of the half-million who have already become accomplished players never dreamed they possessed musical ability. They only wanted to play some instrument—just like you—and they found they could quickly learn how this easy way. Just a little of your spare time each day is needed—and you enjoy every minute of it. The cost is surprisingly low—averaging only a few cents a day—and the price is the same for whatever instrument you choose. And remember, you are studying right in your own home—without paying big fees to private teachers.

Don't miss any more good times! Learn now to play your favorite instrument and surprise all your friends. Change from a wallflower to the center of attraction. Music is the best thing to offer at a party—musicians are invited everywhere. Enjoy the popularity you have been missing. Get your share of the musician's pleasure and profit! Start now!

Free Booklet and Demonstration Lesson

If you are in earnest about wanting to join the crowd of entertainers and be a "big hit" at any party—if you really do want to play your favorite instrument, to become a performer whose services will be in demand—fill out and mail the convenient coupon asking for our Free Booklet and Free Demonstration Lesson. These explain our wonderful method fully and show you how easily and quickly you can learn to play at little expense. This booklet will also tell you all about the amazing new **Automatic Finger Control**. Instruments are supplied when needed—cash or credit. U. S. School of Music, 866 Brunswick Bldg., New York City.

WHAT INSTRUMENT FOR YOU?	
Piano	Piccolo
Organ	Hawaiian
Violin	Steel
Clarinet	Guitar
Flute	Drums and
Harp	Traps
Cornet	Mandolin
'Cello	Sight Singing
Guitar	Trombone
Ukulele	Piano
Saxophone	Accordion
Banjo (Plectrum, 5-String or Tenor)	
Voice and Speech Culture	
Harmony and Composition	
Automatic Finger Control	
Italian and German Accordion	
Juniors' Piano Course	

The
SHADOW MAN

by

Edgar Wallace

The trail of The Shadow Man winds through page after gripping page of mystery and thrills. Follow it with Edgar Wallace—England's greatest master of the detective story—as he unravels the threads which tangled Scotland Yard in the knottiest crime maze of the year.

CHAPTER ONE

Escape

WHEN Mr. Reeder went to New York in connection with the Gessler Bank fraud he was treated as if he had been a popular member of a royal family. New York policemen, who are accustomed to seeing humanity in all sorts of odd shapes and appearances, saw nothing amusing in the old-fashioned frock coat which he kept tightly buttoned, in his square derby hat, or even in his side whiskers. They offered him the respect

Reeder saw the cyclist pause before his door — then came the shots.

which was due to a very great detective. They were less deceived by his seeming timidity and his preference for everybody's opinion but his own, than were their English colleagues.

His stay was a comparatively short one; yet, in the time at his disposal, he glided through the police headquarters of four great American cities, saw Atlanta prison, and two days before he sailed passed through the gates of Sing Sing and inspected that very interesting building, under the guidance of a deputy warden, from card index to death house.

"There's one fellow I would like you to have seen," said the deputy warden just before they parted. "He's an Englishman—a fellow called Redsack. Have you ever heard of him?"

Mr. Reeder shook his head. "There are so many people I've never heard of," he murmured apologetically, "and Mr. Redsack is one of them. Is he staying here—er—for a long time?"

"Life," said the other laconically, "and he's lucky to have escaped the chair. He's broken three prisons, but he won't break Sing Sing—the most dangerous man we have in this institution."

Mr. Reeder rubbed his chin thoughtfully. "I—um—would like to have seen him," he said.

The deputy warden smiled. "Just now he's not visible, but he'll be out tomorrow," he said. "We've had to put him in a punishment cell for trying to escape. I thought you might know him. He's had four convictions in the United States, and he is probably guilty of more murders than any prisoner inside these walls; he has certainly the biggest brain I have encountered in all my dealings with criminals."

Mr. Reeder smiled sadly and shook his head. "I have never yet met—um—anything that resembled a brain in the crim-

NOTE: See page 123 for material on Edgar Wallace, author of "The Shadow Man."—Ed.

inal world," he said, with deep melancholy. "Redsack? What a pity his crimes were not committed in England!"

"Why?" asked the deputy warden, a little staggered.

"He would be dead by now," said Mr. Reeder, and heaved a deep sigh.

Mr. Reeder, waiting for his ship to depart, filled in the time very profitably by glueing himself to the record department at police headquarters, New York, and making himself acquainted with Mr. Redsack.

He was a consistently elusive person. There was no photograph of him, curiously enough, that had not been cleverly distorted by his own facial maneuvers. It was not true to say that he was an Englishman: he had been born in Vancouver, been educated in London, and at thirty had a record that would have made him respected in any criminal circle and nowhere else. Almost Mr. Reeder, albeit reluctantly, agreed with the deputy warden that this man showed evidence of genius. He was clever, he was ruthless. In the bare police records, and even without the assistance of an explanatory dossier, the investigator noticed three samples of the operation of a brilliant mind.

Mr. Reeder sailed at midnight on the following day. As, clad in his gay pajamas, he climbed into bed, he could have no idea that, five decks below him, working in the bunkers, was the man he had left in the punishment cell at Sing Sing.

When the deputy warden had said again at parting, a little regretfully: "Pity you can't see Redsack. He'll be out tomorrow," he unconsciously was a prophet.

IT WAS the most daring and the most sensational escape that Sing Sing had known. It was all the more remarkable because it was entirely unpremeditated. This happened on a dull, wintry afternoon, when a dozen prisoners were at their exercises in the big yard of the prison. They were watching, with some curiosity and interest, the maneuvers of a small naval airship which, caught in a half gale, was tacking over the Hudson in a vain effort to get back on its course. Suddenly, without warning, something went wrong, and the big gas-bag, sagging in the middle, began to make a rapid and oblique descent. Its trail rope came over the wall of the prison yard, dragging along the ground, and the nearest man to it seized it. As he did so, a heavy quantity of ballast was released from the gondola beneath the bag, and the balloon shot up—carrying with it Mr. Redsack.

Whether he intended to assist in tethering the balloon, or whether he saw here the helping hand of Providence, one must guess. But the guards saw their charge carried over their heads, and could neither fire at him or do anything but watch helplessly.

The airship drifted across the Hudson into New Jersey, came low again.

Mr. Redsack dropped. It was near a small village. Close at hand, standing unattended by the side of the road, was a dilapidated touring car. Half an hour later that car drew up before a bank office in a small town ten miles from Jersey City; a man got out, carrying under his arm a double-barrelled shotgun that he had found in the car, and walked into the bank. It was within a minute of the time when the bank closed its doors. There was nobody there but the cashier and the accountant. The latter was going on a vacation and had a suitcase behind the counter. Redsack left with the suitcase, some six thousand dollars, two Colt automatics that he discovered on a shelf under the counter, and the janitor's second-best overalls which he had found in the cellar where he had locked the two bank officials.

At the earliest opportunity he hid the suitcase and its contents under some débris in a ditch, changed into the workman's overalls, parked his stolen car up a deserted lane, and trudged a few miles to the outskirts of Jersey City, where he boarded a car.

He knew that the police would be looking for a man dressed in the accountant's best clothes, and that all the descriptions would favour this apparel. He had no idea where he was going until he came by ferry to New York, and eventually to the pier where an outbound liner was berthed. After that everything was very simple for Mr. Redsack.

Stokers were needed, and money is an eloquent letter of recommendation. He had been assigned his watch and was trimming coal with the greatest industry before the ship pulled out of New York harbor.

If you told Mr. Reeder it was a coincidence that he should at this stage have been brought into contact with one of the most remarkable criminals of our time, he would have shaken his head half-heartedly and in the most apologetic terms have differed from you.

"It is no coincidence—um—that any detective should meet, or nearly meet, any criminal, any more than it is a coincidence that the glass of water you are —er—drinking should at some time or other have been part of the Atlantic Ocean."

When the people in Scotland Yard speculate upon this peculiar happening they always begin with the word "if". "If" Redsack had not been in the punishment cell; "if" Mr. Reeder had only seen him. . . . Quite a lot of trouble might have been saved, and the L. and O. bank was by no means the beginning or the end of it.

That Mr. Reeder forgot about Redsack is unlikely. When he reached England

and went through the files the man's name was familiar. It was inevitable that his record should go down in abbreviated form in his case book, for Mr. Reeder despised the story of no criminal.

But, strangely enough, the name of Redsack did not occur to the man from Whitehall in connection with the L. & O. Bank affair.

CHAPTER TWO

Mr. Hallaty of the L. & O.

MR. REEDER very seldom went to the theatre. When he did he preferred the strong and romantic drama to the more subtle problem plays which are so popular with the leisured classes.

He went to see *Hearts Asunder,* and was a little disappointed, for he detected "the man who did it" in the first act, and thereafter the play ceased to have any great interest for him.

The unpleasant happening of the evening occurred between the first and second acts, when Mr. Reeder was pacing the vestibule, smoking one of his cheap cigarettes, and speculating upon the advisability of recovering his coat and hat from the cloak-room and escaping after the interval bell had rung and the audience had gone back into the auditorium.

There approached him a resplendent man. He was stout, rather tall, very florid. He wore a perpetual smile, which was nine-tenths amused contempt. His small mustache was waxed to a needle point at each end; his stubby nails were manicured and polished; Mr. Reeder suspected that they were faintly tinted. His clothes fitted him all too perfectly, and when he smiled his way up to Mr. Reeder that gentleman had a feeling that he would like to go back and see the second act after all.

"You're Mr. Reeder, aren't you?" he said in a tone which challenged denial.

"My name is Hallaty, Gunnersbury branch of the L. and O. Bank. You came down to see me one day about a fellow who'd been passing dud checks."

Mr. Reeder fixed his glasses on the end of his nose and looked over them at his new acquaintance.

"Yes, I—um—remember there was a branch of the bank at Gunnersbury," he said. "Very interesting how these branches are spreading."

"It's rather funny to see you here at a theatre," smiled Mr. Hallaty.

"I—um—suppose it is," said Mr. Reeder.

"It's a funny thing," the loquacious man went on, "I was talking to a friend of mine, Lord Lintil—you may have met him. I know him personally; in fact, we're quite pals."

Mr. Reeder was impressed. "Really?" he said respectfully. "I haven't seen Lord Lintil since his third bankruptcy. Quite an interesting man."

Mr. Hallaty was jarred but not shaken. "Misfortune comes to everybody, even to the landed gentry," he said, a little sternly.

"You were talking to him about me?" Mr. Reeder spared himself the admonition which was coming. "And—um—what did you say about me?"

For a moment the manager of the Gunnersbury branch did not seem inclined to continue his aristocratic reminiscences.

"I was saying how clever you were."

Mr. Reeder wriggled unhappily.

"We were talking about these bank frauds that are going on, and how impossible it is to bring the—what do you call 'ems—perpetrators to justice, eh? That's what we want to do, Mr. Reeder —bring 'em to justice."

His pale eyes never left Mr. Reeder's.

"A most admirable idea," agreed the detective. He wondered if any helpful advice was likely to be forthcoming.

"I suppose there must be a system by which you can stop this sort of thing going on."

"I'm sure there must be," said Mr. Reeder. He looked at his watch and shook his head. "I am quite anxious to see the second act," he said untruthfully.

"Personally," Mr. Hallaty went on with the greatest complacency, "I'd like to be put in charge of one of these cases, on the basis of the old and well-known saying of which you've no doubt heard."

Mr. Reeder when he was most innocent was most malignant. He was innocent now. " 'Set a thief to catch a thief?' But surely not, Mr.—I didn't quite catch your name."

The man went purple. "What I meant was *'Quis custodiet ipsos custodes'*—a Latin proverb," he said loudly.

Fortunately the bell rang at that moment and Mr. Reeder made his escape. But it was only temporary. When he got outside the theatre that night, after the conclusion of the third and tamest act of the play, he found his banking friend waiting.

"I wondered if you'd like to come up to my club and have a drink?"

Mr. Reeder shook his head. "It is delightful of you, Mr.—um—"

Mr. Hallaty told him his name for the third time.

"But I never go to clubs and I do not drink anything stronger than barley water."

"Can I drop you anywhere?" asked Mr. Hallaty.

Mr. Reeder said he was walking and therefore could not be dropped.

"But I thought you lived at Brockley?"

"I walk there," said Mr. Reeder. "I find it so good for my complexion."

HE WAS not unduly surprised at the persistence of this very self-satisfied man. Quite a number of people did their best to scrape acquaintance with the country's greatest authority on crime against banks: some out of morbid curiosity, some for more personal reasons.

Mr. Hallaty was a type, self-important, pompous, self-sufficient. To Mr. Reeder's annoyance a few days later, when he was eating his bun and drinking his glass of milk at a teashop, the smiling man appeared before him and sat down at the same table. Mr. Reeder's bun was hardly nibbled, his milk remained untouched. There was no escape. He sat in silence, listening to Mr. Hallaty's views on crime, the detection of crime, banking methods and their inadequacy, but mainly about Mr. Hallaty's extraordinary genius, prescience and shrewdness.

"Personally," he said, "I think professional crooks are not clever. They think they are, but when they're matched against the intelligence of the average business man, or a man a little above the average, they're finished."

He chatted on in this vein until Mr. Reeder put down his bun, glared solemnly over his half glass of milk, and said, with startling distinctness: "Will you please go away? I want to have my lunch."

Thick-skinned as the man was, he was taken aback; went very red, apologizing incoherently, and swaggered out of the shop without paying his bill for the cup of tea which had been brought at his order. Mr. Reeder paid it gratefully.

Recalling those two conversations, Mr. Reeder remembered later that most of the enquiries which the bank manager made had to do with systems of search for missing delinquents. When he got home that night he very carefully marked down the name of Mr. Hallaty in a little book the cover of which was inscribed with a big question mark.

Yet it seemed impossible to believe that a man who was so aggressive could be anything but an honest man. Men engaged in the tiresome trade of roguery are suave men, polite men. They soothe and please—it is part of their stock in trade. But Mr. Hallaty was boorish.

He was, as he claimed, the manager of the Gunnersbury branch of the London & Orient Bank, and was a man of style and importance. He had a flat in Albemarle Street, drove his own car, had a chauffeur, a valet and quite a nice circle of reliable friends. He had also a very humble flat in Hammersmith, and this was his official address.

The Gunnersbury branch of the L. & O. was in its way rather important. It carried the accounts of half a dozen big plants on the Great West Road, the Kelson Gas Works, and the Brite-Lites Manufacturing Corporation, and was therefore responsible for very heavy pay-rolls.

ABOUT a month after the teashop talk Mr. Hallaty called at the London office of the Ninth Avenue Bank on Lombard Street, and said that he had a request from the most important of his customers for a large supply of American currency. The customer in question was an Anglo-American concern, and in order to celebrate some new amalgamation the directors had decided to pay a big bonus in dollars. Could the Ninth Avenue Bank supply the necessary greenbacks—fifty-seven thousand dollars, no less?

The American bank, after the way of American banks, was obliging. It undertook to sell dollars to the required amount, and on the Friday afternoon at two o'clock Hallaty called and exchanged English currency for American.

At the headquarters of the L. & O. Bank there was rather an urgent conference of general and assistant-general managers that afternoon.

"I'm worried about this man Hallaty," said the chief. "One of our secret-service people has discovered that he is living at the rate of five thousand a year."

"What is his salary?" somebody asked.

"Just under a thousand."

There was a little silence.

"He is a very careful man," said one. "He may have some very good investments."

The question became instantly urgent, for at that moment came an official with a telephone message from yet another American bank—the Dyers Bank of New York. Mr. Hallaty had just purchased a hundred thousand dollars' worth of American currency. He had negotiated the purchase in the morning, giving as a reason the requirements of the Brite-Lite Corporation. The Dyers Bank had certain misgivings after the departure of Mr. Hallaty with a thousand notes for one hundred dollars tucked away in a kit-bag, and those misgivings were caused by a glimpse which one of the commissionaries had of the contents of the kit-bag—already half full of American notes.

The bank detectives sped to Gunnersbury—Mr. Hallaty was not there. He had the key to the vault, but the detectives had taken with them a duplicate key, which was kept in the safe at the head office.

There should have been, in preparation for the next day's pay-out, some £72,000 in the vaults. In point of fact, there were a few odd bundles of ten-shilling and pound notes.

Mr. Hallaty was not at the flat where he was supposed to live, nor at the flat in Albemarle Street, where he actually lived. His valet was there, and his chauffeur.

The Axford air port had a clue to give. Mr. Hallaty had arrived that afternoon, seemingly with the intention of flying a small Moth airplane which he kept at the port. He was well known as an amateur flyer and was a skilled pilot. When the airplane was removed from the hangar it was discovered that the wings had been slashed, the struts had been half sawn through, and other damage done which made the machine unusable. How it had happened was a mystery which nobody could explain.

Mr. Hallaty, on seeing the damage, had turned deathly pale and had reentered his car and driven away, carrying with him his two suitcases.

From that moment Mr. Hallaty was not seen. He vanished into London and was lost.

CHAPTER THREE

Two Tickets to Norway

IF THE losses to the bank had been £72,000 only, it would have been serious enough. Unfortunately, Hallaty was a very ingenious man, with a very complete knowledge of the English banking system. When accounts came in and were checked, when the clearing-house made its quick report and certain Northern and Midland banking branches presented their claims, it was found that considerably over a quarter of a million of money had vanished.

Three days after Hallaty disappeared, Mr. Reeder came upon the scene. He was in his most apologetic mood. He apologized for being called in three days after he should have been called in; he apologized to the gloomy chairman for the offence of his unfaithful servant; he apologized for being wet (he carried a furled umbrella on his arm) and by inference regretted his side-whiskers, his square bowler hat and his tightly fitting frock coat.

The chairman, by some odd process of mind, felt that a considerable amount of responsibility had been lifted from his shoulders.

"Now, Mr. Reeder, you see exactly what has happened, and the bank is leaving everything in your hands. Perhaps it would have been wiser if we'd called you in before."

Mr. Reeder plucked up spirit to say that he thought it might have been.

"Here are the reports," said the general manager, pushing a folder full of large manuscript sheets. "The police have not the slightest idea where he's gone to, and I confess that I never expect to see Hallaty or the money again."

Mr. Reeder scratched his chin. "It would be improper in me if I said that I hope I never do," he sighed. "It's the Tynedale case all over again, and the Manchester and Oldham Bank case, and the South Devon Bank case—in fact—um—there is here the evidence of a system, sir, if I may venture to suggest such a thing."

The general manager frowned. "A system? You mean all these offences against banks you have mentioned are organized?"

Mr. Reeder nodded. "I think so, sir," he said gently. "If you will compare one with the other you will discover, I think, that in every case the manager has, on one pretext or another, converted large sums of English currency into either francs or dollars, that his last operation has been in London, and that he has vanished when the discovery of his defalcations has been made."

The general manager shivered, for Reeder was presenting to him the ogre of the banking world—the organized conspirator. "I hadn't noticed that," he said, "but undoubtedly it is a fact."

"There are some things—er—gentlemen, to which I am loth to give the authority of my support. Theories which —um—belong to the more sensational press and certainly to no scientific system. Yet I must tell you, gentlemen, that in my opinion we are for the first time face to face with an organized attempt to rob the banks on the grand scale."

The chairman shook his white head. "There are such things as crimes of imitation, Mr. Reeder. When some man steals money in a peculiar way, other weak-minded individuals follow suit."

Mr. Reeder smiled broadly. "I'm afraid that won't do, sir," he said with the greatest kindness. "You speak as though the details of the fraud had been published. In three cases out of five the general public know nothing about these crimes. In no case have the particulars been published or have they been available even to the managers of branch banks. And yet in every case the crime has followed along exactly similar lines. These are the points I make."

He ticked them off on his fingers.

"First of all, a manager or assistant manager in straitened circumstances. Secondly, a very carefully organized plan to draw, upon one given day, the maximum sum of money which can be drawn from headquarters, the changing over of the money into foreign currency, and the complete disappearance of the bank manager, all within twenty-four hours. It is an unusual kind of fraud, for it does not involve of itself any false book-keeping. In several cases we have found that a petty fraud has been going on for some time and has been obviously the cause of the bigger crime.

"Gentlemen—" Mr. Reeder's voice was serious—"there is something very big in the way of criminal activity in London, and an organization is in existence which is not only directing these frauds and profiting by them, but is offering to the men who commit them asylum during their stay here, and facilities for getting out of the country without detection. I'm going to deal with the situation from this angle, and my only chance of putting

a stop to it is if I am able to catch one of the minor criminals immediately before he brings off the big coup. I want from every bank a list of all their suspected staff, and I want this list before the bank inspectors go in to examine the books, and certainly before anything like an arrest is made."

INSTRUCTIONS to this effect were immediately issued, and the very next morning Mr. Reeder had before him in his bureau at the public prosecutor's office a list of bank officials against whom there was a question mark. It was a very small list, representing a microscopic percentage of the enormous staffs employed in the business of banking. One man had been betting heavily, and attached to his name was a list of his bookmakers and what, to Mr. Reeder, was more important, exact details as to the period of time his betting operations covered.

Reeder's pencil went slowly down the list until it stopped before the name of L. G. H. Reigate. Mr. Reigate was twenty-eight and an assistant branch manager. His "offence" was that he had been engaged in real-estate speculation, had bought on a rising market, and for some time past had vainly endeavored to get rid of his holdings. His salary was £600 a year; he lived with a half sister in a small flat at Hampstead, spent most of his evenings at home, did not drink and apparently had no other vices.

The reports were very thorough and there was not a detail which Mr. Reeder did not examine with the greatest care.

He went through the remaining list and came back to Mr. Reigate. Evidently here was a case which might repay his private and personal investigation. He jotted down the address on a scrap of paper and made a few inquiries in the City. They were entirely satisfactory, for on the third probe he found a Canadian bank which had been asked if it could supply Canadian dollars in exchange for sterling, and if the maximum amount could be so supplied on any average day. The inquiry had come not from Mr. Reigate's branch but from a client of the branch. Reeder spread his feelers a little wider, and stumbled on a second inquiry from the same client. He went to the general manager of the head office. Mr. Reigate was known as a very conscientious young man and, except for the fact that he had been engaged in real-estate speculation, the exact extent of which was unknown, there was nothing against him.

"Who is the branch manager?" asked Mr. Reeder.

"His name is Wallat. He is a most excellent fellow, but loses his head at times. But as he always loses it on the side of the bank we have no serious complaints against him."

That week a strange thing happened to Manager Wallat. He received a letter from a man whose name he did not remember, but who had been apparently an old customer of the bank.

I wonder if you would care to take a fortnight's trip to the fjords on a luxury ship? A client of ours has booked two passages but is unable to go, and has asked me to present the passages to any friend of mine who may wish to make the trip. As you were so good to me in the past—I don't suppose you remember the circumstances or even recall my name—I should be glad to pass them on to you.

Now the curious thing was that only a week before the manager had spoken enviously of a friend of his who was making that very trip. He had always wanted to see Norway and the beauties of Scandinavia, and here out of the blue came an unrivalled opportunity.

His vacation was due; he immediately put in a request to headquarters for leave. The request went before the assistant general manager and was granted. The boat was due to leave on Thursday night, but on Tuesday the manager, in a burst of zeal, decided to make a rough examination of certain books.

What he found there put all ideas of holiday out of his mind. On Wednesday morning he called before him Mr. Reigate, and the pale-faced young man listened with growing horror to a recital of the irregularities which had been discovered. At this sign of his guilt the manager, true to his tradition, lost his head, threatened a prosecution and, in a moment of hysteria, sent for a policeman. It was an irregular act, for prosecutions are initiated by the directors.

Panic engendered panic. Reigate put on his hat, walked from the bank, and was immediately pursued by a bare-headed manager. The young man, in blind terror, leaped on the back of an ambulance which happened to be passing, and was immediately dragged off by a policeman who had joined in the pursuit. If the manager had only kept his head the matter could have been corrected. As it was, he charged his assistant with the defalcations, which he admitted, and Reigate was put into a cell.

BANK headquarters was furious. They had been committed to a prosecution and, as a sequel, the possibility of an action for damages. Mr. Reeder was called in at once, and went into consultation with the bank's solicitors. He interviewed the young man, and found him incoherent with terror and quite incapable of giving any information. The next morning he was brought before a magistrate and remanded.

Apparently the magistrate took a serious view, for although Reigate, who was now a little calmer, asked for bail, that bail was put at a prohibitive sum. The young man was taken to prison.

That afternoon, however, there appeared before the magistrate Sir George Polkley, who offered himself as surety. The name apparently was a famous one. Sir George was a well-known north-country shipbuilder. He was accompanied at the police court by a gentleman who gave the name of an eminent firm of Newcastle solicitors. The surety was accepted, and Reigate was released from Brixton prison that afternoon.

At seven o'clock that night Scotland Yard rang up Mr. Reeder.

"You know Reigate was bailed out this afternoon?"

"Yes, I saw it in the newspapers," said Mr. Reeder. "Sir George Polkley stood surety—how on earth did he know Sir George?"

"We've just had a wire from Polkley's solicitors in Newcastle. They know nothing whatever about it. Sir George is in the south of France, and his solicitors have sent nobody to London to represent them. What is more they have never heard of Reigate."

Mr. Reeder, lounging in his chair, sat bolt upright.

"Then the bail was a fake? Where is Reigate?"

"He can't be found. He drove away from Brixton in a taxicab accompanied by the alleged solicitor, and he has not been seen since."

Here was a problem for Mr. Reeder, and one after his own heart. Who had gone to all that trouble to get Reigate released—and why? His frauds, if they were provable, did not involve more than three or four hundred pounds. But somebody was very anxious to get Reigate out of prison with the least possible delay.

Mr. Reeder interviewed the public prosecutor.

"It's all very, very odd," he said, running his fingers through his thin hair. "I suppose it has a very simple explanation, but unfortunately I've got the mind of a criminal."

The public prosecutor smiled. "And how does your criminal mind interpret this happening?" he asked.

Mr. Reeder shook his head. "Rather badly, I'm afraid. I—um—should not like to be Mr. Reigate!"

He had sent for the cowed and agitated manager. He was a pompous little man, rotund of figure and round of face, and he perspired very easily. For half an hour he sat on the edge of a chair, facing Mr. Reeder, and he spent most of that half hour mopping his brow and his neck with a large white handkerchief.

"Headquarters have been most unkind to me, Mr. Reeder," he quavered. "After all the years of faithful service. . . . The worst they can say about me is that I was misled through my zeal for the bank. I suppose it was wrong of me to have this young man arrested, but I was so shocked, so—if I may use the expression—devastated . . ."

"Yes, I'm sure," murmured Mr. Reeder. "You were going on vacation, you tell me? That is news to me."

It was now that he learned for the first time about the two passages for the fjords. Fortunately the manager had the letter with him. Mr. Reeder read it quickly, reached for his telephone and put through an inquiry.

"I seem to remember the address," he said as he hung up the phone. "It has a familiar sound to it. I think you will find it is an accommodation address, and the gentleman who wrote to you has, in fact, no existence."

"But he sent the tickets! They're made out in my name," said the manager triumphantly, and then his face fell. "I shan't be able to go now, of course."

Mr. Reeder looked at him, and in his

eyes there was pained reproach. "I'm afraid you won't be able to go now, and I'm quite satisfied in my mind that you would have been very sorry if you had gone! Those tickets were intended to serve one purpose—to get you out of the bank and out of England, and to give young Mr. Reigate an opportunity of bringing home the beans—if you'll excuse that vulgarity."

Mr. Reeder was both puzzled and enlightened. Here was another typical bank case, planned on exactly the same lines as the others, and revealing, beyond any question of doubt, the operation of a master mind.

CHAPTER FOUR

The Pajama Corpse

AS SOON as he got rid of the bank manager he took a cab and drove to Hampstead. Miss Dora Reigate had just returned from work when he arrived. She had read of her brother's misfortune in the evening newspaper on her way back from her office, and it struck Mr. Reeder that she was not as agitated by the news as the world would expect her to be. She was a pretty girl, a slim brunette, and looked much younger than her twenty-four years.

"I have had no news from my brother," she said. "He is really my half brother, but he and I have been very great friends all our lives, and I was terribly upset by this awful thing."

She crossed to the window and looked out. Not a young lady, Mr. Reeder thought, who very readily showed her feelings. She was obviously exercising great self-control now. Her lips were pressed closely together; her eyes were filled with unshed tears, and he sensed rather than observed the tension she was enduring.

Suddenly she turned. "I'll tell you,

Mr. Reeder." She saw his eyebrows go up and smiled faintly. "Oh, yes, I realize you haven't told me your name, but I know you. You're quite famous in the City."

Mr. Reeder was genuinely confused, but came instantly to business when she hesitated.

"Well, what are you going to tell me?" he asked gently.

"I'm relieved. That is what I was going to say. I've been expecting something for a long time. Johnny hasn't been himself; he's been terribly worried over his land deals, and I know he's been short of ready money—in fact, I lent him a hundred pounds of my savings only last week. I thought, however, he'd got over his worst difficulty, because he returned the money the next day—in fact, more than the money: five hundred dollars at the present rate of exchange is worth nearly a hundred and thirty pounds."

"Dollars?" said Mr. Reeder sharply. "Did he repay you in dollars?"

She nodded.

"In dollar bills?"

"Yes, five bills of a hundred dollars. I put them in my bank."

Mr. Reeder was now very alert. "Where did he get them?" he asked.

She shook her head. "I don't know. He had quite a large sum of money in dollars, a big roll."

Reeder scratched his chin thoughtfully but made no comment, and the girl went on.

"I've always suspected there was something wrong at the bank, and I had an idea that he'd borrowed this money and was putting things right. And yet he wasn't very happy about it. He told me that he might have to go out of the country for a few months, and that if he did I wasn't to worry."

"Was he a cheerful sort of fellow?"

"Very," she said emphatically, "until

the past year, when property went down. He used to do quite a lot of buying and selling, and I think made a considerable sum of money till the slump came."

"Had he any friends in London?"

She shook her head. "No," she said. "There used to be a man who called here, but he was not a friend." She hesitated. "I don't know whether I'm doing him any harm by telling you all this, but Johnny is really a deeply religious man, a man of the highest principles. Something has gone wrong with him in the past few months, but what it is I haven't the slightest idea, unless it is that this slump has driven him desperate and made him do things which ordinarily he'd never dream of doing. He used to have terrible fits of depression, and one night he told me that it was much better that his conscience should be at rest than that he should tide over his difficulties. He wrote a long statement, which I knew was intended for the bank. He sat up half one night writing, and he must have changed his mind about sending it, because in the morning, while we were at breakfast, he took it out of his pocket, re-read it and put it in the fire. I have a feeling, Mr. Reeder, that he was not acting entirely on his own initiative, but that there was somebody behind him who was directing him."

Reeder nodded. "That is the feeling I have, Miss Reigate," he said, "and if your brother is as you describe him, I think we shall learn a lot from him."

"He has been under somebody's influence," said the girl, "and I am sure I know who that somebody was."

She would say no more than this, though he pressed her.

"Can I send him food in prison?" she asked, and learned now for the first time about the bail and Reigate's mysterious disappearance. She did not know Polkley, and so far as she was aware her brother had no association with New-castle.

"But he knows you, Mr. Reeder," she said surprisingly. "He's twice mentioned you, and once he told me that he thought of seeing and having a talk with you."

"Dear me!" said Mr. Reeder. "I don't think he kept his promise. He has never been to my office—"

She shook her head. "He wouldn't have come to your office. He knows your address in Brockley Road." She gave the number, to his amazement. "In fact, one night he did go down to your house, because afterwards he told me and said that at the last moment his courage had failed him."

"When was this?" asked Reeder.

"About a month ago," she answered.

MR. REEDER went back to Brockley that night in a discontented frame of mind. Give him the end of the thread, and he would follow it through all its complicated entanglements. But now he had not even the end of his thread. He had two isolated cases, distinct from one another, except that they were linked together by a similarity of method—and nothing more.

The quietude of Brockley Road was very soothing to him. From near at hand came the gentle whirr of traffic passing up and down the Lewisham High Road, the clanging of car bells, the rumble of lorries, and the shrill voices of boys calling the final editions of the evening newspapers.

In the serenity of his home Mr. Reeder recuperated his dissipated energies. Here he could put in order the vital little facts which so often meant the destruction of those enemies of society against whom he waged a ceaseless war.

He had very few visitors and practically no friends. No neighbor dropped in on him for a quiet smoke and a chat.

He had been invited to sedate family parties during the festive season, but had declined them. And the method of his refusal was responsible for the legend that he had once been in love and had suffered; for invariably his letter contained references to a painful anniversary which he wished to keep alone. It didn't matter what date was chosen for the party. Mr. Reeder had invariably a painful anniversary which he wished to celebrate in solitude.

He sat at his large desk with a huge cup of tea and a large dish full of hot and succulent muffins before him, and went over and over every phase of these bank cases without securing a single inspiration.

Lewisham High Road at that hour was a busy thoroughfare, and nobody saw the extraordinary apparition until a taxicab driver, swerving violently, missed him. It was the figure of a man in a dressing-gown and pajamas, darting from one side of the road to the other. His feet and his head were bare, and he ran with incredible speed up the hill and darted into Brockley Road. Nobody saw where he came from. A policeman made a grab at him as he passed, and missed him. In another second he was speeding along Brockley Road.

He hesitated before Mr. Reeder's house, looked up at the lighted window of his study, then, dragging open the gate, flew up the stone steps. Mr. Reeder heard the shouts, went to the window and looked out. He saw somebody run up the flagged pathway to the door, and immediately afterward a motor-cyclist speeding up the road ahead of a little crowd. The cyclist slowed before the door, and stopped for a second. At first Mr. Reeder thought that the explosions he heard were the backfire of the machine. Then he saw the flame of the third and fourth shot. They came from the driver's hand, and instantly the cycle moved on, gathering speed, and went roaring out of his line of vision.

Reeder ran down the stairs and pulled open the door as a policeman came through the gate. A man was lying on the top step. He wore a dressing-gown of an Indian pattern, and apparently was undressed. They bore him into the passage, and Mr. Reeder switched on all the lights. One glance at the white face told him the staggering story.

The policeman pushed back the crowd, shut the door and went down on his knees by the side of the prostrate figure.

"I'm afraid he's dead," said Mr. Reeder, as he unbuttoned the dressing-gown with deft fingers and saw the ugliness of a violent dissolution. "I think he was shot by the motor-cyclist."

"I saw him," said the policeman breathlessly. "He fired four shots."

Reeder made another and more careful examination of the man. He judged his age to be about thirty. His hair was dark, almost raven black; he was clean-shaven, and a peculiar feature which Reeder noticed was that he had no eyebrows.

The policeman looked and frowned, put his hand in his pocket and took out his notebook. He examined something that was written inside and shook his head.

"I thought he might be that fellow they're looking for tonight."

"Reigate?" asked Mr. Reeder.

"No, it can't be him," said the policeman. "He was fair, with bushy eyebrows and dark mustache."

The dressing-gown was new, the pajamas were of the finest silk. They made a quick examination of the pockets and the policeman produced a sealed envelope.

"I think I ought to hand this to the inspector, sir—" he began.

Without a word Mr. Reeder took it

from his hand, and, to the constable's horror, broke the seal and took out the contents. They were fifty bills each for a hundred dollars.

"H'm!" said Mr. Reeder.

Where had he come from? How had he appeared suddenly in the heart of the traffic? The next hour Mr. Reeder spent making personal inquiries, without, however, finding a solution to the mystery.

A newsboy had seen him running on the sidewalk, and thought he had come out of Malpas Road, a thoroughfare which runs parallel with Brockley Road. A pointduty constable had seen him run along the middle of the road, dodging the traffic, and the driver of a delivery van was equally certain he had seen him on the opposite side of the road to that where he had been observed by the newspaper boy, running not up the hill but down. The motorcyclist seemed to have escaped observation altogether.

AT TEN o'clock that night the chief officers of Scotland Yard met in Reeder's room. The dead man's fingerprints had been sent to the Yard for inspection but had not been identified. The only distinguishing feature of the body was a small strawberry mark below the left elbow.

The chief constable scratched his head in bewilderment.

"I've never had a case like this before. The local police have called at every house in the neighbourhood where this fellow might have come from, and nobody is missing. What do you make of it, Mr. Reeder? You've had another look at the body, haven't you?"

Mr. Reeder nodded.

"And what do you think?"

Mr. Reeder hesitated. "It is a great pity," he said, "that the telephone system is not more universal in this country. I find it extremely difficult to get into touch with people, but I have sent a car for the young lady."

"Which young lady?"

"Miss—er—Reigate, the sister of our young friend."

He heard the ring of the bell and himself went down to open the door. It was the girl. He took her into the little parlour on the ground floor.

"I'm going to ask you a question, Miss Reigate, which I'll be glad if you can answer. Had your brother any distinguishing marks on his body that you would be able to recognize?"

She nodded without hesitation. "Yes," she said, a little breathlessly. "He had a small strawberry mark on his forearm, just below the elbow."

"The left forearm?" asked Mr. Reeder quickly.

"Yes, the left forearm. Why? Has he been found?"

"I'm afraid he has," said Mr. Reeder gently. He told her his suspicion and left her with his housekeeper whilst he went up to explain to the men from the Yard just what he had discovered.

"It was very clear to me," he said, "that the hair had been dyed, the mustache recently removed and the eyebrows shaved." Reeder pointed to the dollar bills lying on the table. "The money was part of the system, the disguise was part of the system. Did you notice anything about the clothes?"

"I noticed they smelt strongly of camphor," said one of the detectives. "I've just been remarking to the chief constable that it almost seems as if the pajamas and dressing-gown had been kept packed away from moths. My theory is that he must have had an outfit stowed all ready for his getaway."

Mr. Reeder shook his head. "Not exactly that," he said, "but the camphor smell is a very important clue. I can't tell you why, gentlemen, because I am naturally secretive."

The body was identified by the distressed and weeping girl beyond any question. It was that of Jonathan Reigate, sometime assistant manager of the Wembley branch of the London & Northern Banking Corporation. He had been killed by four shots fired from a 38 automatic pistol, and any three of the four shots would have been fatal. As for the motor-cyclist, there was none who could identify him or give the least clue.

AT NINE o'clock the next morning Reeder, accompanied by a detective sergeant, made a minute search of the Reigate flat. It was a small, comfortably furnished apartment consisting of four rooms, a kitchen and a bathroom. It had no drawing room, the dining room serving also as a sort of lounge.

Reigate had occupied the larger of the two bedrooms, and in one corner was a small roll-top writing desk which was locked when they arrived.

The dead man was evidently very methodical. The pigeonholes were crammed with memoranda, mainly dealing with the little properties he had bought and sold. These the two men inspected item by item before they made a search of the drawers.

In the last drawer they found a small steel box which, after very considerable difficulty, they succeeded in opening. Inside were two insurance policies, a small memorandum book, in which apparently Reigate had kept a very full record of his family accounts, and, in a small pay envelope, sealed down, they discovered two keys. They were quite new and were fastened together by a flat steel ring. An inspection of these showed Reeder that they were intended for different locks, one being slightly larger than the other.

There was no name on them and no indication whatever as to their purpose.

He examined the keys under a powerful magnifying glass, and the conclusion he reached was that probably they had never been used. At the bottom of the box, and almost overlooked, because it lay under a black card that covered the bottom, he found a sheet of paper torn from a small notebook. Its contents were in a copperplate hand; certain words were underlined in red ink, carefully ruled. It consisted of a column of street names, and against each was a time. Mr. Reeder observed that the times ranged from then in the morning till four o'clock in the afternoon, and that the streets were side streets adjacent to main thoroughfares. Against certain of the times and places a color was indicated: red, yellow, white, pink; but these had been struck out in pencil, and in the same medium the word "yellow" had been written against all of them.

"What do you make of those, Mr. Reeder?"

Reeder looked through the list again carefully.

"I rather imagine," he said, "that it's a list of rendezvous. At this place and at this time there was a car ready to pick him up. Originally it was intended to have four cars, but for some reason or other this was impracticable. I take it that the color means a flower or a badge of some kind by which Reigate could distinguish the car that was picking him up."

Later at Scotland Yard he elaborated his theory to an interested circle.

"What is clear now, if it wasn't clear before," he said, "is that there is an organization working in England against the banks. It is more dangerous than I imagined, for obviously the man or men behind it will stop at nothing to save themselves if matters ever come to a pinch. They killed Reigate because they thought—and rightly—that he was coming to betray them."

CHAPTER FIVE

The Benevolent Brothers

MR. REEDER claimed that he had a criminal mind. That night, in his spacious study at Brockley, he became a criminal. He organized bank robberies; he worked out systems of defalcations; he visualised all the difficulties that the brain of such an organization would have to contend against. The principal problem was to get out of England men who were known and whose descriptions had been circulated as being wanted by the police. Every port was watched; there was a detective staff at every airdrome; Ostend, Calais, Boulogne, Flushing, the Hook of Holland, Havre and Dieppe were staffed by keen observers. No Atlantic liner sailed out but carried an officer whose business it was to identify questionable passengers.

For hours Mr. Reeder wallowed in his wickedness. Scheme succeeded scheme; possibility and probability were rubbed against one another and cancelled themselves out.

At midnight Mr. Reeder rose from his desk, lit his thirtieth cigarette, and stood for a long time with his back to the fireplace, the cigarette drooping limply from his mouth, his head on one side like a cockatoo, and cogitated upon his criminal past.

He went to bed that night with a sense that he was groping through a fog toward a certain door, and that when that door was opened the extraordinary happenings of the past few months would be susceptible to a very simple explanation.

On the following morning Mr. Reeder was in his office when he heard a heavy cough outside his door and the confident rap of the commissionaire's knuckles.

"Come in," he called.

"Dr. Joseph Clutterpeck, sir."

Mr. Reeder leaned back in his chair. "Show him in, please," he said.

Dr. Clutterpeck was tall, rather stout, very genial. He spoke with the slightest of foreign accents.

"May I sit, please?" he beamed, and drew his chair up to the desk almost before Mr. Reeder had murmured his invitation. "It was in my mind to see you, Mr. Reeder, to ask you to undertake a small commission for me, but I understand you are no longer private detective but official, eh?"

Reeder bowed. His fingertips were together. He was looking at the newcomer from under his shaggy brows.

"I am in a very peculiar position," said Mr. Clutterpeck. "I conduct here a small clinic for diseases of the 'eart—for various things. I am a generous man; I cannot 'elp it." He waved an extravagant hand. "I give, I lend, I do not ask for security, and I am—what is the word— swindled. Now a great misfortune has come to me. I loaned a man a thousand pounds." He leaned confidentially across the table. "He has got into trouble—you have seen the case in the papers—Mr. Hallaty, the banker."

He waved his agitated hands again.

"He has gone out of the country without saying a word, without paying a penny, and now he writes to me to ask me for a prescription for the 'eart."

Mr. Reeder leaned back in his chair.

"He's written from where?" he asked.

"From 'Olland. I come from 'Olland; it is my 'ome."

"Have you got the letter?"

The man fished out a pocket-book and from this extracted a sheet of notepaper. The moment Reeder saw it he recognized Hallaty's handwriting. It was very brief.

Dear Doctor,

I must have the prescription for my heart. I have lost it. I cannot give you my address. Will you please advertise it in the agony column of The Times?

It was signed "H."

If Dr. Clutterpeck could have looked under those shaggy eyebrows he would have seen Mr. Reeder's eyes light.

"May I keep this letter?" he asked.

The big man shrugged. "Why, surely. I am glad that you should, because this gentleman seems to be in trouble with the police, and I do not want to be mixed up in it, except that I would like to get my thousand pounds. The prescription I will advertise because it is humanity."

DR. CLUTTERPECK took his departure after giving his address, which was a small flat in Pimlico. He was hardly out of the building before Mr. Reeder had verified his name and his qualifications from a work of reference. The letter he carried to Scotland Yard and to the chief constable.

"Smell it," he said.

The chief sniffed. "Camphor—and not exactly camphor. It's the same as we found in young Reigate's dressing-gown. I've sent it down to the laboratory; they say it's camphor-lactine, a very powerful disinfectant and antiseptic, used in cases of infectious diseases."

He heard a smack as Mr. Reeder's hands came together, and looked up in astonishment.

"Dear, dear me!" said Mr. Reeder. He almost purred the words.

When he got back to his office in Whitehall the commissionaire told him that a lady was waiting to see him. Mr. Reeder frowned.

"All right, show her in," he said.

He offered a limp hand to the girl and pushed up the most comfortable chair for her.

"Mr. Reeder—" she spoke quickly and nervously— "I have found a little pocket-book of my brother's, and the full amount of his defalcations—"

"I have those," said Reeder. "It is not a very large amount, certainly not such an amount as would have justified the trouble and pains they took to get him out on bail."

"And in the pocket-book was this." She put a little cutting on the table.

Mr. Reeder adjusted his glasses and read.

In your dire necessity write to the Brothers of Benevolence, 297, Lincoln's Inn Fields. Professional men who are short of money, and in urgent need of it, will receive help without usury. Repayment spread over years. No security but our faith in you.

Mr. Reeder read it three times, his lips spelling the words; then he put the cutting down on the table.

"That is quite new to me," he said, with a suggestion of shamefacedness which made the girl want to laugh. "I'll have a search made of the newspapers and see how often this has appeared," he said. "Do you know when your brother applied for a loan?"

She shook her head. "I remember the morning he cut it out. That must have been months ago. And then one night, when he had a friend here, I brought him in some coffee and I heard Mr. Hallaty say something about the brotherhood—"

"Mr. Hallaty?" Reeder almost squeaked the words. "Did your brother know Hallaty?"

She hesitated. "Ye-es, he knew him. I told you there was a man who I thought had a bad influence on Johnny."

He saw a faint flush come to her face.

"I was introduced to him at the dance of the United Banks, but he was rather a difficult man to—to get rid of."

Reeder's eyes twinkled. "Did you ever

tell him to go away? It's a very rude but simple process."

She smiled. "Yes, I did once. He came home one night when my brother wasn't in, and he was so objectionable that I asked him not to come again. I don't know how he became acquainted with my brother, but he used to call rather frequently, and the curious thing was that after the time I spoke of—"

"When he was unpleasant to you?"

She nodded. "—he made no attempt to see me, and wasn't apparently interested."

"Did you know Hallaty had disappeared after robbing the bank of a quarter of a million?"

"Yes. It very much upset Johnny; he couldn't talk about anything else for a few days. He was so nervous and worried, and I know he didn't sleep—I could hear him pacing up and down the room throughout the night. He bought every edition of the papers to find out what had happened to him."

Mr. Reeder sat for a long time, pinching his upper lip.

"Does anybody know you found this book and this cutting?" he asked finally.

To his surprise she answered in the affirmative. "It was the caretaker of the flat, who was helping me to turn out one of the cupboards, who found it," she said. "In fact he brought it to me. I think it must have fallen out of my brother's pocket. He used to hang some of his clothes there."

IT WAS late in the afternoon when Mr. Reeder turned into Lincoln's Inn Fields, found No. 297, and climbed to the fourth floor, where a small board affixed to the wall indicated the office of the Brothers of Benevolence.

He knocked, and a husky, foreign voice asked who was there. Presently the door was unlocked and opened a few inches.

Reeder saw a man of sixty, his face blotched and swollen, his white hair spread untidily over his forehead. He was meanly dressed and not too clean.

"What you want?" he asked, in a thick, guttural voice.

"I've come to inquire about the Brotherhood—"

"You write, please."

He tried to shut the door, but Mr. Reeder's square-toed shoe was inside. He pushed the door open and went in. It was a disorderly little office, grimy and cheerless. Though the day was warm, a small gas fire burnt on the hearth. The dingy windows looked as if they had never been opened.

"Where do you keep all your vast wealth?" asked Mr. Reeder pleasantly.

The old man blinked at him.

Though he spoke with a foreign accent, Reeder realized that he was a man of culture. A bottle on the table gave evidence that this gentleman took a kindly interest in raw spirits. There was more than a suggestion that he slept in this foul room, for an old couch had the appearance of considerable use.

"You write here—we are agents. We are not to see callers."

"May I ask whom I have the pleasure of addressing?"

The old man glowered at him. "My name is Jones," he said. "That is for you sufficient."

There were one or two objects in the room which interested Mr. Reeder. On the littered window-sill was a small wooden stand containing three test tubes, and near by half a dozen bottles of various sizes. The little desk was covered with manuscript, and the man's grimy hands were smothered with inkstains.

"You do a lot of writing?" said Reeder.

"Yes, I do writing," said Mr. Jones sourly. "We do much correspondence;

we never see people who call. We are agents only."

"For whom?" asked Mr. Reeder.

"For the Brotherhood. They live in France—in the south of France." He spoke quickly and glibly. "They do not desire that their benevolence shall be publicized. All letters are answered secretly. They are very rich men. That is all I can tell you, mister."

As he went down the stairs Mr. Reeder was whistling softly to himself, and that was a practice in which he did not often indulge, although all his questions and all his cajoling had not produced the address of these Brothers of Benevolence, who lived in the south of France and did good by stealth.

CHAPTER SIX

Miss Reigate Has Callers

IT WAS too late for afternoon tea and too early to go home. Mr. Reeder called a cab and drove back to Whitehall. He was crossing Trafalgar Square when he saw a car pass his, and had a glimpse of its occupant. Dr. Clutterpeck was looking the other way, his attention distracted by an accident which had overtaken a cyclist. Mr. Reeder leaned out of the window.

"Follow that car," he said to his driver, "and keep it in sight. I will see that the police do not stop you."

The car went leisurely through the Mall, up Birdcage Walk, and, circling the war memorial, turned left into Belgravia. Reeder saw the big car stop before a pretentious-looking building, and signaled the cabman to drive in. Through the spyhole at the back he saw Dr. Clutterpeck alight, and, when he was out of sight, stopped the cab, paid him off and walked slowly back.

He met a policeman, who recognized and saluted him.

"That building, sir? Oh, that's the Strangers' Club. It used to be the Banbury Club, for hunting people, but it didn't pay, and then a foreign gentleman opened it as a club of some kind. I don't know what they are, but they have scientific lectures every week—they've got a wonderful hall downstairs—and I believe the cooking's very good."

Now the Strangers' Club was a stranger to Mr. Reeder, and he was interested. He did not attempt to go in, but passed with a sidelong glance. He saw a plate-glass door and behind it a man in livery.

The Strangers' Club formed part of an island site. At the back there had once been a range of mews. Some enterprising builder had purchased this and had erected a number of buildings, tall, unlovely, their only claim to beauty being their simplicity. One of these was occupied by a West End store, which was apparently a dressmaking establishment. The second building had a more sedate appearance. Mr. Reeder noted the chaste inscription on the little silver plate affixed to a plain door, and went on finally to circumnavigate the island, and came back to where he had started.

Clutterpeck's car had disappeared. When he came again abreast of the club, the man in the hall was not in sight. He crossed the road and took a long and interested survey of the building, and, when this was done, he again went round to the back. There was a pair of big gates in that part of the building which bore the silver plate. He found a chauffeur cleaning his car, made a few inquiries, and went to his office not entirely satisfied, but with a pleasant feeling that he was on his way to making a grand discovery.

For his own encouragement he had dispatched wires to various parts of the world, and was waiting for replies.

He had hardly sat down in his office when the telephone rang. "A very urgent message, Mr. Reeder," said the operator's precise voice. "You are through to New Scotland Yard."

There was a click. It was the chief constable speaking. "We've found Hallaty. Will you come over?"

In three minutes Mr. Reeder was at Scotland Yard, and in the chief constable's office.

"Alive?" was the first question he asked.

The chief constable shook his head. "No, dead."

Mr. Reeder heaved a long sigh. "I was afraid of that. The trouble was that Hallaty was too clever. He wasn't in pajamas, of course?"

The chief constable stared at him. "It's curious you should say that. No, he was in a sort of uniform, looked rather like an elevator attendant."

LATE that afternoon a man riding a big and powerful motor-bicycle had passed at full speed in an easterly direction between Colchester and Clacton. He had stopped to ask the way to Harwich, for apparently he had missed the road. After he had gone on a light-hooded motor-van had followed, taking the same direction as the cyclist. A laborer, working in the field, had heard a staccato rattle of shots, and had fallen into the same error as Mr. Reeder had done on a previous occasion. He thought it was the sound of the motor-cycle. He saw the van stop for a short time, and then move on. He thought no more of the matter until he made his way back to the road on his way home. It was then he saw, lying half in the ditch and half on the verge, the body of a stout man in a dark-blue uniform. He was quite dead, having been shot through the back. There was no sign of the motor-cycle, though the wheel tracks were visible on the road, and had swayed off on to the verge. Thereafter they were lost.

Detectives, who were on the spot from Colchester within an hour, searched the road and discovered pieces of broken glass, obviously portions of a smashed lamp. They found also a small satchel, evidently carried by the man, which was empty.

Hallaty's hair had been completely shaved, as had also his mustache. Instead he had a pair of side-whiskers, which were of recent growth. The examination of the clothes showed neither the maker's name nor any clue by which they could be identified, but when the clothes were stripped, it was found that underneath he wore a suit of silk pajamas, similar in texture to that which was worn by the unfortunate Reigate.

Mr. Reeder made a rapid journey through Essex to the seat of the murder. He inspected the body and came back to London at midnight.

Again there was a conference and Mr. Reeder offered his views.

"Hallaty was too clever. They all suspected that he had a plan for double-crossing them. You will remember that he was a pilot and had a machine at the Axford air port. When he went to take out his plane he found that the struts had been cut through and the fabric of the wing was damaged so that it couldn't be flown. That was their precaution. Hallaty had either to go their way, or no way. Even at this eleventh hour he hoped to fool them. That empty case was probably full of loot. Harwich? Of course he went to Harwich. He had a trunk parked there and a passport. He had another at Brighton. You know you can get from Brighton to Boulogne on the pleasure steamers."

"Did you know this?" asked the staggered chief.

Mr. Reeder looked guilty. "I had an idea this might happen," he said. "The truth is, I have a criminal mind. I put myself in the crook's place and, having satisfied myself as to his class of mentality, I do just what he would do, and usually I am right. There isn't a cloak-room at any sea port in England that my agents have not very carefully searched, and Mr. Hallaty's bags have been in my care for a fortnight."

Mr. Reeder was very tired, and welcomed the offer of the police squad car which was to take him home. Tired as he was, however, he took greater precautions that night than he had taken for many years. With a detective he searched his house from basement to garret. He inspected the strip of back garden which was his very own, and even descended to the coal cellar, for he realized that he had made one false move that day—and that was to call at Lincoln's Inn Fields and interview the dirty little old man who had test tubes in his office.

H E WAS sleeping heavily at six o'clock the next morning, when the telephone by the side of his bed woke him. He got up and, to his surprise, heard and recognized the voice of Dora Reigate. It was weak and tremulous.

"Could I see you today, Mr. Reeder ... Soon... I've had a most terrible experience."

Mr. Reeder was now wide awake.

At his request the squad car had been held for him all night. It had remained parked outside his house—not, as he explained, because he was afraid of dying, but because it would have been considerably inconvenient to everybody concerned if he did die that night.

He sat by the weary driver as the car sped through the empty streets.

The caretaker had opened the main doors when Reeder arrived, and was a little scandalized at this early morning call.

"I don't think the young lady is up yet, sir."

"I assure you she is not only up but dressed," said Mr. Reeder.

As he was being taken up in the lift, he remembered something.

"Are you the man who found the small book belonging to the late Mr. Reigate?"

"Yes, sir," said the man. "Rather remarkable finding it. He had a press cutting about some brothers—I didn't rightly understand it."

"Have you told anybody about your finding the book?"

The man considered. "Yes, sir, I did A reporter from a paper came up here and asked me if there was any news. He was a very nice fellow. As a matter of fact, he gave me a pound."

Mr. Reeder shook his head. "My friend, you have no knowledge of papers. If you had, you'd know that a reporter never gives you money for anything. And you told him about the book, I suppose?"

"As a matter of fact, I did, sir."

"And the newspaper cutting?"

The janitor pleaded guilty to that also.

Dora Reigate opened the door to him. She looked very white and shaky, and even now she was trembling from head to foot. She had arrived home the previous night at eleven o'clock. She had been to see some relations of her stepmother and they had kept her till late. She had opened the door with her key, gone inside the flat and was reaching out to switch on the light, when somebody had come out of the hall cupboard behind her. Before she could scream a hand had been placed on her mouth and she had been forcibly held. Somebody had whispered to her that if she did not scream no harm would come to her, and almost at the point of collapse, she had allowed the men—there were two apparently—to blindfold her, and, when this was done, she had heard the light turned on.

She had been led into her sitting room and seated on a chair. It was then that she had become aware that a third man was in the flat. He was a foreigner and spoke with a harsh accent. Even though he had whispered she recognized this, for there had been a little wrangle between two of the men.

Presently she had felt somebody hold her by the arm and pull up the sleeve of her blouse, and immediately afterward she had felt a sharp pain in the forearm.

"This won't hurt you," said the voice that had first spoken to her, and then somebody else said: "Turn out the light."

Though she had been thickly blindfolded, she had realized that the lights were extinguished. The man was still holding her arm and apparently sitting by her side.

"Keep quiet and don't get excited," said the first man. "Nobody is going to hurt you."

She remembered very little after that. When she woke up she was lying on her bed, still fully dressed, and she was alone. The curtains and the blinds had been drawn up and she had a dim idea that as she woke she heard the door close softly. It was then about five o'clock. Her head was swimming, but not aching. She had a queer taste in her mouth, and when she dragged herself to her feet, her legs gave away, and she had to support herself with a chair.

"Did you send for the police?"

"No," she said. "The first person I thought of was you. What have they done, Mr. Reeder?"

He examined her arm. There were three separate punctures. Then he went in and looked at the bedroom. Two chairs had been drawn up by the side of the bed. The atmosphere was still thick with cigarette and cigar smoke. There were the butts of a dozen smoked cigarettes on the hearth. But what interested Mr. Reeder most was something that the intruders had left behind. It was a fountain pen. He handled it gingerly, using a piece of paper, and carried it to the light. The pen was of a very popular make, but it offered a wonderful surface for fingerprints.

When he came back to the girl Mr. Reeder's face was very grave.

"They've done you no harm at all. I don't think they had any intention to hurt you. I was the gentleman they were out for."

"But—but—" stammered the bewildered girl.

Mr. Reeder did not reply immediately. He got on the telephone and called up a doctor he knew.

"I don't think you will feel any bad after-effects."

"What did they give me?" she asked.

"Scopolamin. Its main effect was to make you speak the truth. Not," said Mr. Reeder hastily, "that you ever speak anything but the truth, but rather it was to remove certain inhibitions. The questions they asked you were, I imagine, mainly about myself: what had you told me, how much did I know? And I'm afraid—" he shook his head— "I am very much afraid that you told them much more than is good for me."

She looked at him with wide, disbelieving eyes.

"But who were they?"

Mr. Reeder smiled. "I know two of them. The third may, of course, be the most dangerous of the trio, but I really don't think he matters."

CHAPTER SEVEN

The Strangers' Club

THAT morning there was a swift raid on the premises at 297 Lincoln's Inn Fields, but the raiders arrived too late. They had to break open the door—the room was empty. Apparently there had been a considerable amount of destruction going on, for the gas fire had been dragged out of the hearth, and the original grate behind it was full of black paper. The test tubes had gone, and so had the manuscripts which Mr. Reeder had seen on the desk. Inquiries made on the premises produced very little in the way of information. Mr. Jones had occupied his office for four years. He was believed to be a Swede, and he gave no trouble to anybody. Very few callers came. He paid his rent regularly, and the only adverse criticism that was offered was that occasionally he used to sing in a strange language and in a stranger voice, to the annoyance of the solicitor's clerks who occupied an office immediately below him.

Undoubtedly he drank. They found ten empty gin bottles in one cupboard and fourteen earthenware bottles in another.

After the raid Mr. Reeder took counsel with himself. He had, he realized, sufficient evidence to produce most of the effects which were desirable. He had brought in to him a file dealing with the bank crimes that had been recorded in the past two years, and very carefully he went over the names of the men who had vanished, and with them considerable sums of money.

From his pocket he took the two keys which he had found in Reigate's pocket. If he could find the locks for these, the matter would be developed to its end. Mr. Reeder was very anxious that he himself should fit these keys to the right locks, the more so since he had seen, as he thought, a very likely lock in the queer shop building immediately behind the Strangers' Club.

He fought with himself for a long time. Starkly he arraigned his dramatic instincts before the bar of sane judgment, and in the end he condemned himself and sought an interview with the chief constable to detail his theories.

The chief constable had eaten something which had not agreed with him. It was a prosaic explanation for the fall of a great man, but he was at home, in the doctor's hands, and the deputy chief constable occupied his chair.

It was unfortunate that Mr. Reeder and the deputy chief constable had never seen eye to eye, and that there was between them an antagonism which can only be understood by those fortunate people who have worked in, or watched the work of, a great government department.

The deputy chief was due for retirement. He had a grievance against the world, and every superintendent and chief inspector at Scotland Yard had a grievance against him.

He was a little man, very bald, thin of face, and thinner of mind, and it was his boast that he belonged to the "old school." It was so old that it had fallen down, if the truth be told.

When Mr. Reeder had detailed his theories: "My dear fellow," said the deputy chief constable, "up to a point I am with you. But I will not accept—I never have accepted—the master-criminal theory in any case with which I have been associated. There is a great temptation to fall for that romantic idea, but it doesn't work out. Your other ideas are, of course, fantastical. I happen to know all about the Strangers Club. It is extraordinarily well conducted and every Thursday there is a series of lectures in the basement lecture hall, which have been given by some of the greatest scientists in this country. Dr. Clutterpeck has an international reputation—"

Mr. Reeder was staring at him owlishly. In his soul there was a fierce, malignant joy.

"There can be no question or doubt that there is quite a lot in your theory," the deputy chief constable went on, "but I could not advise action being taken until we have made very careful observations and there's no chance of our making a mistake. Personally, the fact that two men who were defaulting cashiers have been killed, suggests to me that there was a little gang operating in each case, and that somebody has tried to double-cross them."

"And the silk pajamas?" murmured Mr. Reeder.

The deputy chief was not prepared to explain the silk pajamas.

IT SEEMED to Mr. Reeder that the two chief inspectors, who were present at this interview, were not so completely happy about the matter as the chief.

"As it is," that gentleman went on (he was the type of man who always had an after-thought, and insisted upon expressing it) "we may have got into very serious trouble in raiding the office of Mr. Jones. I've been inquiring into the Benevolent Brotherhood, and they are most highly recommended by bishops and other important persons of the church. No, Mr. Reeder, I don't think I can go any further in this matter in the lamentable absence of the chief constable, and, anyhow, a day or two more or less isn't going to make any difference."

"Does it occur to you," asked Mr. Reeder gently, "that two men having been killed, there is quite a possibility of another seven going the way of all flesh?"

The deputy smiled. That was all—he just smiled.

Outside, in the corridor, one of the chief inspectors overtook Mr. Reeder.

"Of course, he's all wrong," he said, "and I'm going to take the responsibility of covering whatever work you do."

Mr. Reeder made an appointment for the chief inspector to meet him after dinner, and alone he went back to the Strangers' Club, carefully avoiding the front. He had to wait for his opportunity, because there were several chauffeurs outside their garages, but after a while he crept along the wall till he came to a small door, inserted first one key and then the other. At the twist of the second the door opened noiselessly.

Mr. Reeder drooped his head and listened. There was no sound. He had expected at least to hear a bell. Taking a flashlight from his trousers pocket, he sent a beam into the dark corridor. It was a little wider than he had expected and terminated, so far as he could see, in a flight of stairs which led up round a bend out of sight. On the left-hand side there was a wide door in the wall. He thrust the light up and saw a powerful electric globe fixed to the ceiling, but there was no sign of a switch; presumably the light was operated from upstairs. He closed the door carefully, tried the second key on the bigger door, but this time without success.

At the appointed time he met Chief Inspector Dance and told him what he had discovered. They sat for over an hour in Mr. Reeder's room, discussing plans. At nine o'clock the inspector left, and Mr. Reeder opened the safe in his office, took out a heavy Browning and loaded it with the greatest care. He pushed every cartridge into the chamber and out again, added a touch of oil here and there, and finally, slipping a spare magazine into his waistcoat pocket, he pressed up the safety catch of the Browning and pushed the pistol behind the lapel of his frock coat.

THE night commissionaire saw him go out, wearing one big yellow glove on his left hand, in which he carried the spare glove. His bowler hat was set at a jaunty angle. There was about him that liveliness which was only discernible in this very quiet man when trouble was in the offing. At twenty minutes to ten he walked almost jauntily up the steps of the Strangers' Club, passed through the swing door and smiled genially at the porter.

That funtionary was tall, broad-shouldered; he had a large round head and a wooden expression.

"Whom do you want?" he asked curtly.

Evidently the servants at the Strangers' Club, though they might be hand-picked for some qualities, were not chosen for either their good manners or their finesse.

"I would like to see Dr. Clutterpeck. He did me the honour to call at my office —my name is Reeder."

For a perceptible moment of time he saw a light dawn and die in the dull eyes of the hall porter.

"Why, surely!" he said. "I think the doctor is dining here tonight, Mr. Reeder and he'll be glad to see you."

He went to a little telephone, pressed a knob.

"It's Mr. Reeder, doctor. He just dropped in to see you."

What the man at the other end of the phone said—and he said it at some length —it was impossible to overhear, but Reeder saw the man step back a little, so that he could look through the glass doors into the street outside.

"No, that's all right, doctor," he said. "Mr. Reeder is by himself. You haven't got a friend, Mr. Reeder? Maybe you'd like to invite him in?"

Mr. Reeder shook his head. "I have no friend," he said sadly. "It's one of the tragedies of my life that I have never been able to make friends."

The man was puzzled. Obviously he had heard a great deal of this redoubtable gentleman from the public prosecutor's office, and he was not quite sure of his ground. He gave Mr. Reeder a long, scrutinizing glance, in which any antagonism there might have been was swamped by genuine curiosity. It was almost as though he doubted the evidence of his eyes.

Evidently somebody called him urgently at the other end of the wire, for he turned suddenly.

"That's all right, doctor. I'll bring him right up. Will you leave your coat here?"

Mr. Reeder regarded him with a pained expression. "It's a frock coat," he said. "I don't think it would be wise for me to go upstairs in my shirt sleeves."

CHAPTER EIGHT

Doctor of Crime

AT THE far end of the hall there was a door. The janitor opened it, switched on the light and disclosed a comfortable little elevator. Mr. Reeder stepped in and turned so quickly that he might have gone in backward. He had expected the porter to follow. Instead the man closed the door. There was a click and a gentle whirr and the lift shot upward. It went up two stories and then stopped, and the doors opened automatically—and there was Dr. Clutterpeck, very genial, very prosperous-looking in his evening dress and his heavy gold watch-guard, with an outstretched hand like a leg of mutton.

"Glad to meet you, Mr. Reeder. This is a great honor. Will you follow me, sir?"

He went ahead, down a narrow passage, then, turning to the right, descended two flights of stairs, which, so far as Reeder could judge, brought him to the first floor. It was obvious that from the first floor which the elevator had passed there was no communication with this part of the building. It was almost unnecessary for the doctor to explain this.

He opened a door and disclosed a beautifully furnished room. It was long and narrow. A heavy pile carpet was evidently laid over a rubber foundation, for the visitor had the sensation that he was walking on springs.

"My little sanctum," said Dr. Clutterpeck. "What do you drink, Mr. Reeder?"

Mr. Reeder looked round helplessly. "Milk?" he suggested, and not a muscle of the big man's face moved.

"Why, we can give you that even." Raising his voice: "Send up a glass of milk for Mr. Reeder," he said. "I have a microphonic telephone in my room. It saves a whole lot of ringing," he added. "But maybe you'd like me to shut it off?"

He turned a switch near the big Empire desk which stood in an alcove.

"Now you can talk and say just what you like, and nobody is going to listen to you. You'll take that glove off, Mr. Reeder?"

"I'm only staying a few minutes," said Mr. Reeder, gravely. "I wanted to see you about certain statements that have been made and which in some way suggest that this club is associated with a benevolent society run by an old gentleman called Jones."

Clutterpeck chuckled. Whatever else he was, he was a good actor.

"Why, isn't that strange!" he said. "I know old Jones. In fact, I've kept the old man alive. That crazy benevolent society! The odd thing about it, Mr. Reeder, is that it is quite genuine. Some people get a whole lot of money out of those poor guys who live in the south of France."

Mr. Reeder inclined his head gravely.

"It has that appearance. In fact, I was speaking with the chief constable tonight. We were discussing whether there was anything sinister—if I may use that expression—about the society, and he took the view that it was quite genuine. I am perfectly satisfied in my own mind that the brotherhood is responsible for giving quite a lot of money to people who felt an urgent need for it."

Clutterpeck was watching him, projecting his mind into Reeder's, taking his point of view—Mr. Reeder knew it.

"The whole thing arose out of the discovery of an unfortunate young man named Reigate," Mr. Reeder continued. "He was shot at my door, and after his death there was found in a notebook an advertisement of this brotherhood. That and one or two other curious circumstances—oh, yes, I remember, two keys we found in his desk—gave the case a rather mysterious aspect."

MR. REEDER was suffering under a great disadvantage. By a curious trick of mind he had entirely forgotten the excuse on which Clutterpeck had called at the public prosecutor's office. Such a thing had happened once before, and he was as a man who was walking over a bridge from which one plank was missing.

"That fellow Hallaty now," began Clutterpeck, and in a flash the reason for the call was revealed. "You remember, Mr. Reeder, the man who owes me money, and who is in Holland."

"He returned," said Mr. Reeder. "He was found shot in Essex. Probably he had come back from the Hook of Holland to Harwich, and now—"

There was a tinkle of a bell and Dr. Clutterpeck opened a panel in the wall which hid a small service lift and took out a glass of milk.

Mr. Reeder sipped at it gently. He had a palate of extraordinary keenness, and would have detected instantly the presence in that harmless fluid of any quantity which was not so harmless; but the milk tasted like milk. He took a longer sip and put it down, and he thought he saw in the face of Dr. Clutterpeck just a hint of relief.

"And now, doctor, I am going to ask

you a great favor. I am going to ask you to show me round your club, about which I have heard so much."

The smile left the doctor's face.

"I'm afraid I can't do that. In the first place, it isn't my club, and in the second, one of the rules of this establishment, Mr. Reeder, is that there should be no intrusion on the privacy of members."

"Of whom you have how many?"

"Six hundred and three."

Mr. Reeder nodded. "I have seen the list," he said. "They are mainly honorary members who are admitted to the ground floor for your lectures. I've yet to have the satisfaction of seeing a list—um—of your members."

Clutterpeck looked at him thoughtfully. "Why, then," he said, "come along and meet them."

He walked past Mr. Reeder, opened the door and stood aside for his guest to pass.

"Maybe you'd like me to go first?" he said with a smile, and Reeder knew that war had been declared, and followed him up the stairs. Again they were in the long corridor, and presently the doctor stood by the door of the lift, and pressed a bell. When the lift came up it was to all appearances the same elevator that he had seen before. It had the same black-and white tiled floor, and yet Mr. Reeder had a feeling that it was a little newer, a little cleaner than when he had seen it last.

As his foot touched the floor, he felt it give under him. Throwing his full weight upon his right leg, he sprang backward. He heard something swish past his head. There was a crash where the short leaden club struck, and, recovering his balance, Reeder lashed out with his gloved hand. Dr. Clutterpeck went down like a log—no remarkable circumstance—for under Mr. Reeder's glove was a knuckle-duster.

For a moment he stood, automatic in hand, looking down at the dazed man at his feet. Clutterpeck blinked up at him, and made a movement to rise.

"You can get up," said Reeder, "but you'll keep your hands away."

Then all the lights went out.

The detective stepped back quickly, so quickly that he collided with somebody, who was behind him. Again he struck out, but this time missed. He was deafened by the pang of an explosion. He was so close to the pistol that the powder stung his cheek. Twice he fired in the direction of the flash and then he suddenly lost consciousness. He did not feel the blow that hit him, but went painlessly down into oblivion.

WHEN the lights went up suddenly, a voice said, "Put on the lights now. Has he hit anybody?"

The bullet-headed porter was looking stupidly at a wrist and arm that were red with blood.

A shorter edition of the porter came into view round the angle of the corridor, and looked at the senseless detective.

Clutterpeck stopped to inspect the wound of the hall porter. "There's nothing to it," he said. "Bind it up with your handkerchief. It's just a scratch. Gee, you're lucky, Fred!"

He turned his attention to the senseless man. There was neither malice nor anger, but rather admiration, in his glance. "Help me get him into the cubby," he said.

In reality he needed no help. He was a man of extraordinary strength. Stooping, he lifted the unconscious Reeder, dragged him through the passage into a little room, and dropped him into a chair.

"He's O. K.," he said.

The little man, who had come from the passage, looked at the detective with an expression of amazement.

"Is that the bull?" he said.

Clutterpeck nodded. "That's the bull," he said grimly. "And don't laugh, 'Baldy.' That guy's put more men in stir than any ten fellows at the Yard.

"He looks nuts to me," grunted Baldy.

"Feed him some water. Here, give it to me."

Clutterpeck took the glass from the man's hand and threw it into the face of the drooping figure. Mr. Reeder opened his eyes and stared round. His glove had been pulled off. The knuckle-buster had disappeared.

"I'll hand it to you, Reeder," said Clutterpeck amiably. "If I'd not been all kinds of a sap, I'd have known you had that duster in your glove."

He felt his jaw and grinned.

"Have a drink?"

He turned the leaves of a table and a nest of decanters rose.

"Brandy will do you no harm."

He poured out a large potion and handed it to the dectective; Mr. Reeder sipped it. Putting his hand to his head he felt a large, egg-sized bump, but no abrasion.

"All right, Baldy. I'll ring for you." Clutterpeck dismissed his assistant. When he had gone: "Let's get right down to cases. You're Reeder. Who am I?"

"Your name is Redsack," said Reeder without hesitation. "You are what I would describe as a fugitive from justice."

Clutterpeck nodded amiably. "You're right the first time," he said. "How far have you got, Reeder? You and me are old-timers and hard boiled. We'll talk it right out, just as we feel, and we're not going to get sour with each other. You went out for a prize and got a blank. There's only one way of treating blanks, Reeder —and that's the way you're going to be treated. Have some more brandy?"

"Thank you, I've had enough."

"Maybe you'd like a cup of tea?"

Clutterpeck was genuinely solicitous.

He was not acting. He had pronounced sentence of death upon the man who had come, seeking his life, but he was entirely without animosity, Death was the natural and proper sequel to failure, because dead men cannot take the stand and testify to one's undoing.

"I think I would like a cup of tea."

Clutterpeck turned the switch and bellowed an order, then switched it off again.

"You can't say you haven't met Clutterpeck," he grinned again.

Mr. Reeder nodded and winced. "No, I met him in Lincoln's Inn Fields—a very unpleasant old gentleman."

"A clever old guy," interrupted Redsack. "In his way as clever as you. I picked him up when I came to England. He was doping then, and sleeping on the old Thames Embankment. He'd been so long away from Holland—he had no friends in England—that I thought Clutterpeck might be as good a name for me as for him, and he didn't care anyway. It's been a grand racket, Reeder. If I clear up tonight we'll go on for a year or two.

"I came to this country with ten thousand dollars. Part of it I brought on to the boat, and part of it I snitched from a passenger's cabin. It was so long since I'd been in England that I didn't know how easy it was. You're all so damn law-abiding here that any big racket, if it looks good, will surely get—"

CHAPTER NINE

Drop of Doom

CLUTTERPECK settled himself comfortably in his chair, but rose almost immediately to open the panel, and took out a cup of tea.

"You can drink that. If you like, I'll drink half of it. Say, these poisoners make me sick. You know what I got the dungeon for in Sing Sing? It was for beating up a guy who had poisoned his wife and mother-in-law. I just hated to see him around. He told them I was trying to escape and that he wouldn't stand by me. But that's ancient history, Mr. Reeder. Drink your tea."

Mr. Reeder drank and put down the cup carefully.

"I wasn't a month in this country before I found a young bank clerk who'd been playing the races and had been snitching money from the bank. He got tight and told me all about it and I saw how easy it was to make big money; so I just organized him, and he got away with a hundred thousand dollars."

He leaned forward and raised a warning finger.

"Don't say I didn't play fair with him, because I did. We shared fifty-fifty. The great thing was to hide him up for a month, and the next big thing was to get him away, and that was hard. I never realized before that England was surrounded by water, and that's where Clutterpeck came in useful. I set him up in some rooms in Harley Street, but he was never entirely satisfactory, because we wouldn't keep him sober. We had one or two narrow escapes with the invalids he was escorting across the Channel." He chuckled as though it were a pleasant memory, and then, with a deprecatory smile: "You know what it is, Reeder, when you and me have to depend on second-class people and not on ourselves. We're so near being sunk that a lifebelt doesn't mean a damn thing."

"When did you start the nursing home for infectious diseases?"

Mr. Redsack laughed uproariously and smacked his knee.

"Say, I wasn't sure whether you knew about that. You're clever. You got it, did you? Why, that happened after one or two of these birds had tried to double-cross us. You see, what we did was to put an advertisement in every paper once

a week. Naturally we had thousands of letters, but we waited till we got a man who could hand in the dough. You've got no idea how bank clerks don't know how to look after money! If he was just an ordinary five-cent man, we passed him on. But you'd be surprised at the number of big fellows—I once had an assistant general manager, who was so old that he couldn't be dishonest. But we got quite a few real smarties; as soon as we picked on 'em, we sent them along a notification that, as a very special honor and on the recommendation of the Lord knows who, they had been elected members of the Strangers' Club. We got a whole range of private rooms. But naturally we didn't want any member to meet another member. We gave 'em good food, free tickets for the theatre. Just made them feel that they were staying with Uncle John. How the hell they thought we did it on ten dollars a year I don't know. But I daresay you find, Reeder, that thieves are mean cusses.

"Once we got them here the Benevolent Brothers started their operations. I was the agent, but I had to make sure that they were men you could trust. I'm not going to give you the long of it, but it was not easy to get the smarties to fall for this grand idea. Most men are thieves at heart, but the thing that scares them is: how am I going to get away without a lagging? They can get the stuff all right, but where is it going to be put? Where will they hide? How will they leave the country without assistance? We provided everything for them: passports, transportation. Why, we even chartered a tug to get that guy, who pulled down a million from the Liverpool bank, from England to Belgium, and he didn't leave from Dover either. He went from London by water to Zeebrugge, and was carried aboard and ashore on a stretcher with so many bandages on his face that half the people who saw him land were crying before the ambulance took him on to Brussels. We made more than half a million bucks out of that, and he is living like a prince in Austria.

"WE GIVE service, Reeder. That's the keynote of our organization—service. We took 'em out of London in ambulances marked 'Infectious Diseases Only.' Can you see any policeman with children of his own stopping them and inspecting the patients? Why, you could smell that camphor dope before you saw the ambulance.

"You guessed right when you made an inspection of our nursing home at the back, and you guessed right when, after you had opened the door, you decided you wouldn't go in. We keep all our runaways snug in that home for a month —sometimes two months, and no harm comes to them. They are out of the country as per contract. Service!"

He shook his head, and used the word lovingly.

"We picked 'em up from the bank, we brought 'em to London, we hid them and we got 'em out of the country, and never had a failure. Hallaty was yellow. In the first place, he didn't bring all the stuff to us, but cached nearly half of it at a small public house in the Essex Road. Then he tried to get away, and naturally we had to go after him. That kid Reigate, he got religious. We thought we had everything set, but he jumped out of the ambulance on his way to Gravesend, and naturally Baldy, who was acting as escort, had to stop him talking.

"I'm glad you didn't come in when you used that key. I shouldn't have had the pleasure of talking to you. We had a machine gun on you, and Baldy was all ready with his motor-cycle to cover up the sound. But you didn't come in, and, honestly, Reeder, I'm glad." He was very earnest. "You're the kind of guy I wanted to meet."

He shook his head, genuinely sad.

"I wish I could think of some other way out for you, but you're tied up to your graft, the same as I am to mine."

Mr. Reeder smiled with his eyes, and finally spoke.

"May I ask whether you plan to let the matter end in this interesting and complicated building, or have you a more spectacular method in your mind?"

Mr. Redsack smiled. "You're a classy talker, Reeder, and I could listen to you for hours. Naturally you would imagine that I'd be thinking of something bad for a fellow who's given me the worst sock in the jaw I've ever had in my life." He touched his swollen cheek tenderly. "But I've got no malice in me. I guess we'll try the grand old American operation that's got so popular since I left the United States. We'll take you for a ride. If you've got any particular place you'd prefer, why, I'm willing to oblige you, Mr. Reeder, so long as it gives me a chance of getting back before daylight."

Mr. Reeder thought for a minute. "I naturally would prefer Brockley, which has been, as it were, and to use an expression which will be familiar to you, Mr. Redsack, my home town, but I realize that this highly populated suburb is not suitable for your purpose, and I suggest, respectfully, that one of the arterial roads out of London would suit both of us admirably."

Then Redsack switched on his loud-speaker and gave an order.

He took from the belt under his waistcoat a large-sized automatic and examined it as carefully as Mr. Reeder earlier in the evening had inspected his own lethal weapon.

"Let's go," he said.

He led the way, opened the door again, and Mr. Reeder passed through.

"Turn right!"

Mr. Reeder followed his directions, and came to the blank end of the passage.

"There's a door there that'll open in a minute," said Redsack encouragingly.

They waited a few seconds. Nothing happened. Pushing past him, Redsack rapped on the wall, and a tiny crack appeared in one corner. It opened wider and wider, and the door swung open.

"Say, what's the idea?" said Redsack loudly, and, even as he spoke, whipped out his gun and fired twice.

It was a lucky day for Chief Inspector Dance. One bullet whipped off his hat; the other went between his arm and coat.

He fired back, but by this time Redsack was flying along the passage and had turned the corridor.

When they came up, halting gingerly to feel their way, there was nobody in sight. They heard the whirr of the lift, but whether it was going up or down they could not tell.

Then again the lights went out from some central control. They could find no stairs.

"Back to where we came," said Dance.

They fled along the passage, through the door, down the steep flight of stairs. These turned sharply, and Mr. Reeder saw what it was. They were out in the mews, but not quickly enough. As Dance fumbled with the lock, they heard two gates open with a crash, the pulsation of an engine and the roar of it as it shot past. By the time they were out in the mews the Strangers' Club had lost its proprietor, janitor and chief attendant.

Dance reported hastily. "I gathered he got you and advanced the time five minutes."

He saw Mr. Reeder rub his head.

"Hurt?" he asked anxiously.

"Only in my feelings," said Mr. Reeder.

BACK at Scotland Yard, a chastened deputy constable was anxious to do all that was possible to correct his error, but the formidable network which was immediately drawn close about London, was established too late. So at five o'clock in the morning a tug left Greenwich and proceeded leisurely down the river, made its signal to Gravesend and passed out into the open sea.

The thing that came between Mr. Redsack and his future appeared in the form of a smoky cloud on the horizon, and a gray hull. From one tiny mast broke a string of little flags. The master of the tug reported to his chief passenger and charter party.

"A destroyer, sir," he said.

"What does he say?" asked Redsack, interested in the nautical drama.

" 'Heave to, I am searching you'."

Redsack considered this. "Suppose we don't?" he suggested.

"He'll sink us," said the alarmed master. "Why shouldn't we let him come aboard?"

"That's O. K. with me," said Redsack.

He turned to the tall janitor, yellow-faced and shivering in spite of his heavy overcoat. "If I was sure they'd take me back to Sing Sing, why, I wouldn't mind," he said. "Sing Sing's kind of a lucky prison to me. But I'm so damned English that it's Dartmoor or nothing, I guess. Or maybe they don't hang people at Dartmoor."

He considered the problem as the destroyer came nearer and nearer, and then he went down to the little cabin and scribbled a note.

Dear Mr. Reeder,

I said last night it was you or me, and I guess it's me.

He signed his name with a flourish, sat down on the hard sofa and took out a cigar. He heard the bump of a boat as it came alongside and an authoritative voice demanding particulars of the passengers.

Mr. Redsack placed his cigar carefully in a little polished stove and shot himself.

Swathed in their frayed and mouldy winding sheets they stood there—row after ghoulish row of withered dead. And on the floor, glistening drops of scarlet. What could these red terror-tokens mean? Why were they there? For even maimed and mangled, mummies never bleed!

THE FOURTEENTH MUMMY

by
T. T. Flynn

Author of "Three-Ring Murder," etc.

"There will be no trial. Neither of you will leave here alive."

CHAPTER ONE

Stool Pigeon's Steer

INSPECTOR Dennis Breen's large hand clamped on "Finger" Sammy's elbow like the jaws of a vise. And Finger Sammy almost fainted. His face was white and scared as he stopped abruptly and whirled around.

A broad smile was on Dennis Breen's face as he surveyed his catch. "If it isn't my old friend, Finger Sammy," he said genially. "A fine morning to be seeing you, Sammy. Where have you been all my life?"

Sammy cast a scared look up and down the street. He was a thin, wispy fellow, gaunt, shabbily dressed. His face was a pasty gray; his eyes were narrow-pupiled, restless.

"Listen, Breen, don't stop me out here on the street this way," Sammy begged. "It's liable to get me in Dutch. No tellin' who's lookin'."

Dennis Breen's fingers dug deep in Sammy's bony arm. "You're in bad already, Sammy—in bad with me. And you'd better worry more about that than what your crooked friends will think."

Finger Sammy's glance went up and down the street again. His mouth worked. His eyes caught Dennis Breen's desperately. "Listen, Breen, I c'n explain. I was gonna get in touch with you. I been out of town. I'm playing on the level with you. Fer Gawd's sake get off the street somewheres. I don't wanna be seen here talkin' to you."

"Now ain't you the nervous little punk?" Dennis Breen said warmly. "You know, Sammy, I've got a good mind to walk you up and down the main stem for an hour or so. Arm and arm with me, Sammy, so everyone will know what good pals we are."

Only a detective like Dennis Breen and a stoolie like Finger Sammy could appre-

ciate what that meant. It was as good as a death sentence. The news would flash through the underworld that Finger Sammy was palling with a cop. Men whose plans had gone awry, who had seen secrets they thought hidden slip into the files of the police, would begin to put two and two together—and the next thing someone would set out with a rod to make sure that Finger Sammy was a danger spot no more.

And Finger Sammy acted accordingly. His pasty face blanched grayer. His stained teeth fairly chattered. "Don't do that, Breen!" he begged. "You know what it'll mean! I won't be no good to you no more!"

"Good to me?" said Dennis Breen in surprise. "Are you any good to me, Sammy? I can't see where you are. Why, I haven't heard a word from you for almost a month."

"I been out of town, I tell you!" Sammy chattered. "There's a hallway up ahead. Let's go in there where we can talk without the whole damn town rubberin' at us."

Dennis released the arm. "All right, Sammy," he sighed. "I'll step in there for a minute. But I don't know—I feel like company this morning. You'd make swell company for a walk. I'm lonesome, Sammy. Mighty lonesome."

But Sammy was already scurrying for the shelter of the hallway, face down, shoulders hunched, as if curious glances were already seeking him out. Dennis strode after him. And in the hallway, safe from prying eyes for the moment, Dennis changed. His hand shot out, gripped Finger Sammy's scrawny neck.

"Now, you little punk!" he said harshly. "What's the idea of fading out on me like you did? Trying to give me the runaround, were you? Thought if you blew the coop I'd forget about you—and that warrant they're holding down at headquarters?"

Finger Sammy twisted under the tight grip. "I didn't take it on the lam!" he protested. "Honest to Gawd, Breen! I'm givin' it to you straight! I got hold of a piece of change and went to Chi to spend it. I thought maybe I could get some work there, but—but there wasn't any, so I came back here."

"You wouldn't work if they shoved it in your face."

"Sure I would."

"All right—all right. Have it your way. I haven't got time to stand here and listen to you lie. What I want to know is, do I get anything out of you? I didn't let you slide away from that warrant because I loved you."

"I only been back two days," Finger Sammy pleaded desperately. "I was gonna call you up as soon as I got anything you could use."

"Then you haven't got anything?"

Finger Sammy gulped. "No," he confessed.

"*Hmmmm.*"

Sammy's eyes wandered away from Dennis Breen's hard gaze. His uneasiness grew.

"You're lying!" Dennis said with finality. "Playing me for a sucker again, Sammy. And you know how far you'll get with that. Come on and start that walk with me." He seized Sammy's elbow firmly.

Sammy twisted away. "Don't do that!" he chattered. "Listen, I'll come clean with you! I got something maybe you can use! I'll shoot the works! I'll show you I'm on the level with you!"

"I thought you had something up your sleeve," Dennis said grimly. "What is it?"

Sammy wet his lips, looked fearfully out the doorway, then back up the stairs. A spare elderly man with steel spectacles and a leather briefcase under his arm turned in from the sidewalk. Sammy wheeled to the wall quickly and hunched his shoulders while the stranger walked up the creaking stairs.

"It's all right. He doesn't know you," Dennis said impatiently. "Out with it."

Sammy heaved a deep sigh as he turned around. "It's this way," he said uneasily. "I was in 'Dinky's' speak last night. You know, that joint down at Harvard and Fourth."

"I know it—and a rotten dump it is. You would be hanging around there. What about it?"

"I was over in the corner half asleep when 'Buster' Moran and a couple of his friends come in," Sammy said hurriedly. "They had a few drinks, an' then sat down an' started to buzz over the table. They didn't pay no attention to me, but I kept my ears peeled to see if there was anything you could use."

"To see if there was anything you could make a dirty dollar out of, you mean," Dennis corrected. "All right, what did you pick up? Moran is a hot customer. If he's up to anything, it's good."

"I didn't get much. They were speakin' too low for me to hear. But just as they got up to go, one of the guys says to Moran, 'Ten tomorrow mornin' at the express office then.'"

"And then what?"

"That's all," Sammy confessed nervously. "I'm on the level with it. But I thought it might be somethin' you could use. Moran ain't interested in the express office unless there's somethin' good there. I was gonna telephone you this mornin' an' tell you."

"It's nine now, and you were going to get me after while and tell me about a ten-o'clock job!" Dennis rasped. "Lying again! You've probably been trying to figure where you can pull a fistful of dough out of it. Sure you didn't get any more? If you're lying to me—"

"That's all, s'help me! I'm straight

with you, Breen! If there was any more, I'd tell you!"

Looking at the fearful little stool pigeon, Dennis Breen decided that he was probably hearing the truth. As long as Finger Sammy told part, he might as well tell all. And he didn't have the guts to pull anything in the way of a double cross. The warrant down at headquarters, taken with Finger Sammy's record, was good for ten years. Sammy wasn't going to take any chances with that, despite the fact that he was so crooked he would cheat himself.

Dennis disliked this part of his profession. But he had long ago learned that a smart detective who was on his job always had a few lines out in the underworld to sift and sort the wash of information continually circulating there. Finger Sammy was a rat. He should have been in prison long ago. But he was more valuable to Dennis Breen and to society as he was functioning now. His petty crookedness was more than offset by the chance that he might prevent a big coup, help catch a killer, put the police straight on a confused trail of some sort. As a matter of fact he had done more than one good turn for society already. Dennis had not really intended to take him for that fatal walk around town. But he knew Finger Sammy's type. They had to be handled roughly or they'd start slipping fast ones over.

"All right," Dennis said. "Lam. And don't try to get in touch with Moran and tell him I'm wise to anything."

Finger Sammy scuttled out on the sidewalk and vanished. After waiting a few moments Dennis Breen walked out too.

THE main express office was down by the union station, at the end of the freight sheds. Here all incoming and outgoing express for the city was collected and distributed. The express delivery wagons served the congested district within a certain radius of the office. Outside that delivery trucks and private cars did the work. During the hours the office was open a constant stream of arriving and departing cars passed through the parking space in front of the express office.

Dennis Breen parked the police car far down the street.

"What time is it?" he asked Lawrence, one of the detectives in the robbery detail whom he had brought along.

"Fifteen of ten," Lawrence said, glancing at his wrist watch.

"Time enough. You stroll down this side of the street and I'll go over and look in the office. If I don't call you, stay back and keep your eyes open. Moran might be up to anything. He probably won't be around, but if he is, let him alone and we'll try to catch him cold."

"Right," Lawrence agreed. He was a tall, thin, angular chap, red-headed and silent. A good man in a pinch. Dennis had felt that he could handle this matter all right, but he had brought Lawrence along to be on the safe side.

Looking, in his plain clothes, like any other square-shouldered citizen in the early thirties, Dennis strolled to the express office. The railroad yards lay back of it. Freight sheds were beyond.

The express office was in the end of a long building beside a spur of track. Down the front of it were doors where trucks and cars could back up and receive their packages. In front of the office door were parking spaces, occupied by half a dozen automobiles.

Dennis took in the possibilities of the place at a glance. Through the windows he could see clerks and customers. Seven or eight men were in there, and a woman. They would be no great bar to armed men carrying out a surprise attack. Valuable shipments often came through the express. Was Moran after something like that?

Outside here everything looked all right. No sign of Moran or any men who might be acting for him. No one standing around who looked suspicious. A peaceful, bustling place of business was the most Dennis could say for it.

He wondered if Finger Sammy had put him on a wrong trail in an effort to stall and get away. The idea creased a frown in his forehead as he went inside.

The office was just as peaceful as the outside. Clerks were weighing packages, making out shipping tags and papers, collecting charges and handing small packages over the metal-covered counter to those who had called for them.

Dennis heard one clerk tell a man: "You can get your box around at the side. Door C. Just show them this receipt."

The hands of a big electric clock on the side wall pointed to exactly ten o'clock. Dennis loosened the service revolver in the leather holster under his arm, to be ready for action if it was needed. He said to the clerk who came to the counter to wait on him: "Where's the manager?"

"Over there at that big desk. Mr. Carter. . . . "

Carter, the manager, was a gray-haired, paunchy man wearing black cloth sleeve protectors and a worn eyeshade. Dennis moved down to the end of the counter where he could talk without being heard. When the manager faced him expectantly, Dennis showed his small badge in the palm of his hand.

"I'm from headquarters," he confided. "Inspector Breen."

"Ah, yes, inspector. Is there something wrong?"

"I don't know," Breen confessed.

"We've got a tip that a well-known crook and some of his men are interested in this place this morning. I don't see any sign of them around, but they may show up. Anything around here that might interest them? Valuable shipments?"

The manager took a pencil from behind his ear and drummed nervously on the counter top with it. "Nothing that I know of," he said. "Practically everything we handle is boxed and packaged, and we have no idea of what it's worth, unless it happens to carry a very large declared valuation. We usually keep an eye on such things. As far as I know there's nothing like that in the place now. Nothing that would appeal to crooks."

"No money or gold, jewels or anything like that?"

The manager smiled, shrugged. "Nothing like that at all. Of course we usually have a few hundred dollars in the safe."

"Better lock it up," Dennis advised.

"Yes, I'll do that. Pardon me a minute, please."

The manager hurried over to a small steel safe in the corner and locked it.

"That's that," he said as he came back. "I don't know of anything else around the place that would pay anyone to come after. Are you sure you haven't been misinformed?"

"I wouldn't take an oath on it," Dennis confessed grimly. "But I've got a hunch I was steered right. Still, if you say there's nothing here worth big money it looks like I'm wrong."

"I'm afraid you are," the manager nodded.

The outer door opened at that moment. Dennis' eyes went to the man who entered. His face remained blank, but he said tersely out of the corner of his mouth: "Maybe I'm right after all! I know that man! Let's see what he wants!"

CHAPTER TWO

The Box at Door D

THE man he indicated was small—smaller than Finger Sammy. His face was narrow and fox-like, shrewd, cunning, keen. A cap was tilted slightly to one side of his head. He wore duck trousers and an old coat. And he went straight to the counter without looking around the room.

A clerk stepped forward to wait on him.

The newcomer fished a printed postcard from his pocket and slid it over the counter. Dennis recognized it as one of the printed forms the express company mailed out for notification that express was waiting to be called for.

The clerk looked at it, asked a question, walked back to the door leading into the big freight shed behind the office. The customer fished out a package of cigarettes and lighted one. He flipped the match carelessly to the floor. He shifted from one foot to the other; his eyes went around the room restlessly. He seemed nervous.

Dennis was only a stride away when the little man's eyes rested on his face. A puzzled expression was followed by a flash of emotion, and then blankness.

"Hello, 'Wee Willie'," Dennis said casually.

Wee Willie Watson's right arm made the barest move toward the inside of his coat. Dennis slid his hand under his left arm quicker.

"Don't!" he advised.

Wee Willie's hand relaxed. His face was still blank. "Don't what?" he asked.

"Reach for it."

"For what. I don't getcha, mister. Who are you?"

"That," said Dennis, "is the great big surprise. Step over here to the end of the counter, please."

Wee Willie Watson hesitated. Dennis watched him fixedly. Wee Willie had served time for one shooting affair. He had been regarded as a bad one with a gun.

Wee Willie shrugged. "I don't get it," he said. "But if it'll make you feel any better, O. K."

He walked down to the end of the counter. Dennis kept close at his heels. The manager had watched the little by-play anxiously. He moved to the end of the counter also. None of the other people in the room had noticed anything unusual, so quiet and casual had everything been.

Wee Willie inhaled from his cigarette, looked at the manager and then at Dennis. "Well," he asked, "what's the idea?"

"I'm from headquarters," Dennis said gently.

"You don't say?" Wee Willie cocked his head on one side and surveyed Dennis through half-closed eyelids. "I thought your mug looked familiar," he said. "What's on your mind?"

"First, we'll have a look inside your coat."

Wee Willie shrugged. "Go ahead. There's a gat there. But I got a permit to carry it. Laugh that off, flatfoot."

"We'll see about the permit," Dennis promised as he located an automatic, looked at it, and thrust it in his coat pocket. "Now what are you doing here, Willie?"

"Getting a box."

"Who for?"

"My boss. I'm working now," Wee Willie sneered at him. "If you think you can crab the job, go ahead. I told the boss I had served a stretch. He's wise, and he says as long as I do my work all right, it's jake with him."

"Jake with me too," Dennis agreed. "We're not trying to make you stir birds any trouble as long as you run straight. Who are you working for?"

"Professor Richfield," Wee Willie answered promptly.

"Who is he?"

"Rich guy who lives out on the north edge of town. One of these fellows who collects things. Goes all over the world and digs up old ruins."

Carter, the manager, said: "I recall the name, inspector. We have quite a few shipments for him. Imported things mostly."

"And so you're after a box for Professor Richfield?" Dennis questioned.

"Yeah," said Wee Willie shortly.

Dennis looked at the manager and lifted his eyebrows. "Phone?" he asked.

"Over there on my desk."

"Come on, Willie," Dennis ordered.

THEY walked behind the counter to the telephone. Dennis looked in the directory, got the number of Professor Adam Richfield, called it. A man's voice answered promptly at the other end.

"I want to speak to Professor Richfield," Dennis said.

"Just a minute," he was told.

It took a minute and a half by the second hand of the big clock on the wall. Then a nasal voice said: "This is Professor Richfield speaking."

"This is Inspector Breen, of headquarters," Dennis said. "Did you send a man to the express office after a package, Mr. Richfield?"

There was a short pause. "Why?" Richfield countered.

"We're checking up on your man here at the express office. He has a criminal record and we want to be sure everything is all right."

"Is he there?"

"Yes."

"Let me talk to him," Professor Richfield said curtly.

Wee Willie Watson took the phone Dennis shoved at him. He kept one wary eye on Dennis as he talked. It was impossible to hear what Professor Richfield was saying. Wee Willie's answers were monosyllabic.

"Yeah," he said. "Yeah. . . . Yeah. . . . It's all right. . . . He thought I was trying to steal something from you, Mr. Richfield. . . . Yeah. . . . Uh-huh. . . ."

Wee Willie handed the telephone back to Dennis with a sly grin. Professor Richfield's voice was calm and cordial.

"I thank you for the trouble you have taken, inspector. It's a pleasure to know the police are so efficient. But I know about the man's record, and I sent him there on a bona-fide errand. You will allow him to carry it out, I trust?"

"Certainly," Dennis agreed.

"Thank you." The receiver clicked up at the other end.

Dennis put the telephone back on the desk with a feeling of chagrin. He had been certain that Wee Willie Watson was the sour spot he was looking for. He paid no attention to the little man's sly triumphant grin. His mind was once more searching for the answer to Finger Sammy's tip.

"Anything else?" Wee Willie asked insolently.

"No."

"Then how about giving me my gat back?"

"Got your permit on you?"

"No. It's at the house."

"I'll keep the gun until we look into that matter of the permit," Dennis told him. "I don't know who issued one to an ex-con and a gunman like you. Bad business. I think we'll have to have it revoked."

"Say, you can't treat me like that! I got a permit, I tell you! I want the rod!"

"Scram!" Dennis said curtly.

Wee Willie hesitated, and then said venomously as he moved off: "I'll see that you get burnt for this, you big flat-foot!"

Dennis didn't bother to answer him. He had more on his mind than trading words with an ex-con. Ten o'clock was well past now. It was beginning to look as though he had come here on a false tip.

The clerk came back, put a slip on the counter for Wee Willie Watson to sign. Dennis heard him say: "You can pick up that box at Door D."

"O. K.," said Wee Willie. He went out.

Everything was peaceful. Dennis said to the manager: "Keep your safe locked all day. No telling what will turn up."

The manager was not so friendly now. "You must have had wrong information," he declared.

"It happens," Dennis replied, nettled.

He cast a look at the customers before the counter and went out. Across the street and down a hundred yards he saw Lawrence loitering casually. Everything was clear outside here too. Dennis shook his head at Lawrence, and then strolled back along the loading platforms.

Express trucks, other trucks and private automobiles were backed up and parked before the platforms. Dennis cased the drivers as he walked back. Everyone looked all right. He found Wee Willie Watson at Door D, watching two of the express-company employees loading a long heavy box into a light panelled delivery truck. The box looked as though it might contain a coffin.

"What's in there?" Dennis asked Wee Willie.

He drew an unfriendly glance. "Listen, this is one time I don't have to answer a cop's questions!" Wee Willie said with hostile relish. "Scram yourself. You got nothin' on me, an' I'm attendin' to my own business. Snort that off, flatfoot!"

"Some day," said Dennis pleasantly, "I'll have the joy of knocking you off for

something, Willie. And then you can work that mouth of yours till it gets a cramp."

"Rats!" scoffed Wee Willie.

Dennis noticed that the box was fastened with bands of wire, sealed with lead. It was liberally plastered with FRA-GILE labels, with customs stamps and seals. It appeared to have passed the borders of many countries.

The men shoved it in the truck. Wee Willie closed the door, walked around to the driver's seat and slipped behind the wheel. The starter whirred; the motor caught. Wee Willie looked at Dennis.

"You give me a big laugh this morning, flatfoot," he grinned. "The razzberry for you, and keep that thick head of yours outa my business after this." He drove off.

DENNIS watched the car roll to the next corner, turn it and disappear. Then with a last glance about he started across the street to Lawrence. But he stopped almost instantly at sight of Carter, the office manager, running toward him.

"Where did that man go?" Carter called to him. "That man you were talking to in the office?"

"Got his box and left," Dennis said, eyeing Carter curiously. "What's the matter? Something wrong?"

Carter stopped, panting. He fished out a handkerchief and mopped his face. "Something seems to be," he nodded. "Professor Richfield just telephoned and asked for his man. He seemed excited, agitated. He asked me to stop delivery on the box consigned to him. Not to let his man take it away. He asked me to get him to the telephone at once. You say he's gone?"

"Yes. Watched him drive away. What was in that box he got?"

"I don't know," Carter said with a last deep breath. He looked worried. He said apprehensively: "I wonder what's wrong?

It's nothing they can come back at me for. You heard Professor Richfield say to give him the box. He signed for it. We couldn't do anything else."

"You're in the clear all right," Dennis agreed. "You say Richfield is on the telephone?"

"Yes—waiting to speak to his man."

"I'll talk to him," Dennis decided. He went back in to the telephone. "This is Inspector Breen again, professor. Your man has left with your box. It was too late to stop him."

Something that sounded like an oath came over the wire. Professor Richfield asked sharply: "You saw him leave?"

"Yes."

"And he got away all right? No trouble of any kind?"

"No."

Richfield hesitated. "All right," he said. "I merely wanted to give him further orders. Thank you."

The receiver at the other end clicked down before Dennis could ask any questions. He thought of ringing back, and then shrugged the idea away. If Richfield wanted to explain anything he had had the chance. It was his business whether he wanted his box delivered or not. Perhaps he had been thinking over Watson's record and decided that he could not be trusted with a valuable shipment.

Nevertheless as Dennis went outside again the incident bothered him. It was decidedly queer. He felt there was something extraordinary behind it. He would have liked to know what it was.

Lawrence had crossed the street, was standing at the corner of the building. "Lot of running around over here," he said as Dennis joined him. "Thought I might be needed."

"False alarm," Dennis said. "Seen anything suspicious?"

"Everything looks all right."

"Too good," Dennis admitted. "I don't understand it. I'd have sworn that punk who tipped me off didn't have the guts to pull a phony. But it's beginning to look like he did. I'll give him the works when I get my mitts on him. I thought for a minute a while ago I had the thing sewed up. Wee Willie Watson came in for a box. He's done time. Used to be a bad one. But he's got a job, and his boss cleared him. And now his boss just called up all excited and asked them to hold the box. Didn't want it delivered to Watson. It doesn't make sense. One minute everything's jake—and the next it's wrong. I wonder what made him change his mind so quick."

"Something wrong?" Lawrence hazarded.

"Can't be much. He knew who I was, and he didn't say anything was wrong. He did ask me if there had been any trouble of any kind. Sounded like he was expecting something to happen. When I told him nothing had he stalled about wanting to give Watson some orders, and hung up."

"Queer," Lawrence agreed. "What was in that box he took away? It looked like a coffin from across the street."

"I thought the same thing," Dennis nodded. "He wouldn't tell me. He had a cop wrong for once in his life and he made the best of it. Suppose we climb into the car and cruise around a little.'

"What's that!" Lawrence exclaimed. "Wasn't that a couple of shots?"

Dennis heard them also. Two faint but distinct reports. And it wasn't an automobile backfiring. "Trouble!" he guessed sharply. "Come on!"

CHAPTER THREE

Who'd Steal a Corpse?

DENNIS led the way at a run to the police car. In his efforts to start it quickly he flooded the still warm carburetor. It took several minutes to get the motor running. Then they shot down the street, careened around the corner, and raced in the direction from which the shots had come.

Dennis slammed on the brakes sharply as he passed the next corner. A block down the side street people were running. The machine stopped with shrieking tires, leaped back in reverse, and swung into that side street. A moment later they drew up beside a small closed delivery car, angled in to the curb.

"Wee Willie Watson's car!" Dennis rapped to Lawrence as they came up.

Half a dozen people were gathered around it. A bushy-haired, elderly German was speaking excitedly, gesticulating violently as he talked. Dennis shoved to his side and looked in the front seat. Wee Willie Watson was calmly leaning back in the corner behind the wheel, noticing nothing.

Dennis swore under his breath as he peered in. A stream of blood was still oozing down Wee Willie's face from a small round powder-marked hole in his forehead. A second hole had been blown through his lower jaw. Wee Willie Watson would never razz another cop, never run afoul of the law again. He was dead.

Dennis wheeled to the excited old German. "Who did this?" he demanded.

A violent shrug. Further waving of hands. A stream of excited German answered him.

"Talk English!" Dennis ordered loudly.

More German was all he got. A young boy translated: "He says he was sitting inside his window in that house there, mister. He heard two shots. He looked out and saw two autos standing here. Some men were at the back of this one. They took a big box out and put it in the other car and drove away."

Dennis hurried around to the rear of the truck. Using his handkerchief, he gingerly turned the door handle and looked inside. The large box that Wee Willie Watson had carried away from the express platform had vanished.

Dennis closed the doors, leaving his handkerchief over the handle. He asked the little group of curious who had gathered: "Anyone else know anything about this? Did you get a description of the other car? Its license number, or what the men in it looked like?"

A woman who said she lived across the street volunteered excitedly that the other car had looked something like the one they were standing by. No one else had seen it, so quickly had everything happened. Neither of them had gotten the license number of the other truck. And they could tell little about what the men looked like.

Dennis made his decision quickly. "It's got a five or six minute start on us," he said to Lawrence. "We haven't got a chance to run it down. No use wasting the time. Run in one of these houses and report it. Have a general alarm sent out to watch for a car something like this one."

As Lawrence ran to do that, Dennis herded the curious back from the truck.

"And the first one who touches that handkerchief on the back-door handle will get a run-in as quick as I can call the wagon!" he promised them.

Lawrence came back, panting. Dennis had been doing a lot of thinking.

"I should have known this might happen," he said to Lawrence. "I noticed he was nervous, as if he was afraid of something. He started to reach for his gun when I accosted him. Perhaps he'd have had a chance if I had left it on him."

"Maybe he'd have had a chance and maybe not," Lawrence said dubiously as he inspected the body on the driver's seat. "Whoever got him, got him plenty. Say, inspector, do you think—"

"I was," Dennis agreed. "I'm wondering if this isn't the tip-off play. I'll have

Moran rounded up as quick as possible."

"If we knew what was in that box," Lawrence hazarded.

"I'll call the owner and find out. It must be something pretty valuable."

"Must have been, to rate murder," Lawrence agreed.

THEY stayed there until a homicide detail came shrieking down the street and took command of the situation. Dennis pointed out the door handle and asked that it be photographed for fingerprints.

"Wee Willie Watson's his name," he said to Lieutenant Sardi, who had charge of the squad. "Used to be a slick gun. He's on the level now. At least he claimed he was. I talked to his boss over the telephone. Here's his rod."

"You saw him before this happened?" Sardi asked, taking the automatic.

"Over in the express office. Got a tip something was due to be sour here around ten o'clock. While I was waiting this Watson blew in. Made a reach for his gat when I eased up behind. Then claimed he had a permit to carry it. Told me he was going straight now. I called his boss and got the same dope. So Willie took his box and blew. He got this far."

Sardi was a hefty man, chunky and alert. "What about the box?" he asked quickly.

"Looked like a coffin to me."

"Huh? Coffin? You handing me one?"

"Straight," Dennis assured him. "You've seen the shipping boxes they use?"

"Uh-huh."

"Well, it was like one of those. I asked the little shrimp what was in it, and he gave me the razz. He knew I didn't have anything on him—couldn't even ask him to open the box—and he made the most of it."

"Coffin," Sardi repeated blankly. "You don't think there was a body in it?"

"Search me," Dennis said cheerfully. "Might have been."

"Who'd want to cop a stiff? Hey, Mc-Guinness, run them people back! This ain't a free show! Lady, go down to the morgue if you got to rubber at nasty things!"

"You never can tell what anyone'll want to cop," Dennis sighed. "My tipster said Buster Moran was interested in something around the express office at ten. He didn't show up. No one did. This is the only thing that happened."

"It's enough," Sardi grunted. "So Buster Moran's got a thumb in this?"

"Maybe not."

"I'll jerk him in anyway," Sardi promised. "Who's the guy the box was going to?"

"Professor Richfield. Lives out on Berkeley Drive, on the north side. Wee Willie said he was an archaeologist. Collects old things—relics and so on. The manager in the express office knew of Richfield. Said a lot of stuff came through for him. Mostly from foreign countries."

"Well, that angle sounds all right," Sardi said. "Them things are worth jack, too. Museums and people who collect, pay ungodly prices for 'em."

"There's your case," Dennis grinned with a wave of his hand. "Something valuable came through, and someone else was wise and copped it."

"Eight to one you're right," Sardi nodded. "This wasn't an old score someone settled. If they'd just come out to knock Watson off, they wouldn't have bothered to take his box."

"Unless they figured there was something valuable in it," Dennis suggested.

"There you go, crabbing my case all up," Sardi grumbled good naturedly. "If one thing ain't right, you'll furnish another, eh? Ralph, what did you find on that door handle?"

"A couple of pretty good prints and some smudges," the fingerprint man said, carrying his case to the seat of the car. "Say, this stiff sure leaked blood, didn't he?"

"They all do," Sardi assured him. "Look on the corner of the windshield and around the steering wheel. Whoever plugged him was on the running board. Both of the wounds have powder marks around them. Where'd you phone in from, inspector? I think I'll call the owner of that box and see what was in it."

"Don't bother. I'll do it," Dennis offered. "I'll telephone headquarters and have a general snatch sent out for Buster Moran and any men close to him."

LAWRENCE took Dennis to the house where he had telephoned headquarters. The members of the household were out in the street, staring with morbid curiosity. The two headquarters men walked in the hall to the telephone. Dennis called in and requested that Buster Moran be picked up at once.

"You may get a line on him at Dinky's speakeasy at Harvard and Fourth," he suggested. And then he called Professor Richfield's number once more. The same voice answered the telephone. "I want to talk to Professor Richfield," Dennis requested.

There was a short pause. "Who is this?"

"Inspector Breen, of headquarters."

"What do you want?"

"Professor Richfield," Dennis snapped. "Ask him to come to the telephone. It's important."

"Professor Richfield isn't here."

"Where is he?"

"He went out. He didn't say where he was going."

"When will he be back?"

"I can't tell you, sir."

"What was in that box your man got from the express office a little while ago?" Dennis asked shortly.

"I—I don't know," the other answered uncertainly.

"I'll call back," Dennis informed him.

"Is there anything wrong, inspector?" the man at the other end questioned hurriedly.

"What could be wrong?" Dennis countered.

"I—I don't know. I just wondered, since you are from headquarters."

"Who are you?"

"I'm the butler, sir."

"I'll call back and talk with the professor," Dennis said. "Ask him to wait when he comes in."

"Yes, sir."

Dennis slammed the receiver back on the hook. To Lawrence he said with a frown: "I don't like the way that fellow talked. He was too curious to know if there had been trouble. So was Professor Richfield. It looks to me like they were expecting something to happen. That must have been why Richfield called the express office in such a lather. They're covering up, trying to hide something. I think I'll run out there and talk to this Professor Richfield face to face. I'm getting curious. Go back to headquarters with Sardi's men and help look for Moran. I'll come in as quick as I can. I think if we get Moran we'll have this case boxed."

Dennis climbed in the police car and drove out to Berkeley Drive, a tree-bordered street on the extreme north side of the city. A street that was not straight, that threaded a leisurely, winding way between low knolls and small wooded hills. There were houses close to the road, and houses set well back, small lots and sizable patches of ground.

Dennis drove slowly, watching the house numbers. Professor Richfield's place proved to be one of the larger ones. It sat on the sloping side of a hill, a huge three-story frame house surrounded by three or four acres of land. The place was heavily wooded, towering trees spreading wide. There was so much shade the house and grounds seemed mantled in deep gloom.

And Dennis got a shock as he rode leisurely by. Standing at the back corner of the house, watching the road, was a thin, gaunt, shabbily dressed figure. It moved quickly back out of sight. But there was no doubt in Dennis' mind as to who it was.

He had seen for an instant his stool pigeon, Finger Sammy!

Dennis drove past the grounds without stopping. But he was suddenly tense, alert, wary. What was Finger Sammy doing out here? Why had he dodged back behind the corner of the house so quickly? Had he recognized the police car and the driver? What was he nervous about?

It began to look as if Sammy's presence explained that second call at the express office. Warned of impending trouble, Professor Richfield had tried to prevent his shipment from leaving. But why hadn't he said something about it when Dennis spoke to him over the telephone? Why had he been so secretive? And why had Sammy come out here?

Sammy must have known more than he had told. Must have known who Moran was after. And he had held back that knowledge for some reason.

"The dirty little rat!" Dennis growled to himself. "I'll make him sweat for that!"

THE road curved around the base of the hill. Dennis passed out of sight of the big gloomy house and yard, then pulled over to the side and stopped. Leaving the car there, he cut up through the trees to the top of the hill, and came down again toward the back of the big house. Garage and outbuildings were between him and the house. Sammy had disappeared; no one was in the yard. Shades

on the lower floor were drawn down. It looked a gloomy, deserted place.

His shoes crunched on the gravel before the garage as he strode swiftly to the back porch. He noticed that the garage was large, capable of housing three or four automobiles.

The banging of his fist on the back screen door broke the deep quiet that hovered about the place. No one answered. Dennis knocked again, and kept on knocking until the back door opened. A girl peered out—a pretty girl, one of the most striking Dennis had ever seen. She was dark and vivid, standing out against the gloomy background of the house and grounds like a marsh flower in noisome shadows. Well dressed too, in a light summer sports suit. Dark, slumberous eyes surveyed him inquiringly.

Dennis removed his hat. Before he could speak, she asked: "What do you want?" And her voice was low, vibrant, pleasing.

"Is Professor Richfield here?" Dennis asked.

A jade necklace around her white throat quivered as she shook her head. She came no further out of the doorway. She seemed to be standing there uncertainly, poised to slam the door if he made an overt move. The screen door was locked, preventing him from opening it unless he kicked it down.

"I am Inspector Breen, of police headquarters," Dennis explained.

A startled shadow of emotion passed across her face. It might have been fear, might have been something else. Then her dark eyes regarded him fixedly. "Yes," she said slowly. "What do you want, inspector?"

"I came to see Professor Richfield."

"He isn't here."

"I'll come in and wait for him," Dennis said promptly.

"I'm sorry," she informed him. "I

can't let you in. Uncle told me not to admit anyone unless he was with them."

"I don't want to stand out here and wait," Dennis said patiently.

"Then you'll have to go away."

"This is police business. I can't wait. Will you let me in?"

"I can't do that," she refused.

She looked frightened for a moment. He saw her hand clenching tight on the door until the knuckles stood out white and vivid against the slight tan of her skin.

"You have a man in there I want to see," Dennis told her.

"A—a man?"

"Yes."

"Aren't you mistaken? There's no one in here but me."

"I saw him a few minutes ago. Standing at the corner of the house."

"You must have been mistaken, inspector."

"Where did he go?"

"I didn't see anyone. If—if there was anyone out there it must have been an intruder who left at once."

But she didn't have the control over her voice and face that she should have had. She was lying. Dennis was sure of it as his eyes searched her face. A slow tide of color welled up in her cheeks. Her eyes held his for a moment, and then dropped.

Why was she lying? She looked as if deceit were entirely foreign to her. And yet—she was lying! Coldly, deliberately, Dennis asked: "Are you sure you are the only person in the house?"

Without meeting his glance, she nodded silently. Then, as a second thought, said flatly: "I have a gun here, in case I need it."

This was not getting anywhere; it was maddening. He had no search warrant to enter the house. He could break in and prove that she was lying but it might

make trouble. This household had done nothing to justify that as far as he knew.

"Where did your uncle go?" Dennis demanded.

"I don't know," she said. A tiny frown creased the smooth skin between her eyes. She was not able to hide the fact that she was worried.

"When is he coming back?"

"I—I don't know. Perhaps not until evening."

And Dennis again got the impression that she was lying. She knew well enough, and was hiding it behind false statements. They troubled her too. Dennis mastered his irritation. There seemed small chance of gaining anything by standing outside the screen door and telling her she was lying. There were more ways than one to get at a thing. He had the gift of patience. He could wait.

"All right," Dennis said evenly. "Tell your uncle I was here. I can't spare the time to come back today. I'll telephone him, or he can call headquarters and ask for me. Good day."

But as he strode down the graveled driveway, ignoring the way he had come, Dennis swore under his breath. That girl had blocked him neatly and effectively. Finger Sammy was in that house or about the place, he was certain. If Sam had fled back over the hill Dennis would have met him, seen him. The girl had known about that too. She had baldly lied about it.

Midway to the road Dennis turned suddenly and looked back at the house. It was a trick that he had worked before. His watchful eyes caught the quick drop of a curtain falling into place. Someone in that house had been furtively watching him go.

The whole thing puzzled him. Why this air of mystery and evasion? Why was Finger Sammy hiding from him? Dennis had always prided himself on his judgment of people. He could usually tell the good from the bad; he could spot a crook almost as far as he could see one. That girl looked honest and above-board. And yet—she had not been.

If there was trouble, why didn't they come frankly to the police with it? Finger Sammy's entrance into the matter tangled every idea that occurred to him.

Meanwhile murder had been done. It had to be cleared up. Dennis conned the chances of getting Buster Moran as he drove swiftly back to the center of town.

CHAPTER FOUR

Mummies Don't Bleed

BACK at headquarters Dennis learned that the general alarm had produced no results yet. Moran had apparently slipped into the labyrinths of the under-world and vanished. He might stay there for days, weeks—might leave town. "We went to Dinky's place the first thing," Sardi said disgustedly. "Not a crumb there. Dinky won't talk for anything but a sweating, an' I doubt if he would then. He gets his standing by keeping a close mouth. He said he didn't know anything about Moran, and stuck to it. Admitted Moran had been in there with a couple of strangers last night, but said they were just three customers to him and he didn't pay any attention to them."

No suspicious-looking light delivery truck had been picked up. As Sardi pointed out, the truck was probably hidden safely in some garage before the general alarm got out. Every trail they had run to earth had vanished.

"The prints on the door handle of that truck belong to the dead fellow," Sardi continued gloomily. "Not a thing on the truck that will do us any good. We've got the bullets that killed him, but they're no good until we got the gun they were fired from."

Dennis had been tilted back against the wall in a chair. The legs of his chair thumped to the floor now. "I wonder if Moran owned a car in his own name."

Sardi shrugged. "Might have."

"Be back in a few minutes," Dennis said, and hurried out.

The city license bureau was on the floor above. Dennis went up there, drafted a clerk and started a hurried search through the automobile license records. Buster Moran's real first name was not known to the police. He might have given any one. There were a dozen Morans listed. Dennis copied them all on a sheet of paper and went back to Sardi.

"If Moran's got a car in his name, we'll locate it," he said. "Where's Lawrence?"

"Still out."

"We might as well go together," Dennis decided. "Moran is a tough egg. If he knows we're after him for murder, he's liable to put up a scrap."

It was slow, patient work, the kind from which real success usually sprang—this running down first one name, and then another, to make certain each address could not have been used by Buster Moran. Some they were able to eliminate in a moment or two of talk. Others they had to check and verify with inquiries nearby.

Three of the addresses were garages. Suddenly Dennis said: "I've got a hunch it'll pay us to skip some of these names and hike over to the Owl Garage. I know one big bootie who has a lot of car work done there. If they work for one crook they're apt to take on more. This Jacob Moran who gave that as his address ought to stand a lot of checking."

The Owl Garage was a small, dirty, dark place located on the fringe of the wholesale district. A ramp led down from the street level into the cavernous interior. Several trucks and automobiles were parked in stalls against the walls.

A dim lamp burned over a repair bench at the back, and another light on an extension cord was visible under the front end of a touring car. The sound of a hammer striking metal came from under the car.

Dennis went back there and bent down. "Who's the boss around here?" he called.

A grease-smeared face peered out at him. "Joe Cohen," the mechanic replied. "He stepped out for a minute. He'll be right back."

Dennis lighted a cigarette in calm disregard of the NO SMOKING sign overhead. He had hardly done that when a dapper little man in a blue dust coat came briskly down the ramp.

"Something for you gentlemen?" he called.

"You Cohen?"

"Yes. Sure. That's me."

Dennis palmed his badge and showed it to Cohen. "Police," he said briefly.

MR. COHEN looked warily at them. The corner of his nose twitched slightly. He threw out his hands in exasperation. "What now? I ain't done nothin'! Don't tell me you're here to make trouble! Always it's trouble, an' there ain't a more law-abiding fellow in town than me. Ask anybody that knows me if I ain't a—"

"Wait a minute!" Dennis broke in. "Who said we were trying to make trouble? You'll be all right if you come across with the right dope."

Cohen eyed him distrustfully. "What's the right dope?"

"Just a few things about this Jacob Moran who keeps his car here," Dennis informed him casually.

Cohen's eyelids drooped the merest bit, veiling his look. "That guy? I can't tell you nothing about him. He did keep his car here for a few weeks, but he took it away. That's all I know about him."

"And where's Buster keeping it now?"

Cohen tried to look innocent. "Is that his name?" he asked.

Dennis looked around amiably. "I see you're not keeping up with the fire regulations, Cohen. They could make you a lot of trouble for that."

"A man can't do everything!" Cohen cried in anguish. "Here I am trying to make a living, an' just gettin' by, an' you come around talkin' about fire regulations! Ain't it enough, I ask you, that we got a depression an' no business, without bein' hounded for a little thing like that?"

Dennis smiled grimly. "Nobody's hounding you—yet. Now if you were to do us a favor, we might feel the same way about you."

Cohen was no fool. But he was unwilling to talk. He weakened however as Dennis sent a searching look around the shadowy interior of the garage. "Sure, I do you any favors I can," he assented hastily.

"Jog your memory about Moran and his car. Where is it?"

"Honest, it ain't here any more!" Cohen insisted. "He ain't kept it here for months."

"Come on—kick through! Where does he keep it then?" Dennis snapped. "Play ball, or you'll be sorry. We want a line on Moran quick."

Cohen sighed, looked around, lowered his voice. "You keep this confidential?" he begged.

"Certainly."

"Well then, I took a new battery over to his car about a week ago. He's keepin' it in a little private garage just off Grand Street. You go to Sixth, an' in the middle of the block you turn into the alley an' go halfway back. There's an old brick building there. It used to be a bottling plant, but they've took the machinery out an' turned it into a garage.

An' that's all I know about it if I die an' lose my business for saying so."

"Have you got a telephone?" Sardi demanded.

Cohen shrugged.

"I just wanted to tell you that if they know we're on our way over there, you might have some trouble after all," Sardi promised as he turned to the door with Dennis.

Ten minutes later the police car parked fifty feet down the alley from the bottling plant. It was a long, one-story brick building, old, battered, in disrepair. A large pair of sliding doors filled the end. One of the doors had a smaller one set in it to admit pedestrians.

Dennis tried the knob of that door. It opened with the rusty grating of unoiled hinges. He stepped in, hand ready on his gun. Deep gloom filled the interior, broken somewhat by the illumination that came through the open door.

"Here we are," said Dennis with satisfaction.

Three machines were parked inside. A coupe, a large powerful sedan—and a small light delivery truck with an enclosed body. The truck was nearest the door, directly in front of them.

The garage seemed deserted. No one challenged their presence. Dennis went to the truck door and opened it expectantly. The inside was empty.

And as he stared in it with acute disappointment, Sardi uttered an oath. "There's blood all over the floor here!" Sardi exclaimed excitedly. "Fresh blood!"

THERE it was by the side of the truck, beneath Sardi's pointing finger. A dripping trail of fresh blood that led toward the back and ended in a little pool against the side wall. It was easy to read that a man had been wounded, had staggered back toward the car, and had fallen against the wall.

But where was the body now?

They both had their guns out now. They went over every corner of that garage. A solid brick fire wall separated this back part of the long building from the front. The only way to get out and in was through the doors that had admitted them. And they were the only ones in the garage.

Sardi peered under the truck. "What's this?" he said.

He knelt, reached under, and pulled a small dark object out. And as the light fell on it, Sardi uttered a gasp and dropped it.

"Holy cats!" he choked. "Will you take a look at that? Am I seeing things, or is that a head?"

Sardi's explosive words, the look of horror on his face were so intense that Dennis sprang to see what was the matter. An oath of surprise broke from him too as he saw the thing Sardi had pulled out from under the truck.

It was a head.

A human head, lying there on the floor, withered, dry, ghastly. The eyes were cavernous sockets. Dark, discolored parchmentlike skin stretched rigidly over the skull bones. The dry dead lips were drawn in a tight, fixed smile, a smile that seemed to mock them both in those dim and dirty surroundings.

"Is—is it real?" Sardi gasped. "Gosh, ain't that a sweet package for a guy to pull out of the dark?"

Dennis knelt by the ghastly-looking thing and touched it. "It's real," he declared.

Sardi mopped his face. "Where did it come from?" he anguished. "Where's the body. How'd a thing like that ever get in here? Lord, what a hall of horrors this dump turned out to be. Fresh blood and old human heads, an'—an'—"

"And a couple of scared cops," Dennis chuckled. "Sardi, do you know what this is?"

"It's a head, ain't it?"

"Sure. But what kind of a head?"

"A human head. You said so yourself."

Dennis sighed. "Sardi, if I didn't know you were a good cop I'd wonder how such a bonehead ever got in the department. Take a good look at it. Did you ever see a head like this before?"

"Well," said Sardi doubtfully, "in a museum once I saw a mummy with a mug which wasn't no better than this one."

"And there you are," said Dennis, getting to his feet. "A mummy. What is it Professor Richfield collects?"

"Old things."

"Exactly. He's an antiquarian. And that box Wee Willie Watson got from the express office this morning looked like a coffin. It could have held a mummy case very easily."

Sardi took a deep breath. "If that ain't fast head work, inspector," he admired. "Do you think that guy got a mummy out of the express office?"

"This is where the stolen box wound up," Dennis pointed out. "And here is a mummy's head on the floor. All fresh and ancient."

"That blood on the floor didn't come out of the mummy," Sardi declared.

"And the mummy didn't pick up his box and walk out with it either," Dennis said gravely. He chuckled as Sardi looked at him suspiciously. "Moran, or some of his men, hijacked a mummy, we'll say. They brought it here. They took it out of the box. And then—trouble hit 'em. Someone was wounded. The mummy disappeared. And the wounded man or men went too."

Sardi scratched his head. "Will you tell me," he asked plaintively, "why any-

one would want to cop a mummy? They couldn't sell it. Any ham could finally trace it down. A mummy ain't no good for anything. And yet one guy we know of is knocked off. Maybe some more—all on account of a mummy!"

"That's the little question we have to solve," Dennis sighed. "First, we want a line on what happened here. That fire wall cuts off the front of the building from this part. But an auto had to drive up to the door to carry the case away. If we can find someone who saw it there, we might get a line on it."

"We won't," Sardi prophesied.

"We'll try anyway. Come on."

THE two of them went up and down both sides of the alley, knocking on doors, prying into the backs of shops, stores, and two restaurants; asking if anyone had heard shots, or had been out in the alley while a car or men were around the back of the garage.

No one had heard shots; no one had seen anything. It appeared that the alley was a lonely and deserted land into which people rarely ventured and in which they had no interest. In other words the quick intensive hunt for a clue fizzled and flopped.

They met at the end of the alley, where it debouched into the street.

"Not a nibble," Sardi confessed.

"Dry pickings," Dennis agreed.

"What next, inspector?"

"God knows," said Dennis. "Stand still, Sardi! No—don't look around!"

Sardi froze. His face was a study. "What is it?" he begged.

Sardi's back was to the length of the alley. He had not seen the automobile swing in from the next street and stop with a jerk before the garage. A man got out, hurriedly opened the door and stepped inside.

"Come on." Dennis snapped. "Somebody just went in there!"

Sardi wasted no time in idle questions as they ran along the alley. The automobile was a modest coupé that might have belonged to any respectable citizen of the town. But the man who violently opened the door and plunged out into Dennis did not look like a respectable citizen.

"What the hell!" the stranger swore as Dennis' arms clamped around him. "Leggo, damn you!"

Dennis clasped him close in a loving embrace. "Look what the little birds dropped for us!" he chortled. "Frisk 'im, Sardi!"

Sardi had already slid in behind and dropped a hamlike hand roughly on the writhing stranger's neck. "I got him," Sardi said with satisfaction. "Frisk him from the front, inspector."

They worked with the precision of a well-drilled team. It was all over in a few moments. Dennis took a revolver off the captive.

"Now ain't this a sweet toy?" He admired it.

"And him carrying it around in broad daylight too," Sardi grieved, shaking his captive by the nape of the neck playfully, until the other's teeth threatened to loosen. "I'll bet he's a bad man."

"Hey, what the h-h-hell! Lay off-t-that, damn you!" the stranger stuttered angrily.

He was a pudgy, smudgy little fellow, needing a shave and a haircut. His skin was pasty white, with an unhealthy yellow tinge. His pants were baggy at the knees, and his fingernails clamored silently for a manicure.

"He swears," Sardi sighed as he whirled the prisoner around to the open door. "I know he's bad now. Inside, mister." Sardi booted the captive callously through the doorway with his knee, still keeping hold of his neck.

"You got no right to do this to me!" the prisoner wailed angrily. "I haven't done anything. You lousy cops think you can get by with murder! Leggo my neck!"

Dennis stepped inside too and fingered the revolver meditatively. "I wonder if we could get by with murder in here," he said to Sardi. "I'll bet we could. A good sock on the head with this ought to do it, and we could drive away in his car."

"We could stow him in the truck there and nobody would find his body for a long while," Sardi nodded gravely; and then his shoulders shook and his chest heaved as he chuckled. "Wouldn't it be a joke on Moran if he drove around town with a body in the back of his truck?"

Dennis cocked the revolver deliberately and grinned. "I can see Buster's face now. You know, I believe we could shoot him and no one would hear it. The alley's empty now."

The prisoner looked wildly into their faces. His pasty pallor increased. "You guys are kiddin' me," he begged hoarsely.

"Sure. We're only kidding you." Dennis agreed amiably. "Take him over to the side of the truck there, Sardi. We won't have to lift him so far to get him in."

"You can't do this!" the prisoner choked. "What's the idea? Who are you two?"

"We catch bad men," Sardi declared as he shoved the prisoner to the truck. "You're one, ain't you?"

"I don't know what you're talkin' about! I'm a salesman! I came here on business!"

"What do you sell?"

"Men's and ladies' hose! I can prove it! My sample case is out there in the car!"

SARDI cast a troubled glance past the captive's shoulder. Dennis saw Sardi was worried for fear they were working this grim and frightening farce on an innocent man. But one look at the captive made Dennis sure they had little to fear on that score. Nevertheless he stepped out to the car beyond the door and looked inside.

A leather sample case rested on the seat. When he opened it he saw that the case was filled with samples of silk and woolen hose. It held an order book too, with a notation printed in ink on the inside cover—Property of Joe Conte.

Dennis took the case into the garage. "Is your name Joe Conte?" he asked the captive.

"Yes!" the other nodded violently.

"What were you doing in here?"

"I—I stepped in to see if there was anyone in here who wanted to buy some socks. I call on people that way."

"And give a little sales talk with this gun?"

"No! I carry that in case I get into trouble at night. I have to go in some pretty tough places to get money," Conte explained hurriedly. "I came in here and saw that thing—that head—on the floor, an' I got out as quick as I could."

"Did you have an appointment with Buster Moran?"

"Who's he?" Conte asked blankly. "I never heard of him. No, sir—I never heard of him! Is he the guy who owns this place?"

Conte's eyes shifted away from Dennis' steady stare. His statement made Dennis certain he was lying. The sample case was a puzzler though. Conte evidently did sell stockings. The case showed signs of much wear. But why the gun, and the visit to this place?

"Ever been here before?" Dennis asked him.

"No!"

Dennis hefted the revolver suggestively. "Sure you've never been here? And you don't know Moran?"

"No! I tell you I never heard of him!" Conte insisted loudly.

"I'll bet I can help his memory," Sardi volunteered, balling a big fist.

But Dennis ruled that out with a shake of his head. He wanted to go deeper into this before any such extreme measures were used. He didn't believe in them anyway.

"I'll ride down to headquarters with him," he told Sardi. "You get a piece of paper and wrap it around that head and bring it along in our car. The coroner won't need to look at it. The death occurred before he was appointed."

Conte protested excitedly: "You can't arrest me! I ain't done anything!"

"You'd be surprised what we can do," Dennis assured him. "Scram out in that car of yours and drive to headquarters. And no monkey business."

Conte slid sullenly behind the wheel of his car and drove off silently. At headquarters Dennis booked him on a charge of carrying concealed weapons. Conte was a changed man now that he was away from the fear of personal violence. He became loud and vociferous in his demand to see his lawyer.

"Who is your lawyer?" Dennis asked curiously.

"Leo Garrity," Conte stated. Fear was gone from him. He seemed almost jaunty as he showed unclean teeth in a derisive grin. "Just tell him Joe Conte, the sock salesman, is in here and wants him. He'll be right over."

LEO GARRITY—one of the biggest criminal mouthpieces in town. Dennis had found out what he wanted. Conte's choice of a lawyer placed him. He looked at the little man with more respect —grimmer respect. Leo Garrity's services came high. A door-to-door salesman such as Conte claimed to be would never be able to afford the services of a lawyer like Garrity. Unless there was something crooked about him. Dennis was certain now that he had struck a hot trail. He reached for a telephone and called Garrity.

"We've got a sock salesman at headquarters by the name of Joe Conte," he said. "Booking him on a charge of carrying a concealed weapon. He said to send for you. How about it?"

"I'll be right over," Garrity answered briskly, without asking any further questions.

Conte sneered as Dennis hung up. "Well?" he demanded.

"He'll be over," Dennis said.

"Yeah? I told you so!" Conte lit a cigarette and swaggered to a chair.

Dennis watched him thoughtfully. Leo Garrity hadn't even asked a question. There was money involved in this case in some way. Garrity wouldn't make a move for his own father without big money.

Sardi came in, gingerly carrying a bundle wrapped in grimy papers. "Here it is," he said distastefully. "It rolled out of the papers once and I'll swear it winked at me. I'm going to take a couple of men back to that joint and look it over." He went out.

A few minutes later Leo Garrity came in hurriedly. He was a short, sleek, pompous and vain fellow, with a brain as keen as a sharpened blade. Conte was still sitting in the chair. He started up eagerly as Garrity entered. Garrity waved him back and paid no further attention to him. His attitude was almost contemptuous.

"Suppose you get bail set for him and I'll arrange it," he said briskly to Dennis.

"Maybe we don't want him admitted to bail," Dennis said calmly.

"You can't help yourself," Garrity informed him bluntly. "This is a bailable charge, and as his attorney I insist on it. Otherwise I'll jerk him out on a habeas-corpus writ."

Nevertheless Garrity looked surprised when Dennis nodded agreeably and said: "All right. You win. Take him before Judge Brown and have bail set. I'll be up there in a minute."

When lawyer and client were out the door on their way to Judge Brown's court on the third floor, Dennis said under his breath to Pratt, behind the counter: "Have that guy tailed when he goes out."

Pratt nodded understandingly, and Dennis went up to court too. There they quickly got a hearing before Judge Brown. The judge looked at the revolver Dennis showed him, asked the prisoner a few questions, heard Conte's voluble explanations and denials that he had been doing anything wrong, and set bail at three hundred dollars.

A bondsman quickly made the bail on Garrity's say-so. Lawyer and client walked out together. And there was a sneering smile on Conte's face as he turned away from Dennis.

Dennis was thoughtful as he walked back into the front office. Pratt said: "You let that guy slip away easy. Didn't you want him bad?"

"I'd rather get a line on him," Dennis replied. "Give a crook rope, you know, and he'll do something with it. I figure this is a case where a lot of loose rope is needed."

"Say," said Pratt, remembering suddenly, "while you were up in court a man named Richfield called in. He said you wanted to see him, and he would show up here in a few minutes to talk to you."

"That's a break," said Dennis. "I'll be glad to see him."

CHAPTER FIVE

Enter the Professor

PROFESSOR Adam Richfield proved to be a tall, spare, ascetic-looking man with carefully brushed hair beneath a sober black hat, and peering eyes that gazed unwinkingly through precise eyeglasses balanced on his bony nose. He came into the office carrying a leather briefcase which he laid on the counter as he shook hands with Dennis. A limp, pallid shake it was, too, a shake that seemeu to fit the professor's rather unctuous voice.

"I'm sorry I missed you at the house, Inspector Breen," he smiled thinly, taking a rather gaudily bordered silk handkerchief from his pocket and polishing his glasses vigorously. "I ran over to the Sheridan Museum for two hours to chat with the curator of their Egyptian section. And when I got back I found that my man had not come from the station with the box I sent him to get, and that you had been there on police business."

Professor Richfield set the glasses firmly on his nose with both hands and peered through them with a troubled look.

"May I ask, Inspector Breen, if there is anything wrong?" he questioned anxiously. "Watson should have been back hours ago with that box. I can't think what may have detained him. It's queer—mighty queer, taken in connection with your telephone call from the express office. I don't know what to make of it. It has me worried. That's why I drove in here to talk with you personally."

"What was in that box your man got from the express office?" Dennis queried.

"A mummy, inspector."

"It's a queer shipment to be receiving," Dennis commented.

Professor Richfield nodded. "Yes, I quite agree with you. Queer for anyone but a museum to be receiving. But you see I get many queer things. The study and collection of ancient relics is my hobby and my profession. Fortunately I am blessed with enough of this world's goods to indulge in it; and I supplement my income in no mean way by disposing of part of my importations to museums and other collectors at a handsome profit. That mummy, for instance, I had hoped to sell to the Sheridan Museum after I had kept it for a time in my own collection. Professor Courtney Hyde of their Egyptian section had virtually assured me that the budget this year would allow the purchase of a good mummy to round out their collection."

The professor's friendly smile gave way to anxiety again.

"Do you think Watson could have betrayed his trust and stolen that mummy? Although I can't see what he could do with it."

"No. He didn't steal it. He was stopped on the street, killed, and the mummy stolen from him," Dennis said calmly.

Professor Richfield started back. "What? You can't mean that! Surely you're joking, sir!"

"It's the truth."

"Why, this is ghastly! Terrible! I don't know what to think of it! Indeed I don't. Who did it, inspector?"

"We don't know."

"But surely, sir, you have some idea who it was? You must get the men! And why did they steal a mummy? They can do nothing with it! You can't mean to tell me they murdered poor Watson over a thing like that!"

"All we know is that the man was killed and the box he carried in his truck was taken."

Professor Richfield was gripped by a

sudden thought. "Perhaps this is an old underworld feud," he suggested. "You see, I know all about Watson. He was frank with me. Perhaps they didn't know what they were taking."

"We've thought of that—and it doesn't seem to hold water," Dennis told him. "Who knew that shipment was coming in, professor?"

"No one. I don't think Watson even knew what he was sent to get."

Two plainclothesmen came in, and Dennis took his man back in the inner office and sat down in a chair.

"Why did you call the express office and try to stop Watson from leaving with the box?" he asked abruptly. His eyes riveted on the professor's face as he waited for an answer.

"I don't wonder that you ask that, inspector. The truth is, I had another errand I wanted Watson to do first. I had purchased a wall case from a second-hand dealer, and wanted it out at the house at once. There wasn't room in the truck for both, and I wanted Watson to bring the wall case out first."

IT WAS a frank and convincing explanation—yet Dennis was certain it was not true. It didn't explain the professor's agitation at the time, or his request about getting away without trouble. But Dennis gave no sign of his inner thoughts. He smiled blandly.

"That's understandable," he agreed. "What about Finger Sammy Jackson?"

The professor did not bat an eye. "Who?" he asked with a puzzled look.

"Finger Sammy Jackson, the man I saw out at your house when I was there."

"Ah—that has puzzled me," the professor confessed. "Marta, my niece, told me that you had asked about a man she knew nothing about. Granting that your eyes did not play you tricks, inspector, who was the man?"

"A crook," Dennis said bluntly.

"*Hmmm.*" The professor shook his head in a puzzled manner—then brightened. "I have it!" he exclaimed. "The man must have been a friend of Watson's, who slipped around there to see him. He was probably afraid to knock at the door and inquire, and was lurking around outside waiting for Watson."

That explanation had not occurred to Dennis. Was it true, he wondered. Then he thought of the furtive glance he had surprised through the front window. Dennis sighed to himself. No matter which way he turned he met baffling mystery.

The office door opened. Pratt looked in. "I thought you'd like to know, inspector. The eighth precinct just telephoned in and said one of the patrolmen found a dead body in a patch of weeds off Sherry Road. Harris, their plainclothesman, has identified it as Pete Crosby, a pal of Buster Moran's. His head was bashed in. Been dead two or three hours."

"Another one!" Dennis groaned. He slid a glance to Professor Richfield—and surprised more than a flicker of interest.

The professor pressed his thin lips together. "Isn't there an unusual run of criminal activity today?" he questioned.

Dennis nodded. "Plenty." It was on the tip of his tongue to spring suddenly the name of Buster Moran, but he did not. He excused himself and stepped out into the outer office, closing the door behind him. The two plainclothesmen were still there, talking.

"Lay out on the sidewalk and tail this fellow I'm talking to," Dennis ordered them.

He was lighting a cigarette as he returned. "We're doing all we can to recover your property and solve the killing of your man," he stated. "I think we'll make some progress. If we could get our hands on this Finger Sammy who was hanging around your place, he might be able to give us a clue about Watson. I'm inclined to think you're right. Finger Sammy must have made a special trip out there to warn him of some trouble."

"Quite right," Professor Richfield beamed, getting to his feet and tucking his briefcase under his arm. "You'll send out a general alarm for him, I suppose?"

"We know where he hangs out," Dennis smiled. "We'll watch those places. He'll probably show up this evening."

Professor Richfield smiled too. "I hope so. Now inspector, I think I shall offer a reward of a hundred dollars for the recovery of the mummy. And another hundred for the apprehension of Watson's killer. It isn't much, but it may stimulate some of your men to greater efforts."

"They appreciate little things like that," Dennis beamed. "Two hundred dollars is a lot of money to a dick. I'll spread the word."

"And if you find out anything, let me know at once," the professor begged, offering his hand once more. "I'm tremendously interested."

"We'll keep in close touch with you," Dennis promised heartily—and grinned to himself as his visitor's long lean figure went out. Those two men waiting outside would certainly keep in very close touch with the professor.

A few moments later Dennis was issuing orders that Finger Sammy was to be picked up and brought in as soon as sighted.

His next move was to call the Sheridan Museum and ask for Professor Hyde, the curator of the Egyptian section. "Is Professor Adam Richfield still there?" he asked that gentleman.

"Why, no, sir. He hasn't been here for several days," the curator told him.

"I was informed that he was spending part of the afternoon talking with you, Professor Hyde," Dennis said gently.

"There must be a mistake," Professor Hyde returned. "I haven't seen Richfield for days. Who is this talking, please?"

"Western Union," Dennis lied shamelessly. "We are trying to deliver a telegram. Thank you."

He hung up, well satisfied. Richfield had lied about being at the museum. Where had he been while he was away from his house? And why had he lied?

HALF an hour later Sardi was back from the garage. "We got some good prints off the automobiles," he said with satisfaction. "And that ain't all. Look at this. I found it in the door pocket of one of the cars." Sardi laid an order book of the Paree Hosiery Company on the desk.

"So Conte was lying," Dennis said thoughtfully. "I had a pretty good idea he was."

"Let's work on him and get the truth out of him," Sardi suggested.

"I let him go."

"Huh? You let him go? Why?"

"Leo Garrity came over and bailed him out. I had a man tail them away."

Sardi whistled softly. "Leo Garrity, eh? He comes high."

"That's why I let Conte go. There's something big behind all this. Richfield came in too, and said the stolen box contained a mummy. We were right there. He's offered a reward for its recovery."

"How much for the head alone?" Sardi asked practically.

"I didn't tell him we had it. He lied to me about where he was this afternoon. There's something queer about him, too."

"Any bird who'd import a mummy is queer," Sardi grumbled. "Listen, we're not getting anywhere with this case. I hear they found one of Moran's buddies dead. That's tied up with this. I'll bet my hat. It makes two knocked off today. As soon as the papers get hold of a few facts they'll start the ballyhoo. We've got to make an arrest that'll stick."

Dennis grinned as he took a cigar from a box in the desk drawer. He bit off the end and scratched a match. "I'm hoping," he said.

"Hopes won't get us anywhere," Sardi snorted.

The buzzer from the outer office rang, signal that someone was on the telephone. Dennis answered it, listened for a few moments, and said: "All right. Keep an eye on him." Then he hung up and said to Sardi: "That was a report on Conte. He left here with his lawyer. They went to the corner, talked rapidly for a few minutes, and then separated. Conte went from there to the office of the Paree Hosiery Company, and he's still there. They've got an office on the third floor of the Mutual Bank Building."

"I'm going to get a line on that outfit," Sardi promised. "Socks don't pay enough to hire Leo Garrity." He went out.

Another hour passed. The afternoon was rapidly drawing to a close. Twilight was falling. Dennis sat in his office conning every angle of the affair, trying to chart a course that would lead to the truth. And more and more he began to believe that the truth would be startling.

Sardi came back in and threw himself down in a chair. "I checked on that sock outfit. They're a local concern. Buy their stuff in big lots with their names on the labels, and sell it out from house to house through peddlers. The head of it is listed as Albert Strauss. They never borrow money and they seem to be in a pretty good financial condition. At least the credit association has nothing against them. They've been doing business about two years. No one seems to know much

about the company, or about Strauss who owns it."

"He may be all right," Dennis admitted. "But that doesn't say that everyone who works for him is."

The door opened and the two detectives Dennis had sent after Professor Adam Richfield came into the office.

"Here they are!" Dennis greeted. "I've been waiting for you two birds. What did you find out?"

"He got in an auto down the street," Stone, the oldest of the two, said. "There was a fellow at the wheel. Mike's car was parked a little ahead of it, an' we got out after them all right. They went across town, and the driver went into a speakie just off Eighth. He came out with another man, an' the three of them drove around town for a while. They stopped finally and all three of them went into the Mutual Building. Mike got up the stairs almost as fast as the elevator, and saw them go into an office on the third floor. The sign on the door says Paree Hosiery Company."

"Well, fairy godmothers and goldfish!" Dennis breathed. "Also bless my heart! Professor Richfield went into the Paree Hosiery Company, did he? And then what?"

"All three of 'em stayed there about ten minutes," Mike said. "Then they got back in their car and went out on the north side to a house on Berkeley Drive."

"A big frame house set back in a lot of trees?" Dennis guessed.

Mike nodded. "They all went in, and they looked like they were staying for a while, so we pulled out."

"Sardi, do you get that?" Dennis grinned. "Conte and Professor Richfield got together."

"They say oil and water don't mix, but looks like they did this time," Sardi grunted. "I don't get it. What business would this professor have with Conte?"

"Don't know, but he had some," said Dennis, getting up. "And that's where we come in. Let's get to work."

"It's supper time," Sardi objected.

"Not for us."

"Where you going?"

"To the Paree Sock Company," Dennis grinned. "And we won't talk socks."

CHAPTER SIX

Smooth as Silk

THE office of the Paree Hosiery Company was closed. There was not even a light inside the opaque glass of the door. After six the Mutual Building seemed deserted.

Dennis fished in his pocket and brought out a huge bunch of keys. "Here is where an honest cop commits a little breaking and entering," he said to Sardi. And he tried keys in succession until he found one to fit the door. They walked in. Dennis calmly felt for the light switch and turned on the light.

"We look honest now," he chuckled. "Wipe that anxious look off your face, Sardi. It isn't as bad as that."

"It won't be so hot if we're caught in here without a search warrant," Sardi gloomed.

"We'll arrest ourselves for them," Dennis comforted.

A glass showcase filled with samples of socks and stockings stretched in front of them. The wall behind it was covered with shelves piled high with cardboard hosiery boxes. Several chairs stood on each side of the door. And at one end of the rear wall a door gave entrance into a private office.

"Nothing phony about this place," Sardi pointed out.

"And that's why I'm curious about it, my boy. I wonder what we have in the back."

They entered a plainly furnished office with a wooden desk near the windows and a large stout steel safe against the opposite wall. There was a table, and some magazines, a leather-covered couch and a deep easy chair. Two telephones were on the desk. And over the desk, looking benignly down upon them, was a large framed copy of the Stuart portrait of George Washington.

Dennis squinted at it. "They must be all right, with George watching everything they do," he murmured. "Now you take this safe . . . " He walked over to it as he spoke. "They must make a lot of money to need a safe this big."

Dennis fingered the knurled combination knob. "Wish there was some way of getting inside it, Sardi. I'll bet we'd be surprised ourselves."

"You can't get in there," Sardi argued.

"That's why I want to," Dennis grinned.

Sardi jumped as one of the telephones rang loudly.

"You need your supper. You're getting nervous," Dennis chided. He went to the telephone and lifted the receiver. "Paree Socks," he said genially.

A woman's voice, sharp and strained, burst out: "Thank God! I called a few minutes ago and couldn't get anyone! Listen, I want a pair of silk stockings right away."

"Uh—sorry, but we can't get them to you right away," Dennis replied. "You see, this is after hours."

"I thought you never closed until midnight!" she stormed at him. "Listen, I'm all out of stockings! I've got to have a pair right away or I can't last out the night! I'll pay you double price for them! Do you hear me? Double price! But send them up immediately! Miss Alice Donnelly, 341 Platton Arms. Better make it two pairs. I've got the money right here."

The voice coming over the wire sounded very close to hysteria. So strained, so tense, so near the breaking point that Dennis feared an explosion even as he talked.

"All right," he agreed hastily. "We'll get you some stockings. What size and colors, please?"

"Don't kid me!" the woman said hysterically, and slammed up the receiver.

"Whew!" Dennis breathed as he hung up. "That's a sweet one. And it's got me guessing. She'll have kittens unless we bring over some stockings right away. She'll pay double price for them, and won't give size or color."

"Maybe she's kidding you," Sardi suggested.

"Not that woman," Dennis said gravely. "She's in a bad way. It's another queer thing. Let's take her over some. I saw a sample case back of the counter in there."

Dennis took the leather sample case, which looked very like the one Joe Conte had carried. He looked for the order book, and found that it resembled Conte's also. Taking a box of ladies' sheer silk hose from a shelf, and the sample case, Dennis went out with Sardi, locking the door behind him.

THE Platton Arms was a big modern apartment house in a well-to-do part of the city. Five stories high, it covered the whole block, with wings and landscaped courts.

Sardi grumbled as they went in: "It looks to me like a dame living here would have all the stockings she needed. She wouldn't buy them from a peddler anyway."

"Right as always," Dennis agreed. "But she evidently does, just the same."

An elevator took them to the third floor. A long walk through wide halls brought them finally to a solid wooden door numbered 341. Dennis knocked.

The door was snatched open before his knuckles left it. "Come in," a husky, strained voice ordered.

The woman standing back to admit them was clad in an expensive silken kimono. Her hair was down in an untidy mess. Her thin face looked as though it needed washing. And more—it was strained, drawn. Her mouth and nose were twitching nervously. Her fingers kept closing and unclosing spasmodically. And her narrowed eyes surveyed them suspiciously.

"What are two of you doing here?" she demanded warily.

"Breaking in a new man," Dennis explained calmly.

"I've never seen you before either."

"I've never been around in this neighborhood," Dennis answered. "You said you had to have service right away, and we were the only ones in the office."

Her eyes searched his face, dropped to the black sample case he carried. She seemed reassured as she closed the door and led them into a small living room. It was as untidy as she was.

"All right, let me have it," she jerked out, opening a table drawer and taking out a wad of bills.

Dennis laid the box of stockings on the table. "You didn't say what size and color, miss. Will these do?"

She snatched the box open, pawed through the stockings. Her face twisted with anger. She threw it on the floor. "Don't kid me!" she shrilled. "I'm getting the jerks already! Give me the stuff! Hurry!"

She was half sobbing. In her excitement she seized the black sample case from Dennis and opened it with trembling fingers. Her hand darted down inside to a secret pocket that Dennis had not noticed. And it came out holding a small flat paper-wrapped packet. She snapped off a rubber band, opened the paper and poured a dash of white powder on the back of her hand. She sniffed hungrily at it.

Both Dennis and Sardi stood frozen, watching her. Both knew what they were witnessing. That packet held heroin—"snow" in the argot. The woman was an addict who had gone too long without her drug. She had been tottering on the edge of the horrors that would inevitably follow if she did not get her dose.

But now a magic peace began to come over her. The harsh, strained lines in her face started to smooth out. The trembling of her hands passed. Her shoulders came back from their slump. She lifted a hand and brushed at her hair. She took a deep breath of relief, laughed shortly.

"That's better," she remarked. "Lord, I was getting the jerks. I thought I had enough to do me, but I didn't. And when I called the office, no one answered. I'll take another deck while you're here."

Without asking permission she fumbled in the sample case, brought out another packet. She stripped off three bills and thrust them into Dennis' hand.

Sardi started to say something, and then did not as Dennis gave him a warning glance. Dennis pocketed the bills and looked into the sample case. There were four more packets in the little concealed pocket. He closed the sample case.

"Call us any time," he said gently as he turned toward the door.

"Sure. I've been doing it for a year," she said nonchalantly. "Your service is good. Here, better take your stockings."

"You can have them," Dennis said from the doorway. "And I hope they fit."

Not a word passed between Dennis and Sardi until they were in the police car. And then Dennis said dreamily: "I knew there ought to be something interesting in that safe. No wonder Leo Garrity jumped when I called him about Conte. Sock peddler my eye! They're probably rolling in

coin. It's big, Sardi. Big! Think of it! Their peddlers covering the whole city. Orders coming in over the telephones. And everyone who sees their delivery men thinking nothing but socks. What a bunch of saps they've made out of the whole department."

"That office is probably crammed with the stuff," Sardi speculated eagerly. "We can get a search warrant and an order to open that safe, and have it all in a few hours."

"Whoa! Not so fast. We've got other things to do too. There have been two killings today. We've got to walk softly or we'll lose out on them. Are you forgetting that Brother Adam Richfield visited that office?"

"I was wondering about him," Sardi confessed. "What do you suppose he was doing there? Buying snow?"

"We'll go ask him," Dennis said.

STREET lights were few and far between out on North Berkeley Drive. Dark shadows lay thick and heavy. Dennis drove slowly past Professor Richfield's home. Thin streaks of light at many windows showed the big house to be brightly lighted inside. Dennis cut the motor at his earlier stopping place. Leaving the car, they climbed the hill as Dennis had done before, and came cautiously down toward the back of the house.

The moon had not yet come up. A dark scud of clouds across the sky hid most of the stars. The flashlight from the police car lighted their way to the top of the hill, but from there they picked a slow and uncertain way in the darkness. Twigs snapped under their feet. A wind rustled the foliage of the big trees around the house. Those were the only sounds about them.

The big garage loomed up before them. Beyond was the massive rise of the house, its curtained windows seeping threads of light into the black night. The place seemed doubly lonesome in the darkness.

Their feet scrapped softly on the gravel of the driveway leading past the house. Dennis used his flash once, for an instant. The brief stab of light showed three cars parked at the side of the drive before the house. He swore at himself and hoped no chauffeurs were in those cars. Evidently such was the case, for no sign of life followed. But something else did.

A woman screamed inside the house.

"What the hell!" Sardi uttered at his side in a startled voice.

Dennis felt his heart stand still for a moment as that muted cry for help came sharp and desperate to his ears. Someone was being hurt, was mortally afraid. And in the next moment he threw aside all pretense of secrecy abandoned the idea of looking the place over carefully before they showed themselves. Switching on the flashlight, he ran for the long, wide front porch, with Sardi pounding after him.

As they reached the corner of the porch a window crashed out above it. Glass showered over the roof. A shaft of light streamed out into the night. Dodging back and looking up, Dennis saw a big figure plunge out of the window, scramble across the porch roof, drop legs and torso over the edge. It hung there for a moment and then kicked out, landing heavily on the ground.

The flashlight in Dennis' hand picked out the man clearly. "That's Buster Moran!" Dennis rapped to Sardi. He grabbed for his service revolver.

Moran staggered to his feet. Dennis got one good look at his contorted face. It was streaked with blood. His chest was heaving. And his hands were manacled together!

"Moran—come here! What's the matter?" Dennis called, forgetting that Moran could not see him in the darkness.

Moran ducked and dashed toward the street, holding his manacled hands in front of him for balance. Three steps he took—and then there was a dull *pop* close to Dennis. Moran staggered, lurched forward, and fell flat on the ground.

He tried to struggle up. He got to one knee, to his feet. He took one wobbling step and went down again. From the ground he called in a hoarse bellow of defiance: "All right, you damn rats—come and get me! I can take it!"

He had been shot. There had been no gun fired. But—that *pop*...

Dennis heard Sardi give a strangled grunt behind him. He whirled to see the cause. One glimpse he caught of a shadowy figure standing over a huddled man on the ground. And another one—right beside him. Before Dennis could move something struck his head a terrific blow. The night burst into a whirl of flying lights, and Dennis didn't even know that he fell...

CHAPTER SEVEN

House of the Withered Dead

THAT *pop* he had heard close to him must have been a revolver with a silencer attached. As Dennis came to, that thought was running through his mind.

Something was rubbing his face violently. He stirred, opened his eyes. Everything was black. The rubbing on his face stopped. He tried to move his left arm and found that the wrist was attached to something.

A husky whisper spoke against his ear. "You all right, inspector?"

"Guess so," Dennis muttered. "Where are we?"

"Somewhere in Richfield's house, I guess. They got our guns and flashlight. But I had a fountain pen flash inside my coat an' they didn't get that. I can see a barred window from here."

"That's the wing on the north side of the house," Dennis muttered. "Saw it this afternoon." He tried to sit up, and a drag on his wrist helped.

"We're handcuffed together," Sardi informed him. "Used your handcuffs, I guess. I didn't have mine with me."

"What happened?" Dennis asked. His head ached badly. He was still a little groggy.

"Somebody cracked us from behind. They musta carried us in here. I didn't come out of it more'n five minutes before you did. This place is silent as a tomb. I couldn't get up and look around unless I carried you. I been trying to bring you to so we can get some action."

"Flash your light around."

Sardi did that. They were in the corner of a long, wide, high-ceilinged room. A window close to them was barred stoutly. A high wooden-backed case shut off their view of the rest of the room.

"We're locked in tighter than the Siamese twins," Sardi said disgustedly. "And if you ask me, we're in a bad way. Richfield knows you. He wouldn't do this if he figured we were going back to headquarters tonight."

"Or any other night," Dennis added. "That was Moran who jumped off the roof. They shot him. We know too much now to be let loose. Let's see what chance we have to get out of here. Wait—I've just thought of something! Let me see if my billfold is still on me."

"Fat chance you'll have to bribe your way out!" Sardi said gloomily. "And they got your keys. I've already searched you for them."

Dennis gave a grunt of satisfaction as his free hand located his billfold. He pulled it out, placed it on his knees in the darkness and fumbled in it with his free hand.

"Here it is," he said with relief.

"What?"

"An extra key to these cuffs. I lost a key once and had to have the cuffs filed off a prisoner. I decided not to do that again, so I always carry an extra key in my billfold. They didn't find it."

"Well, I'll be jiggered!" Sardi exploded under his breath. "If you've got a key, use it quick! We'll get somewhere after all."

Dennis fumbled in the dark, located the keyhole—and the cuffs clicked free. Sardi stripped them off. They got to their feet.

"They took our guns," Sardi said under his breath. "If we had them it would be a cinch."

They moved out from the corner where they had been dumped. Sardi's flash winked across the room. "Barred windows there too," he said bitterly. "No wonder they left us in here alone." And then Sardi gasped, almost bleated. "Look at th-that!" he stuttered. "What kind of a place are we in?"

The small beam of the flash had moved on past the window and come to rest against a long, narrow wooden box standing upright against the wall. And standing in the box was a still, silent figure swathed tightly in layer upon layer of discolored cloth wrappings. The head was unwrapped—and straight into the light faced a withered, dried, ghastly face. Empty eye sockets stared toward them. Still lips seemed pursed to speak, and yet the silence of centuries lay on them.

Dennis felt the short hairs at the back of his neck prickle. A cold chill went down his spine. The chill air of this musty room seemed suddenly to reek with horror.

With an effort he threw off the feeling. "That's only a mummy," he chuckled drily. "Look, there's another beside it. And another. . ."

"The whole damn wall's filled with them!" Sardi gulped.

AND he was right. As the flash swept down the long wall they saw case after case standing there with their ghoulish contents, the lids leaning against the wall beside them. There must have been a score or more—mummy after mummy. Some of the boxes were closed. Most of them were open. Dennis took the small flashlight and led the way softly down the row. It was eery, uncanny. Death seemed to be the motif of this room.

He directed the flashlight out into the room, saw that it was filled with many glass cases whose shelves held strange, rare objects. At the moment it was impossible to identify them.

The end mummy case was closed. Dennis tugged at the lid, and it came out easily. He uttered a smothered exclamation as he looked inside. "This one's got no head," he said tersely. "It must be the one that was at Moran's garage."

He set the lid against the wall. Standing upright in the case was perhaps the most ghoulish object of them all—a headless body. Its discolored wrappings were in a sad state, dirty, oil-splotched, with many lengths hanging free at the sides.

"Funny that head came off that way," Dennis muttered thoughtfully. "You wouldn't think it could."

He touched the body experimentally, gave it the slightest tug. And it swayed out and started to fall. Dennis pushed back hard, and was amazed to find how light the body was. There was no weight to it at all. With sudden curiosity he laid both hands on and pulled it out.

"For Pete's sake, watch out!" Sardi begged. "What's the idea?"

For answer Dennis laid the body face down on the floor and turned the flash on it. What he saw caused him to bend down and pull at the wrappings, bringing a groan of horror from Sardi. For Dennis opened a section of the back. The wrappings had been slit, the back had been cut, and carelessly pushed back in. The interior of the body was hollow.

Dennis bent lower and shoved the flash inside. Then thrust his hand in and felt around.

"Listen," Sardi pleaded hoarsely, "are you going nuts?"

"Papier mâché," Dennis chuckled.

"Huh?"

"The body is made out of papier mâché," Dennis told him.

"That head wasn't!" Sardi insisted firmly.

"No. That was real," Dennis admitted. "But I'll bet a hat it was attached to this papier mâché body. That's what made it come off so easily."

"What's the idea? That don't make sense. Do you mean somebody's been faking bodies?"

"Looks like it."

"What for?"

"I'm beginning to get an idea why," Dennis told him. "Let's see if the rest of these are fakes too."

The next mummy was papier mâché also, with a slit back and a human head. A tug loosened the head from its neck socket. But the next mummy was real. It was heavier, had not been tampered with. Hurriedly Dennis went down the line—box after box. In thirteen cases he found two more real mummies. The rest were of papier mâché, and their backs had all been opened.

The next box—the fourteenth and last but three—was closed. "See if the lid will come off," Dennis urged.

Sardi stepped to it and gave a tug. The lid stuck, then came off as Sardi jerked hard, rocking the case with the force.

"God! Look at that! Catch him!" Sardi gasped.

Tipping forward, stiff and lifeless, was

a human figure dressed in modern clothes. Dennis saw it in time to catch it, push it back to an upright position in the box. White and staring, the face looked out at them. Rigid and stiff in the box it stood. And the face was familiar.

Gazing at them with sightless eyes, Finger Sammy Jackson stood there, stiff and cold and dead.

"This is murder!" Dennis said through his teeth. "They killed him!"

"Like they're gonna kill us," said Sardi. He put the lid back in place and said through his teeth: "Like hell they will! Now we know for sure what we're up against. Let's see what we can find around here to scrap with!"

"Wait. I want to look at the rest of these." Dennis examined the three remaining boxes, but they were the same sort of cases that the first ones had been. He was frowning thoughtfully as he turned away from them and joined Sardi in a search for something with which they could fight.

A CASE of ancient Egyptian weapons solved the problem. The door was unlocked and opened easily. With a grunt of satisfaction Sardi reached in and plucked out an ancient bronze-headed battle axe. Dennis selected a bronze sword, short and wide and heavy. A deadly thing if used right.

Dennis had no illusions. Murder had been done, and another death or so wouldn't make the penalty any worse. Sardi and himself would never be allowed to leave this place alive. They knew too much.

With the weapons in their hands they made a tour of the big room. All the windows were barred with steel outside, and the windows themselves were locked. Dennis took the flashlight and examined one closely. He chuckled suddenly, took

the bronze sword, and pried the window open a few inches.

"Why do that?" Sardi grunted. "We can't get out that way."

"I think we can." Dennis chuckled again.

"How?"

"Wait and see."

"Listen, if we got a chance to get out of there, let's do it now! We can't afford to wait until they come in and stop us!"

"I think we can," Dennis repeated.

The words were hardly out of his mouth when the big room was suddenly illuminated. A key grated in the door lock.

"Quick!" Dennis snapped. "Get away from this window! Hide that axe!" He put the bronze sword down behind the nearest case hurriedly.

"I ain't gonna let this axe go!" Sardi protested.

Dennis settled that objection by grabbing the axe from Sardi's hand and putting it with the sword. And then he caught Sardi's arm and dragged him away from the spot.

They were standing in the middle of the room, Sardi red-faced and swearing under his breath, when the big door at the end of the room opened. The tall spare figure of Professor Adam Richfield entered, flanked by two men whose hands were thrust menacingly in their coat pockets. At sight of Dennis and Sardi standing there with their hands free the two men snatched short automatics from their pockets. Professor Richfield stopped short.

"Come in and make yourselves at home," Dennis invited genially. "I found another key to my handcuffs in my clothes and unlocked the cuffs. Richfield, do you always treat guests this way?"

Richfield said something to the two men, and then came forward slowly. They followed him. Obviously he was taking no chances. He adjusted his nose glasses on his bony nose and coughed.

"It was regretable," he said in his unctuous voice. "But of course when you come slipping around in the night, you must expect to be treated as common intruders. My men had no knowledge to the contrary."

Dennis waved that remark away carelessly. "Naturally," he agreed. "And now that you see the mistake, I know how you must regret it. Suppose we get out of this chamber of horrors and have the talk we came for? By the way, this is Lieutenant Sardi, of our homicide bureau. He specializes in murders."

Professor Richfield's eyes rested on Sardi contemplatively. "Very interesting," he murmured.

"Now, that little matter of Moran," Dennis went on pleasantly. "I wonder if we might talk to him?"

"I'm afraid not," the professor regretted with a shrug. "You see, he is badly wounded."

"What's going to happen to him?" Dennis inquired bluntly.

"I'm afraid he won't pull through." Professor Richfield took off his nose glasses and polished them carefully. "Most unfortunate," he sighed. "If the man had not made a break to get away he would probably be all right at the present moment, save for slight lacerations he incurred this afternoon."

"When you and your men raided his garage and took back your mummy," Dennis finished.

"You're a very astute man, aren't you, inspector?" Professor Richfield queried coldly.

"Pretty smart, if I do admit it," Dennis agreed. "I can tell you, for instance, that Moran's men hijacked your truck and stole your mummy. And you went to his garage at once and took it back. That's where you were, my friend, instead of at

the museum. And in the little scrap one of Moran's men was killed. You disposed of him by tossing him in a lot full of weeds out on Sherry Road."

"Yes, very astute," the professor murmured. But there was no warmth in his tone. Rather it had chilled. His face was set and hard.

"I wonder what you think of this," Dennis smiled. "You're tangled up in the dope selling over at the Paree Hosiery Company."

Sardi groaned. "For God's sake close your trap!" he breathed out of the corner of his mouth. "You're only making it worse! We won't have a chance now!"

"Do you know anything more?" Professor Richfield asked with dangerous politeness.

"Why, yes—if you care to hear it now. Finger Sammy Jackson tipped you off that Moran was going to hijack your truck, only he was too late for your call back to the express office to stop your man. And in return to Finger Sammy you dealt out murder, and stood him in that box over there. I might add, professor, that you're a pretty cold-blooded customer, and I'll get a certain degree of satisfaction in seeing you draw the death sentence."

THAT shot went home. The professor's face twisted in a spasm of anger. But it smoothed out quickly. "No doubt you will," he agreed. "Do you two bright headquarters men know anything else?"

Sardi's fingers were digging into Dennis' arm, importuning him to stop this rash and reckless talking. Sardi could see clearly what it was doing. And the sight was not calculated to ease his apprehensions.

But Dennis went on with a calm grin.

"I can make a pretty good guess that will be easy to prove. Your mummy importations have been a pretty smooth idea, professor. I'll have to take off my hat to you as the first man I ever heard of who made a mummy work."

"Eh? What's that? Work?"

"Exactly. I wonder just how much dope you've brought into the country since you figured out that method. Who would ever think of looking inside a mummy for smuggled goods? Not I."

The professor's face grew livid. His voice shook. "I see you have been prying around in here."

"Uh-huh. *Papier mâché* mummies and genuine mummies," Dennis agreed with a chuckle. "If you hadn't put us in here I don't know whether I'd ever have been dippy enough to guess that. But it's good. I'll bet the jury will think so too. One exhibit, together with a few facts, and they'll see the light."

Professor Richfield took off his glasses and put them back on again. The two men at his side had been listening in scowling silence. Their eyes were riveted on Dennis and Sardi fixedly.

"I suppose you know you're not going to leave these grounds alive?" the professor said harshly.

"I've been wondering," Dennis murmured. He seemed to be enjoying himself. But Sardi was not.

"You needn't wonder any longer," Richfield said with a sudden rush of viciousness. "And now that you've guessed so much I'll tell you the rest. It may make you feel better to die with a complete case in your hands—that you can't use! Yes, I've been using mummies to smuggle drugs in. And I will continue to do so. You see all this?" He gestured around the room.

"Charming collection," Dennis murmured. "I'm rather astonished to see it belonging to a dope seller."

Richfield winced. He had a thin skin about it after all.

"I wasn't always in this business," he said heatedly. "I spent years at my studies and collections, until my income was cut off. And then one day in Spain I was approached by a friend who suggested I could collect a large sum for letting a few small packages go along in one of my cases. I did it. It was easy. In a year I was handling my own shipments, and finally I gathered men around me to dispose of what I brought in. Some of the mummies were genuine. I sold them to museums. But those of *papier mâché* I had made to order in Germany, fitted with aged heads from dissecting rooms, and used to round out my collection here."

"Very nice," Dennis murmured.

"For a time I sold drugs wholesale to Moran," the professor continued. "But we had a quarrel and I refused to let him have any more. He had built up a large trade behind his silk-stocking business with its dummy owner. His supplies ran low and he couldn't get any more right away. In some way he found out I had a shipment due today and decided to take it. This Jackson heard them talking about it last night. He came to me this morning and offered to sell the information. I agreed to buy it, and when I found out what it was, I tried to stop the case at the express office until I could send in some guards.

"But I was too late. Moran's thugs killed my man and got the case. We met them in the garage. They tried to fight. One of them was killed, unfortunately. We brought Moran here. Jackson knew you had seen him here and was frightened. I could see that as soon as you got your hands on him he would tell everything he knew. His mouth had to be closed."

"Oh, obviously," Dennis agreed drily.

"So," said Richfield, unruffled, "as long as things had reached that point, we decided to take over Moran's business. I went there this afternoon and told his manager we would issue supplies and handle the money after this. He saw the light, and agreed to come here with some of his men tonight and talk it over. In fact they're still here. In some way Moran got loose upstairs and ran through the hall, knocking down my niece. He broke the window and tried to escape, unfortunately for him."

"Decidedly so," Dennis said in the same dry tone. "This niece of yours, professor, is she in the game with you?"

"Certainly not. She has only been with me a few months, just since her father died. She was very distressed about having to lie to you this afternoon, but I had given her strict orders, and she obeyed them, without understanding their significance."

"I'm glad of that," Dennis sighed. "She looked straight to me. I'd hate to have to send her to trial with you."

PROFESSOR RICHFIELD removed his glasses again, and this time polished them long and slowly. Meticulously Richfield replaced the glasses on his nose.

"You know of course that there will be no trial, that neither of you is going to leave here alive. In fact, while those fools are arguing over money I think we will make certain of everything and end it now."

"They know at headquarters we came here," Sardi broke in angrily.

"But no one in this house has seen you here this evening," Richfield informed him blandly. "And when you are found, if ever, it will be a long distance away. Boys, shoot them if they move a step nearer you. And as soon as I get to the door, you may dispose of them as you see fit."

As the professor turned away and Dennis looked into the set, expressionless faces of the two gunmen, a qualm of uncertainty struck through him for the first time. Suppose his plans had gone wrong. Suppose instead of stalling for time he had only succeeded in pushing Sardi and himself into certain death.

Sardi's face was white. His fists were clenching.

"Don't rush them," Dennis warned.

"I'm not going to stand here and be shot down like a dog!" Sardi declared hoarsely. "Why did you work your mouth that way, Breen? You knew it'd end this way!"

"I was hoping it wouldn't," Dennis said.

The professor reached the door. He turned around, hand on the knob. "All right, boys," he said. He opened the door.

At that moment an automobile engine roared up the drive outside and stopped before the house. Running steps pounded across the porch. A heavy fist knocked loudly.

Professor Richfield stepped swiftly back inside and closed the door. He was disturbed. "I wonder who that is!" he exclaimed sharply as the knocking sounded again. "Everyone is here."

The front door opened. A heavy voice called: "Anyone in here? This is the police."

Dennis laughed. "A squad of them, professor. Too bad you kept your burglar alarm in working order."

"B-burglar alarm?" Professor Richfield spluttered, his face paling.

"Yes," Dennis chuckled. "You had all the windows of your museum here wired. So I opened one of them and set off the alarm. I've been waiting for the squad to show up. Your confession was interesting—and helpful. Thanks."

Sardi drew a great breath of relief. "I'll bet Finger Sammy Jackson over there in the box is getting a kick out of this!" he exclaimed.

And Professor Adam Richfield had no answer to make to that.

The PHANTOM NUGGET

by

Fred MacIsaac

Driver didn't believe in ghosts—he knew such things could never be. But talking with a man who has been murdered for more than a year is enough to whiten anybody's hair, turn the gills green with terror.

I AM the sort of man who never forgets a face and I have trained myself to remember names because it is useful in the real-estate business. People like—well never mind that. The fact is, that when I came on deck after dinner on the night before the steamer Samantic reached New York, and found someone sitting in the deck-chair next to mine, I realized immediately that there was something familiar about him.

He was a portly person with a large head, partially bald, a massive nose, a bulging forehead fringed with shaggy eyebrows and deep-set eyes. He wore dinner clothes and, as a shirt stud, he had a gold nugget almost as big as an olive—a bit of bad taste, I thought.

He held an unlighted cigar in his hand and he was regarding it gravely as I dropped into my chair. He did not appear to notice my arrival.

As it annoys me not to place a person, I studied him covertly and, by and by, remembered him. His name was Horace P. Wharton, and I had met him six months before at the home of my friend, Harry Wharton, who lives a couple of doors away from me in Bayside, Long

Island. I recalled that he was connected with the Holstead Bank on lower Broadway, first vice-president, I think, and he didn't let you forget it. A heavy garrulous person with a keen sense of his own importance. If it wasn't for the fact that, obviously, he didn't recall me and it would be a feather in my cap to show how I remembered names and faces, I wouldn't have spoken to him. Besides, it was the last night on board and he would have no further chance to bore me. It was rather curious that I hadn't set eyes on him during the voyage, but I supposed he was a bad sailor and had stuck pretty close to his cabin.

"If I am not mistaken," I said, "you are Mr. Horace P. Wharton of the Holstead Bank."

He lifted his head and gazed at me out of his deep-set eyes. I observed then that his cheeks sagged and there were dark circles beneath the eyes.

"You are not mistaken," he said in a ponderous bass voice. "Nor am I in the habit of forgetting faces—or anything else. You are George Driver and you are in the real-estate business. I met you at the house of my nephew in Bayside, two years ago."

"I'm surprised that you remembered me. I'm nobody in particular. You are very prominent, Mr. Wharton."

"Ah, thank you."

"Haven't seen you before during the voyage."

"No. I've been ill."

"I trust you're better."

"Yes."

"Been abroad long?"

"A few weeks only, or is it a few months or years?" He laughed whimsically. "One loses track of time."

"Come now," I protested, "there's a big difference between weeks and years."

He nodded. "True. I suppose a minute seems a year to a man in prison and a year a minute to one in paradise. Do you expect to see my nephew and his wife soon?"

"Within a day or two after landing. We are neighbors in Bayside, you know."

"Ah, yes. I remember. You will please

Grant deftly slipped handcuffs upon his wrists.

to give them my regards. And, do you happen to know Samuel Thomas, the broker?"

"I think I've heard of him. Never met him."

"Well, if you do, present my compliments."

"But, you'll be more apt to meet him than I."

"No. I am not remaining in New York. I am called elsewhere immediately."

"Been abroad for pleasure, eh?"

"I never do anything for pleasure," he said gravely. "Would you like to know what I have been doing abroad?"

"Why, really, it's none of my business," I stammered, much embarrassed.

"Ha," he ejaculated with a staccato laugh. "Well, I am sure you will be discreet. I shall tell you. I have been compounding a felony."

I was so astounded that I could not answer.

"How long have you been abroad?" he asked.

"Nearly six months. No business, you know, so I took my savings and gave myself a long vacation."

"Just as well perhaps. Mr. Driver, in case you are ever tempted to commit a crime, do it in a big way. Sometime ago, a trusted employee of my bank embezzled nearly seven hundred thousand dollars."

"It doesn't seem possible!"

"It did not seem so to us until we discovered the shortage. Unlike most dishonest bank employees, this man did not speculate with the money. He carried it all away with him. As you know, banking institutions have an excellent system of crime detection. It is very seldom that an absconder escapes our detectives for any length of time. This man did. And the loss came most inconveniently. We set the usual machinery in force without result. After months had passed and no trace of the scoundrel had been found,

our president received a communication from abroad making what might be termed an offer in compromise. This rascal proposed to return to us half a million in exchange for immunity.

"Under ordinary circumstances we would have refused to deal with him, you understand, but our bank stock is closely held and the stockholders would have to make up the loss. Two hundred thousand would burden them less than seven hundred thousand. We decided to compound the felony. In exchange for a signed release from the bank, this thief would turn over to us half a million in cash but his conditions were peculiar. An officer of the bank was to be in the Savoy Hotel in London upon a certain night. He would be accosted and led to the hiding place of the embezzler. I need not tell you that compounding a felony, either for an individual or a corporation, is a crime."

"Look here," I said nervously. "Ought you tell me this?"

"I am trusting to your discretion," he said with a half smile. "I was chosen for this mission. I took an express ship to Plymouth. I was at the appointed place at the appointed time. A stranger came to me and called me by my name. I went with him in a cab to Croydon where we took an airplane and rose in the darkness into the air. I have only a vague notion of where we landed. It was a private landing field about two hours from London. I suspect that it was in Yorkshire. I was taken in a motor car to a small cottage and met this brazen thief face to face. He turned over to me five hundred thousand dollars in crisp new United States treasury notes. I gave him the paper which made it impossible for us to prosecute him without rendering the officers of the bank liable for compounding a felony. I was taken back to London as I came and I immediately took this ship back to New York. I consider that I have successfully accomplished a degrading mission, Mr. Driver. Tomorrow, the money which I have here, will be back in our vaults."

"Good heavens, you don't mean to say you have half a million in cash with you! Of course it is in the ship's safe."

"I could not deposit such a sum without declaring it. Nor could I express it. Absolute secrecy is necessary."

"Do you think it discreet to confide in me," I said hotly. "I won't be able to sleep a wink tonight."

"Ah," he said solemnly. "I do not fear you, Mr. Driver. The money is here in this brief case which you see in my lap. It has never left my hands since I received it."

I LOOKED wildly around. We were alone on the dimly lighted deck. Fortunately no one else had heard the man's insane revelation. Half a million dollars! If I hadn't been a law-abiding citizen, myself, I would have been tempted. I was returning to a shattered business. I had foolishly spent most of my savings abroad. It was evident to me that Wharton had been drinking, though he looked sober as a judge. The thing had been preying on his mind. He had hidden in his cabin during the voyage and, unable to stand it any longer, had come on deck and babbled to the first person who happened to be alone with him. He must have been hitting the bottle heavily for four or five days.

"It's beginning to get chilly," he declared, "and, as we dock early, I think I'll go below."

"I promise to keep your confidence," I mumbled. "For heaven's sake take care of yourself."

"Good night," he said. He heaved his bulk out of the chair with an effort and walked forward in the direction of the entrance to the main companionway. My eyes followed him. As he came to the lighted entrance, a man stepped out and spoke to him. Wharton greeted him cordially, his brief case swinging in his right hand, and then, instead of going inside, he walked forward with the other man out of the light from the companion entrance and they faded from view. I had obtained a glimpse of his friend. He was a tall slender man with features that were clean cut like a cameo. He wore a tail coat, and had a thick crop of black hair.

I sat for a few minutes, pondering over the remarkable tale he had told me. It was inexplicable that a bank official who had taken such extraordinary precautions to conceal the collusion of his bank with an absconding official, should open up to a comparative stranger. The only explanation was that he was drunk as a lord.

A moment later I saw something gleaming on the deck at my feet. I stooped and picked up the nugget which had served as a shirt stud. It had broken loose from its fastening.

While it had no great intrinsic value—there could not have been more than twenty dollars worth of gold in it—he would not have worn it if it had not some sentimental value to him. I rose and went aft along the deck expecting to meet him as he circled the deck house, but it was evident that the pair must have entered the companionway on the opposite side for I made a complete circuit without encountering him.

I went inside and sought the purser's office.

"Can you tell me the number of Mr. Wharton's room?" I inquired.

The purser picked up a passenger list. "Stephen Wharton?" he asked.

"No, Horace P."

"Only one Wharton on board," he said.

I opened my mouth and closed it again. I had nearly made a *faux pas.* Wharton, of course, was traveling incognito. It was in keeping with his mission. Well, I'd see him on the pier in the morning and give him his stud.

However, I did not see him on the pier. My bags were quickly delivered but I had the bad luck to secure a conscientious customs officer who refused to accept my valuation of a number of gifts I had purchased abroad and who sent for an appraiser. By the time I had argued with him and had been forced to pay a hundred dollars more duty than I had counted upon, most of the first-class passengers had run the gauntlet and escaped.

That didn't annoy me much because I could always turn the nugget over to his relatives in Bayside or I could deliver it to him at the bank the first time I passed that way.

For no reason, my name was published among the passengers on the steamer, and when I reached my house that night I found a note from the Whartons which invited me to dinner the following evening.

THE Whartons were very nice people whose pretty little home, like my own, was subject to a mortgage, and the family consisted of Harry, his wife, Maud, and a daughter Sally who was so pretty that I would have fallen in love with her long ago if it had been likely to do me any good. There was a young man named Woods who was sweet on her, at the dinner, and a couple named Yates who lived on our street.

Cocktails were being served when I arrived.

Mrs. Wharton greeted me archly. "George," she demanded, "are you still a bachelor?"

"Most certainly."

"Engaged?"

"No, indeed."

There was a burst of laughter led by

Sally, and Mrs. Wharton looked dismayed.

"Oh," she said, "I was certain that you would meet a nice girl during the trip."

"In fact," said Sally, "there was a bet on. I took the negative because I knew you were in love with me."

This was most embarrassing. Modern young folks don't care what they say nor how they hurt a person.

"While I did not, positively, associate with any young woman during the voyage home," I said to turn the subject, "I had the pleasure of meeting a relative of yours."

"Didn't know we had any left," observed Harry Wharton. "Who the deuce was it?"

"Horace P. Wharton, the banker."

The effect of my statement was as if I had tossed a bomb at the family. The pop eyes of Harry became poppier. Mrs. Wharton became very pale and it looked as though Sally was going to burst into tears.

"You must be mistaken," said Wharton. "He can't be—how do you know it was Uncle Horace?"

"Because he sent you his regards and explained that he would not be able to see you as he would be in New York only a very short time."

"I feel as if I were going to faint," said Mrs. Wharton, and she dropped into a chair.

"When and where did you see him?" persisted Harry.

"Last night on the Samantic. We had quite a long conversation."

The maid servant announced dinner and the hostess pulled herself together and marshalled us into the dining room. It was obvious that I had been so unfortunate as to bring up a subject which distressed the Wharton family, but how was I to know that they would not be delighted to hear from their relative.

However, as soon as we were seated, Sally brought the subject up again.

"Did Uncle Horace tell you where he had been and what he had been doing?" she demanded.

"Yes, but in strictest confidence. Didn't you know that he had gone abroad?"

Wharton laughed mirthlessly. "To tell you the truth we didn't know what became of him. He disappeared a year ago. Of course we haven't talked about it."

"And, as he is our only relative and has a lot of money, we fondly hoped that he was dead," said the candid Sally. "The breaks are against us, mother."

"Why do you say disappeared?" I inquired.

"That is exactly the word for it. He resigned from the bank without letting any of us know and went away without notifying us. The first we heard about it was when his valet came to tell us that Horace had been gone two months and had left no money to pay the rent or to pay the man's wages beyond that period. I went to the president of the bank who told me that Uncle had severed his connection with them and he had no idea where he had gone. His accounts, however, were in perfect shape. I paid off the valet, sent his goods to storage, and have been looking after his property since."

"And we have been fondly hoping that we would learn of his death and his property would be our property," declared Sally.

Mrs. Wharton wiped away a tear. "I was very fond of Uncle Horace," she stated.

"Well," I said heartily. "He's alive and kicking and you'll hear from him quick enough, no doubt."

Conversation languished after that. Knowing the circumstances of my friends, I could sympathize with their point of view. Horace, being anything but a lovable character, always had figured to them as a prospect and his reappearance was a great disappointment to them.

After dinner we played bridge until eleven and then the party broke up.

NEXT morning I dropped in at the Holstead Bank which is not far from my office and asked to see Mr. Wharton. In my vest pocket reposed the lost nugget. I inquired for him of one of the officers whose desk was just inside the main entrance and he stared at me in astonishment.

"Mr. Wharton has not been connected with us for a long time, sir," he said.

"But he was in yesterday, wasn't he? He told me night before last he was coming here."

He gazed at me with a perplexed expression.

"If you wait, I shall inquire," he said and, leaving his desk, crossed the outer office and disappeared through a mahogany door.

In a moment he was back and smiling at me propitiatingly.

"Would you mind accompanying me?" he asked. "Mr. Williams, our president, would like to speak with you."

I followed him into the private office and found there a tall, thin gray man with a white brush mustache and sharp blue eyes.

"You inquired for Mr. Wharton," he said sharply. "He has not been with us for some time."

"So I have been informed."

"But for some reason you supposed you would find him here today."

"That is true. He expected to be here."

"You mean you have seen and talked with him? When and where?" he demanded.

"We were fellow passengers on the Samantic which arrived yesterday morning."

"And what caused you to think he would be here?" he asked eagerly.

"Why, he spoke of having successfully accomplished a mission for the bank."

"Successfully— Good God! Please sit down Mr. er—"

"George Driver, sir."

"You are sure he was on the Samantic?"

"I know him and he recognized me. Called me by name."

"This is most astonishing, most astonishing. So he is in New York, is he?"

"The reason I came in was to return to him an article which he dropped after talking to me. I'll be obliged if you will turn it over to him when he arrives."

I handed him the nugget. Mr. Williams took it and closely inspected it.

"I've seen it a hundred times," he declared. "Mr. Driver, I am very anxious to find him. I will make it worth your while if you can locate him."

I smiled knowingly. "That, I can understand. With what he carries around on his person—"

Williams frowned. "What on earth are you talking about?" he demanded.

"Wasn't he abroad on a mission for the bank, sir?"

"Certainly not. Of course not."

"Then why are you so anxious to see him?"

"Why he is an old friend, an—er—an associate. And—frankly, Mr. Driver, he walked out of the bank a year ago and has never been heard of since. We feared foul play. I am greatly relieved. Did he say where he was going?"

"Only that he had very little time to spend in New York."

The man clenched his hands until the knuckles grew white.

"It is of supreme importance to us to locate him," he said earnestly. "Mr. Driver, what did he tell you about this alleged mission?"

"He said he had gone abroad upon a secret assignment. That he had crossed to London, met a certain person, transacted his business and taken the next ship for New York."

"But that would have taken him over and back in three weeks."

"So I assumed."

The bank president pushed back his chair and rose and came around his chair and placed a hand on my shoulder.

"Mr. Driver," he said gravely, "this is incomprehensible to me. Just now I denied that he was on a mission for the bank. What he told you was true but—" he paused dramatically—"he sailed from New York just three weeks over a year ago and never has been heard from since."

Although I knew that he had been away a year because the Whartons had told me so, I confess that the manner in which Williams said this caused a shiver to penetrate my marrow.

"But he talked—" I stammered— "as though there had been no delay."

"And he said he had been successful?"

"Yes."

"It is very strange. Exactly what did he say to you?"

"Well, if you must know, he said that he had compounded a felony."

"How dared he—that isn't true!"

I shrugged my shoulders. "Well," I said, "that's all the information I can give you."

"Wait, wait." He paced the room and finally paused in front of my chair.

"Mr. Driver," he said slowly. "It often happens that a bank has to make terms with a successful embezzler. It is against the law of course but, if the theft is not reported, there is no comeback. We sent Wharton abroad to receive from a thief the sum of five hundred thousand dollars, part of his loot, in exchange for a quitclaim. We had been forced to conclude that Wharton either had made off with the half million received from this absconder, or, as is more likely, had been killed by him after turning over the quit-claim and receiving the money.

"The situation was that we could not bring his disappearance to the attention of the police without admitting our own offense."

"So you thought it best to let a murder go unpunished?"

"If I had been the messenger and Wharton had been at my desk he would have done exactly as I have done."

"Well, don't worry about it. He is alive and well and you're going to get your half million."

"That is great news," he said without enthusiasm. "But where has he been for a year? And how do you happen to know all this? Why should he tell you that he had compounded a felony? That was the height of indiscretion."

"I assumed that he was drunk, though he didn't appear to be under the influence."

"He should have been in yesterday if he was on the Samantic. Can I rely upon your discretion, Mr. Driver? Are you a great friend of his?"

"A mere acquaintance."

"The less reason why he should have confided in you. There is a possibility that he plans to make off with the money; that he remained abroad as long as he could stand it, and hoped to slip into America and lose himself."

"In that case why tell me his story?"

"I can't understand that. Will you give me your address? We'll try to run him down quietly. We may need you. If there is anything this bank can do for you—"

"I am very glad to be of service in any way, sir."

DURING the next week I was grilled successively by the bank detectives and the head of the biggest private agency in New York. Before the Samantic left port they swarmed over her and questioned her ship's company but they were unable to discover under what name Wharton had crossed the ocean nor could they find a steward on the ship who remembered a person resembling the photographs of the missing man which were shown to them.

My description of the individual who had joined Wharton at the exit from the companionway and walked around the deck with him fared no better, but that was due to the fact that I could give them no distinguishing marks. While I would know him again if I saw him, I couldn't draw an adequate word picture of him.

No taxi-driver was found who would admit driving Wharton from the pier. No customs man remembered him. No hotel clerk could recall renting him a room nor had he put in an appearance at the apartment hotel where he had formerly lived. He had come ashore, unseen, and vanished into thin air.

As weeks passed, I set my business on its feet and concentrated upon it and, as the going was very hard, I dismissed the Wharton matter as much as possible from my mind. The bank detective called on me at the end of a month and accused me of making up the yarn out of whole cloth and I was compelled to order him out of my office. If it hadn't been for the nugget in his possession, Mr. Williams of the Holstead Bank would have taken the same attitude, but that stumped him. And, as nobody but the directors and Wharton knew that a felony had been compounded, he couldn't explain away my knowledge of it.

It must have been five or six weeks after the incident that I became aware that I was shadowed wherever I went and that men were watching my house in Bayside. And I found evidence that my office safe had been opened and its contents inspected. For a time I was too stupid to comprehend why I should be the subject of such attentions, but the awful truth burst upon me one night when I was lying in bed.

They suspected me of making away with Wharton and stealing his five hundred thousand dollars. I did not sleep that night and first thing in the morning I called upon Williams and demanded an accounting.

"Are you responsible for the watch that is being kept on me?" I demanded.

He flushed, hesitated and admitted it.

"Then you think I am responsible for Wharton's disappearance?"

"Mr. Driver," he said candidly, "I don't know what to think. If all passengers on the Samantic had not presented themselves and passed the immigration officers when the ship reached port, I am afraid you would be in a very serious situation at this moment. As it happened, you left a broad trail from the ship to your office and then to your home, upon the day you landed, and we have satisfied ourselves that you were not in Wharton's company that day or evening. But if the police knew what you have revealed to me, and had been notified that Mr. Wharton's disappearance since the Samantic landed caused us to suspect anything, you would be under arrest at this minute. You see, you were aware that he had a fortune on his person and your circumstances are not very good."

"If I were guilty, should I have come to you and told my story?"

"That, of course, is a point in your favor."

"Much obliged," I said bitterly. "I want you to call off your sleuths or I'll go to the police and accuse your bank of compounding a felony. I'll tell them everything, Mr. Williams—everything."

He wrung his hands. "I implore you,

do nothing of the sort. As a matter of fact we are already convinced of your innocence and I'll notify the detective agency to call off its men."

"You'd better," I said hotly, and I left without saying good day.

MY shadows disappeared, to my great relief, and business began to pick up. I managed to list an apartment house on Park Avenue which was for sale at an absurd price, if any price is absurd these days, and, if I succeeded in selling it, I would earn enough in commissions to live well for two or three years. And it looked as if I had a bite, for the day after I listed it I had a phone call regarding it, and the caller said he would drop into my office at four in the afternoon.

I had everything ready and had cleared my desk for action when the customer put in an appearance. My stenographer ushered him in and I affected to be very much occupied and didn't look up for a minute. When I did, I was looking at the man who had walked the deck with Horace Wharton.

"Mr. Driver," he said, "I am interested in the apartment house at 1111 Park Avenue."

That was sufficient good news but my satisfaction went deeper. At last I had found somebody to corroborate my statement that Wharton was a passenger on the Samantic.

"How do you do, sir," I said cordially. "While we haven't met, I believe we were fellow passengers from Europe a few weeks ago."

"You are mistaken," he said. "I haven't been abroad for a year."

"But—but it seems to me that you were on the Samantic with me on the May trip."

He smiled pleasantly. "You mean May, a year ago. I returned upon her upon that occasion."

"No. I saw you on board on the trip which ended May eighteenth."

"Wrong," he said good-naturedly. "I landed from Europe on May nineteenth a year ago. I've been too busy to go abroad this year."

"I must be mistaken," I said dubiously. But I was sure I wasn't mistaken; I know faces. However this was a customer and the customer is always right.

"What is your name, may I ask?"

"Samuel Thomas."

Samuel Thomas! The man to whom Wharton had especially requested me to present his compliments if I should happen to encounter him.

"Glad to know you, Mr. Thomas," I said blandly. "I recently met a friend of yours."

"Whom?"

"Horace P. Wharton."

I was watching him closely. I saw the man turn green. He wet his lips with his tongue and his eyes became opaque.

"Recently, did you say?" he stammered.

"Quite recently."

He walked to a window, apparently interested in some air, outside.

"That's odd," he remarked without turning. "Heard he had resigned from his bank and left town a year ago. Where did you see him?"

"I may have been mistaken," I replied. "I thought I saw him on the Samantic on my last trip."

"You must have been. I'm not feeling very well, Mr. Driver. If you don't mind I'll discuss the building another time. I'm a bit off my feed. Good afternoon." His agitation was so great he couldn't conceal it.

As soon as he had left, I picked up my phone and called the steamship company's passenger office. When I had been connected, I asked if they would inform me whether Samuel Thomas had been a passenger upon the Samantic's May trip from Europe.

After a minute's delay they reported.

"No person named Samuel Thomas was on board," said the clerk.

I hung up, nonplussed. But, come to think of it, Wharton would not have sent the man his regards if he were a fellow passenger. Yet he had not seemed surprised when Samuel Thomas, or his double, joined him at the companionway.

And the perturbation of Thomas when informed that I had met Wharton was hard to explain. The fellow had been frightened. I had seen fear painted on his face. And he had come into my office to talk business and had departed without discussing the deal. He had departed in a great hurry, claiming to be ill. When he had entered he was the picture of health.

For no reason, a chill began to run up and down my spine. Cold sweat broke out upon my brow and my hands got clammy. He had been on the ocean on the Samantic one year ago on the eighteenth of May. And Wharton had been away from New York one year and three weeks on the eighteenth of May of this year. If he had sailed to London, accomplished his mission and returned upon the first ship, Wharton might have been on board the Samantic a year before, with Thomas. He might have been sitting in a deck chair with him and walking the deck with him on the eighteenth of May. And he might have confided to Thomas.

I rushed to the washstand and let cold water run upon my head, but I couldn't shake out of me the superstitious terror which possessed me. Taking these suppositions as a hypothosis, then the man who had sat beside me on the eighteenth of May was a ghost.

Being a solid, hard-headed person, I didn't believe in ghosts and it was insane to credit that the substantial citizen who had talked to me in a confidential manner was a visitor from the other world.

He had broken his stud when lifting his heavy figure from the chair, and I had the nugget to prove that he was Horace Wharton in the full flesh.

AFTER a night filled with disagreeable dreams, I presented myself at the Holstead Bank at ten o'clock and was admitted at once to the presence of Mr. Williams.

"You have news," he exclaimed. "Bad, by the look of you."

"I've got to settle a certain natter or go mad," I replied. "Did Wharton go to Europe under an assumed name?"

"You forget the passport regulations. His baptismal name was Peter Horace Wharton and he booked as P. H. Wharton. Wharton, being a common name, did not identify him with this bank. Why do you ask?"

"I'll tell you later, if there is anything to tell."

When I went into the steamship office I felt like an idiot and as I ran my finger down the list of first-class passengers on the Samantic upon the trip which ended in New York on May twentieth, 1930. I was trembling like a leaf. If the name of P. H. Wharton did not appear there, I would be rid of an insane obsession, but it was there.

And under the "T's," just above, was the name of Samuel Thomas. "Can you tell me if this passenger, P. H. Wharton, was lost at sea?" I asked stupidly of the clerk.

He smiled. "We don't lose many passengers at sea, sir," he replied. "Wait till I look at the duplicate of the immigration report."

He returned in five minutes still smiling.

"Mr. P. H. Wharton appeared before the immigration officials when the ship reached port and was passed ashore by them," he said.

I wiped my brow and sighed with deep relief. I had been laboring under the fantastic notion that Wharton had been on the ship with Thomas and that Thomas had robbed him and thrown him overboard, which meant of course that it was Horace Wharton's ghost which had sat in the deck-chair beside me and which had been met at the companionway by the astral body of the living Samuel Thomas. And this dreadful incident had taken place on the anniversary of the murder and at the hour of its occurrence.

My reason told me that there are no phantoms and that dead people stay dead but the fancies of the best men get beyond their control now and then and I was no exception to the rule.

I was so relieved to learn that Wharton had walked ashore alive and well that I forgot, for the moment, that it did not explain his appearance on the ship a year later nor his insistence that I communicate with a man I did not know and present his compliments. And I did not appreciate, for a few minutes, the importance to the Holstead Bank of the discovery I had made.

I hastened back to President Williams and confessed to him the psychosis which had sent me to the steamship office and told him the result of my investigation.

He grew very pale when I admitted my obsession—few men can hear a tale bearing upon the supernatural without being somewhat affected by it—but he quickly recovered.

"That's all nonsense, of course," he declared, "but it has served a useful purpose. It never occurred to me to watch lists of passengers upon incoming steamers, because I knew that Wharton would come to the bank as soon as he landed, and fully two months passed before we became alarmed here at his non-appearance. And, all the time, the scoundrel was back in America with our five hundred thousand dollars."

"I don't believe he is a scoundrel," I declared. "I tell you he was absolutely sincere on the steamer when he told me that the money had never left his possession and would be in the bank next day."

"But he wasn't on the steamer. You have just proved it."

Again that quake of terror shook me. "Then it was a ghost that I saw, do you think?" I asked weakly.

Williams shook his head limply from side to side. "I don't know what to think about that."

"I'll land in an asylum if this mystery isn't cleared up," I said desperately. "Look here, do you think he had amnesia, recovered, found himself in London and returned to New York as he originally intended, unaware that a year had elapsed?"

"In that case what has become of him and the money? Driver, are you certain that Thomas was alarmed when you mentioned Wharton?"

"I swear the fellow was terrified when I said I had seen Wharton recently."

His thin lips came together in a hard straight line.

"We'll investigate Mr. Thomas," he declared. "It may be that your suspicion that he killed Wharton has a foundation in fact, but that he robbed and murdered him after they landed from the steamer."

"In which case I did see a ghost," I remonstrated.

"No, no. You dreamed meeting him. The strangest truths are often revealed in dreams."

I scowled. "And I suppose I dreamed the nugget, too."

He ran his hands through his gray hair. "Good God, I'll be as crazy as you are pretty soon," he blurted. "Go to your office and try to put the affair out of your mind. I'll set the detectives on Thomas."

"Keep me informed," I pleaded.

"Of course, of course."

I WENT to my office but, as a business man, I was of no earthly use. The face of Horace Wharton kept floating before my eyes and I fancied that his fallen cheeks and the haggard eyes were the features of a dead man. How I got through the next few days I can't tell you but I survived them and rushed to the office of the president of the Holstead Bank upon receipt, at last, of a phone message from him.

It was some slight satisfaction to find that Williams had changed for the worse in the interim. His cheeks were hollow and his eyes had dark circles beneath them.

"I want to talk to you about Samuel Thomas," he said solemnly. "I have had a report on him from Dunn's and from our detective agency. For some years he had been a junior member in the brokerage firm of Hart and Jones. That firm went to the wall in the panic of October, 1929. Thomas saved enough from the wreck to go to Europe. He returned on the Samantic in May, 1930. Within a week after landing he began to operate in Wall Street through the office of Lessups and Company. He had ample funds. He bought stocks on margin in ten-thousand lots.

"I have a copy of his first order. It was for five thousand shares of Amalgamated Metals upon a thirty-point margin. He sold out after a twenty point loss, but immediately sold short ten thousand shares of Consolidated Motors and recouped to some extent. During the first month, the total of his buying and selling orders amounted to two hundred thousand dollars. I believe he was using money which belonged to this bank."

"He came into my office to discuss buying an apartment building worth a million and a half," I stated. "If I hadn't been obsessed by this nightmare, I might have sold it to him and made seventy-five thousand dollars."

"Your nightmare may be the means of getting back our money, Mr. Driver. I haven't told you all. We have found two passengers who crossed on the Samantic with Thomas a year ago and who remember seeing him in Wharton's company."

"Which proves nothing."

"We have your evidence of his perturbation—"

"If you think of accusing Thomas of murder," I said ironically, "I am a very bad witness because I shall have to testify that I saw Wharton alive and well a few weeks ago. I don't think you can convince the jury that I saw a ghost."

The bank president placed the points of his fingers together, crossed his legs and leaned back in his chair and fixed me with a hard eye.

"Driver," he said, "a desperate man takes desperate chances. I own fifty-one per cent of the stock of this bank. I lost millions in the collapse of the stock market. I was forced to borrow money to make good to the bank fifty-one per cent of the seven hundred thousand defalcation. If I can recover part of it, I shall pull through, otherwise I am finished. I shall not be able to meet notes which the directors have been compelled to call. In a few minutes, Samuel Thomas is coming into this office. He has loans on securities from this bank and supposes I want to talk to him about them."

"Do you expect him to admit anything?" I asked sceptically.

"You will step into my secretary's office where you will find Grant, head of our detective bureau, whom you know. You will enter here with him when I ring. You will only answer questions asked you directly by me. Will you oblige me?"

"Certainly, only it seems absurd."

"Go in there now, please."

I shrugged my shoulders and passed into the other office. While it was I who had talked to a ghost, I thought I had myself better in hand than Williams, head of a tremendous financial institution.

Grant, the detective who had accused me of faking the whole thing and whom I had ordered out of my office, greeted me with a grin and offered me a cigar. I was incapable of smoking. We waited in silence for ten minutes when the buzzer sounded.

"Zero hour," said Grant. "Come on."

He opened the door and entered the president's office. I followed him.

THOMAS was sitting opposite Williams. He appeared to be perfectly self-possessed and in amicable conversation with the banker. As we entered he looked up casually, saw me and paled perceptibly.

"What is the meaning of this?" he demanded. "Mr. Williams, I thought—"

Grant bore down upon him, grasped his hands and deftly slipped handcuffs upon his wrists.

"I arrest you for the murder of Horace P. Wharton," he said gruffly.

"Take these things off! This is an outrage! I don't know anything about Wharton," he shouted.

"You're going to the chair for killing Wharton and robbing him of five hundred thousand dollars," asserted the detective firmly.

"It's a lie! Mr. Williams, look here! This man saw Wharton a few weeks ago. He crossed with him on the Samantic. He told me so."

"But you told him it wasn't possible," Williams retorted sharply. "And you knew it wasn't possible because you killed Wharton a year ago."

With his wrists fastened together, Thomas dropped back into his chair.

"You'll have a fine time proving it," he said scornfully.

"We've got people who saw you do it," lied Grant. "And what do you think of this for a piece of evidence? Found it in your apartment, Thomas."

He opened his big hand and there lay, glittering, the golden nugget.

The eyes of Samuel Thomas looked upon it. "Good God!" he muttered. "It isn't so! It can't be so! You never found it! You didn't find that thing in my apartment! How could you?" His voice ended in a shriek.

"And why couldn't we?" demanded Grant harshly.

Thomas writhed in his chair. He lifted his locked wrists above his head and brought them down upon the glass top of Williams' desk with such force that the steel cuffs broke the plate glass.

"I'll tell you why you couldn't," he bellowed. "Because the damn thing went down with him into the sea. I saw it gleaming as he struck the water. It couldn't come up! My God, it couldn't come up!"

"Confession," exclaimed Grant. "You gentlemen heard him."

"It's another stud," wailed the half-demented man. "It's a plant! I tell you I saw that thing sink down, down, down, into the black water."

He was positively gibbering with terror as he rocked in his chair and then I was, myself, engulfed in a wave of superstitious horror and my teeth began to chatter and my hair stood on end and my eyes blurred and I felt myself falling.

I recovered consciousness upon a couch in Mr. Williams' office and he was sitting in a chair beside me.

"Feel better?" he asked solicitously. "You fainted."

"Where are they?"

"Grant took him away."

I began to shake. "He killed Wharton. The nugget went to the bottom with him," I mumbled. "And Grant found it in his stud box. But I gave it to you."

"I told you I was desperate. I had it planted in his stud box."

I pressed my hands against my head which was bursting.

"But Wharton landed from the Samantic on that trip."

"No. Thomas secured his own landing card, reentered the salon, presented himself before another inspector, gave his name as Wharton and carried off the dead man's card. He had Wharton's effects sent to the pier, again passed himself off as Wharton, and carried them away with his own luggage."

"All of which means that I did see a ghost. I won't believe it. I dare not believe it!" I protested wildly.

"Thomas believes it," he said solemnly.

"Because the nugget sank with Wharton and came up again. And Wharton with it. Oh, my God!"

To my indignation Williams began to laugh, a hysterical sort of laugh.

"I'm going to prove to you that there are no ghosts," he said. He rose, crossed the room and opened a door and into the office walked Horace P. Wharton. I am ashamed to admit that I screeched in mortal terror and Williams had to grasp my shoulders and force me back on the couch or I might have jumped through a window.

"He's alive!" he shouted. "In the flesh, Driver. Take my word for it."

Wharton's pale lips parted in a ghoulish smile. I swear he looked more like an apparition than he had on the Samantic. "How do you do, Mr. Driver?" he asked heavily as though speech were an effort.

"Sit down, Horace," commanded Williams. "You're still weak. Snap out of it, Driver. You see I had another shock for

Mr. Thomas if the first one failed to work. Tell him your story, Horace."

Wharton waved his hand wearily. "You tell him," he requested.

WILLIAMS seated himself and I sat up on the couch and stared dubiously at Horace P. Wharton.

"Thomas robbed Wharton and threw him overboard," stated the bank president. "When Wharton came to the surface he was alongside a piece of wreckage to which he clung for twelve hours or more. He was out of his mind at the last and, when he came to, he was being landed in St. Malo by a French fishing schooner.

"He had pneumonia and they kept him in a French hospital for three weeks. After he was released, he was still in an enfeebled condition and sort of clouded mentally. He brooded over a robbery which was a result of his indiscretion in telling Thomas that he had half a million in cash which had no legal owner. Furthermore he forgot his long faithful service and assumed that his tale would not be believed by us at the bank. He supposed we would think that he had secreted the money. He had a letter of credit on London upon which he drew and went to the south of France where he brooded for many months.

"In the end, the thought that Thomas was enjoying his ill-gotten gains caused him to consider coming back to New York. He knew that we dared not prosecute him and, if he could appear before Thomas as one from the dead, he might frighten the criminal into making restitution.

"Well, he booked on the Samantic under an assumed name. He kept to his cabin—"

"Just a minute. Your detectives showed photographs of him to the crew."

"I haven't had a picture taken for twen-

ty years," said Wharton in a low tone. "Of course they didn't recognize me."

"Upon the last night he ventured on deck—"

"I had been drinking heavily," explained Wharton. "It was the anniversary of the night that Thomas threw me overboard."

"He sat in an empty deck chair and you happened to have the chair alongside of his."

"Mr. Driver," said Wharton, "I was in an excited state. I think I had a hallucination that I was back a year, returning with the money. When you recognized me, I babbled. I had Thomas on my mind and I told you to give him my compliments. I meant it satirically since he supposed he had murdered me and I was on my way to confront him. After I left you I walked halfway round the deck and then I carried my empty brief case to my cabin."

"Hold on. I distinctly saw Thomas meet you and you walked on deck with him."

"I've been puzzling over that," asserted Williams. "I can't explain it satisfactorily but Horace's mind was full of what had happened a year before. Thomas did come out of the deck house and walk with him on the fatal night and it may be—I don't know—it seems incredible—but his brain waves may have created the apparition which you saw. Some form of unconscious hypnotism."

"It's hard to believe," I demurred.

"Anyway he did not miss his nugget stud. Next morning he went ashore with the other passengers—"

"I had a hangover," admitted Wharton.

"He left the pier, was unable to get a taxi, walked half a block, attempted to cross the street, carrying his suitcase and was struck by a truck and taken to a hospital by the driver. Two ribs were broken and he received a blow on the head which was serious. There was nothing in his luggage to identify him. Our inquiries, of course, necessarily had been discreet."

"I realized in the hospital," declared Wharton, "that I wouldn't get anything by confronting Thomas. We couldn't arrest him for the theft and my appearance would relieve him of the murder charge. I got out yesterday and came to see Williams and told him my story.

"You had prepared the way for him, Driver," said Williams, smiling. "I hid Horace, planted the nugget in Thomas' apartment and got him here under a pretext. If the nugget hadn't broken him, Wharton's apparition in the presence of three witnesses would have done so."

"You can charge him with attempted murder, of course," I said thoughtfully.

"He has confessed to murder. Being unaware that Horace is alive, he will return the bank's money in return for an agreement not to prosecute him for murderous assault. Incidentally you'll get a check for $25,000, Driver."

"I can use it," I admitted. "I'd swap it for a credible explanation of how I saw Thomas on the Samantic."

"Some sort of unconscious hypnotism by Wharton—"

"I'll take the check," I told him, laughing. "Since Thomas is alive, it certainly wasn't his ghost which appeared to me. I'll consult a psychologist—"

"By the way," asked Wharton. "Have you seen my relatives?"

I laughed again to think of the consternation in Bayside.

"Yes." I replied. "They were delighted to hear of your return."

He smiled complacently. "They were always very fond of me," he stated.

There he lay—Big Joe Rudnicki—staring with sightless eyes at the shambles that had been the Hot Shot Club. No one had seen him die, no one could find a clue—the trail was cold. But Brinkhaus specialized in cold trails, and if there was no clue he had it tailormade.

"Brinky, you fool—stop!" The police phaeton pulled up.

TAILORMADE CLUE

A Sergeant Brinkhaus Story

by
Frederick Nebel

Author of "Murder on the Loose," etc.

CHAPTER ONE

Three Missing

THE place was a wreck. A table stood upside down; the cloth that covered it was a sodden ruin. Amid a chaos of broken glass and shattered crockery an attenuated vase still stood erect and sprouting an artificial poinsettia. A chair that had been hurled, now hung from a wall-light. A rowdy foot had punctured the jazzband's bass drum. Glass ground underfoot glinted like tinsel on the dance floor. Splotches on the walls marked the death of flung bottles.

The Hot Shot Club was a shambles.

Flannagan, the owner, walked up and down near the archway leading to the lobby. Eight paces, then back again; then eight again. Completely bald, his head looked like an oiled skull. He held his head erect—but with an effort. In the unnatural silence of the club the drumming of his rubberless heels beat an endless monotone like the sound of jungle tom-toms. He was the only one who moved.

The waiters stood around like images. The guests—sixty-odd—sat on chairs detached from tables, from groups. One man sat dazedly in the center of the dance floor patting the left side of his face, though it was on the right side that a gash bled.

Members of the jazzband sat by their instruments. The saxophonist held his sax in position as if ready to play at a moment's notice. The drummer sat with his sticks braced on his knees.

A uniformed cop—Patrolman Traviglano—stood framed in the archway, his arms folded, his head turning from side to side like a robot's as his eyes watched the endless pacing of Flannagan.

Once he spoke. "For cryin' out loud now, Jerry, don't get all steamed up."

"Steamed up, eh? Steamed up, eh?" Flannagan's voice was tight like a drawn string.

Yellow-haired Inspector Peter Larsen came quietly into the lobby. Traviglano saluted casually and stepped aside and into the club proper. Larsen appeared in the archway idy drawing off pigskin gloves. A brown ulster had its collar up around his neck. A brown fedora sat neatly on his head. He stood cruising his blue-gray eyes around the club.

"Hello, Jerry."

"Hello, inspector. Get a load of this."

Larsen nodded tranquilly.

Traviglano said: "Over there," and started across the dance floor. Larsen followed amiably toward a mound of chairs and an overturned table. Traviglano stopped, jerked his chin, said: "Pipe it."

Larsen peered between the table and the mound of chairs.

"I didn't want to move anything," Traviglano said.

"Thanks, Mike. Move 'em now, will you?"

Larsen himself grabbed the table and slid it farther out onto the floor. Traviglano moved the chairs.

A woman choked an outcry.

Larsen dropped to one knee, felt the man's pulse. There was no pulse. He moved the eyelids with a forefinger. He saw the hole in the dress shirt and the darkness around the hole. The man was big, lumpy, fortyish. Alive, his face would have been bloated. It was not a good face even dead. There were many rings on his fingers.

"Jerry," Larsen said, rising, "did you get a doctor?"

"There was one in my guests." Flannagan signaled a man who was already on his way over.

"Floom is my name, inspector. Death was instantaneous. He was shot through the heart."

Silence fell again and then sturdy shoes creaked across the floor and the squat, dumpy figure of Brinkhaus moved beneath the lights.

He said: "Josephs is here, boss. And Gatlin."

Deputy Medical Examiner George Josephs came in with his bobbing, happy walk. Rotund, immaculate in dress, he had round little bright eyes and cherubic cheeks.

"Well, well, Peter, what have we here?"

"A dead man," Larsen said.

"My, my!"

ASSISTANT District Attorney Wells Gatlin, small, dark, bitter-mouthed, streaked in importantly, shoved Flannagan out of the way, sideswiped Josephs and bent down over the dead man. He took one look. Then he straightened, pivoted, glared truculently all around and demanded: "Who did this?"

Larsen was in quiet conversation with Flannagan. Gatlin hopped to the center of the floor and shouted: "Who murdered this man? Quick!"

No one answered. A woman began crying. Gatlin rapped his heels across the floor and stood over her, his fists knotted.

"Madam, I will not be side-tracked by feminine tears. I am from the district attorney's office."

A man rose. "She's my wife. This—this has upset her. Quite naturally."

"And who are you?"

"My name is John Carveth."

"Who killed that man?"

"I don't know."

Gatlin snarled: "Oh, you don't know! I suppose you were in two other places when this happened. I suppose—"

"Please, please," sobbed the woman.

"Madam—"

Came Larsen's low soft voice. "Mr. Carveth, you may sit down. Mr. Gatlin, I am handling this investigation."

Gatlin tautened. "I am from—"

"Yes, the district attorney's office." Larsen nodded with mellow irony. "And I happen to be in charge of the detective division. Please mind your place until I've completed the investigation."

"You wouldn't be trying to be funny, would you?"

"No—anything but funny."

Brinkhaus and Josephs were kneeling on either side of the dead man.

"Direct to the heart," Josephs said. "Most direct."

"Close," Brinky supplemented. "Lookit the powder burn on the boiled shirt. I'm beginnin' to know this guy."

"Really!"

"Yeah. Oncet when me and Ogglecarp were pals we had to call on him oncet. Rudnicki's his real name—Josef Rudnicki

—one o' them Slovaks or somethin' or a Polack maybe. He's in big time—or would you say he useter be? Yeah—'Big Joe the Beef' some called him, though he didn't like that monicker worth a damn."

"Oh, you mean Big Joe the Beef!"

Brinkhaus got up, his hard woolen pants clinging to his legs, his garters showing. "Boss—"

"Yes, Brinky," Larsen said, coming up.

"He's Joe the Beef. He's—" Brinkhaus stopped, stepped around Larsen and went creaky-shoed across the floor to a table at which two men sat. "Hello, boys."

The two men stood up, walked past Brinkhaus and did not stop until they reached Larsen. Larsen turned and looked at them. Their faces remained immobile. One was big and broad and thatch-browed. The other was quite as tall, slim and pale and strangely handsome, impeccably clothed in a tux with dull lapels.

This one said quietly: "Joe got it."

"Hello, 'Swan'," Larsen said. Then he looked at the thatch-browed man. "Hello, Krieger."

"Joe got it," Krieger rumbled.

"You guys were with him?"

They nodded.

FLANNAGAN let the flood-gates open. "Joe was kind of drunk. Just kind of. At about eleven the place was jammed. Everybody's happy. This dead guy and these two guys are sitting right here—there was a table right here. A jane and a guy come in. I take a second look at the jane because she looks a knockout. Got an angel face and stands right out. The guy's with her is a bit soused. I get 'em a table way over there behind them palms. They're in here about ten minutes when the band cuts loose. The jane and the guy get up and dance and I'm watchin' the jane because she's such a swell looker and can she dance! Don't ask!

"A big crowd is on the floor when I

see this dead guy push his way through and grab the girl by the arm. I can't hear what he says, the band is makin' so much noise. The young guy pushes this guy away and starts to dance again and this guy comes back at him and tries to get the girl away. I turn to call Buck, me bouncer; and when I look around again the young guy is takin' a swing at this dead guy. Other folks stop dancin' and shift. The jane yells. The lights go out. A guy roars and then—*bang*—a gun goes off.

"Then hell busts loose. Everybody starts crowdin' around. Women fall down and guys start swingin' on general principles. Things start to fly. People start makin' for the door and some get out. I finally find the light switch and turn on the lights and—and—here this guy is. And—and the young guy—and the jane—" he threw up his hands—"are gone. And lookit me place. Just look at it!"

Gatlin demanded: "Why didn't you stop him?"

Larsen said quietly: "Who turned the lights out?"

"I—I don't know," Flannagan gasped.

"Where's the switch?"

"Back in the hallway. Back there. The hall goes to the ladies' room and the men's room. I don't know who the hell turned the lights out. I wish to God I knew."

"How many people ran out?"

"Well, inspector, they didn't go far. They only went as far as the sidewalk. and then after a coupla minutes Buck ran out and told 'em to come back or they might get in Dutch. So they all came back. All but the jane and the young guy, And—and another guy."

"Know him?"

"No. He come here alone. A little guy with eyeglasses on. And a sandy mustache. Harmless-lookin' guy. He danced a few times with one of our hostesses."

"His hat and coat in the check-room?"

"No. He didn't have an overcoat. He only had a hat. He didn't check it."

"Where was he sitting?"

Flannagan pointed. "At that little table —right by the hall that goes back to the rest rooms."

Larsen turned to The Swan and Krieger. "You know that guy came in with the girl?"

"No," said The Swan. "Never saw him before."

"I want the truth."

"You're getting it." The Swan's eyes were amber and steady in his pale narrow face.

Larsen clipped: "How about the girl?"

"I never checked up on Joe's women."

"What makes you think she was Joe's woman?"

"Because he went out after her. Give me a hard one."

Larsen smiled, humorlessly. "If you're thinking of going after that guy yourself —I mean you too, Krieger—think again."

The Swan's smile was equally humorless. But he didn't say anything.

Brinkhaus cleared his throat. "Boss—"

Larsen turned.

Brinkhaus was holding a hat and an overcoat. "These are his, boss."

"Whose?"

"The guy with the gal."

Gatlin rasped: "I wish, Larsen, you would interrogate these people here so that I can."

"Go ahead."

Gatlin was caustic. "I thought perhaps you might object if I took the initiative."

"I don't intend quizzing sixty-two persons."

"What!"

"The only ones that interest me are the three that aren't here. Go ahead, Gatlin. Enjoy yourself."

CHAPTER TWO

Overcoat Clue

DEAD. Joe the Beef was dead. Big Joe Rudnicki—forty-one years, three months and a day old. The underworld had known him as a man who went in strong for hard liquor, soft women and the mailed fist in the furtherance of his business. He'd plowed his way up from the bottom by means of the gun, brass knuckles, graft and an ability to take punishment and come back for more. He'd had guts. Plenty. Even the cops will tell you that. Each year he'd contributed two thousand dollars to the Fund for Policemen's Widows. Only those on the inside track know that he helped build the South Side Orphanage. He'd lived a wild, tempestuous life; brute force had been supplemented by an uncanny ability to touch dross and turn it into gold. During the last year of his life rumor had been circulated that he was going soft. Some wiseacres had said, "The hotter the coal the quicker it burns out." Thereby springing an epigram worthy of the Chinese and, in the light of his death, quite prophetic.

Brinkhaus came into Larsen's office reading the morning paper. "Would I be asked," he said, "I'd say I never seen such slush in all my borned days. 'Big Joe Rudnicki, Don Juan of the Underworld.' I knew Joe. Kind of liked him. But would I be asked again, I'd say Don Juan 'd muscle over in his grave should he read slush like this. Joe was a bruiser. He had guts. It ought to end there— Nice day, boss."

Larsen was staring into space. "We've got to get the guy that did this, Brinky, before Joe's gang get him. They'll crucify him. I didn't like the look in The Swan's eyes. It meant something, I don't just know what."

"Looks like Joe was lookin' for a push in the mug when he grabbed that jane."

Larsen said: "I don't think it was premeditated murder. In fact, I'm sure it wasn't."

"Might ha' been. Them lights went out. The little guy disappeared. Everything went off like a clock. There wasn't a hitch anywhere."

Brinky folded his paper. "He left his hat and coat."

"What good are they? No labels in either."

"That's what I come in for early, boss."

"What?"

"To borry that coat."

Larsen squinted. "What's on your mind, Brinky?"

"Should you lend me that coat, I'll git started."

Larsen grabbed the phone, made a departmental call. "Harry, this is Larsen. When Brinky comes down give him that overcoat."

The day was bright with winter sunlight, sharply cold, the air clear as the toll of a bell. Brinky walked away from headquarters with his broad shoes a-creak, a woolen muffler that Mom had knitted and heavy woolen gloves that Mom had knitted also. He walked with the side-to-side roll of a heavy, stocky man. Five-feet-nine of him encompassed two hundred and five pounds. The muffler jutted up from the back of his collar and almost touched the brim of his flat-crowned brown fedora. Over his arm he carried, neatly folded, a heather-colored overcoat.

In Plummer Street he visited a small tailoring shop. When he came out he boarded a street car and rode ten blocks, got off and entered another tailor's. From this shop he walked four blocks across town consulting memoranda he held in his hand. This was another tailoring shop, and from it he walked five blocks north to another. In two and a half hours he called on fourteen shops. At eleven-twenty he walked into the fifteenth. It was a large establishment on the second floor with broad windows overlooking North Harkness Street.

A man said: "Yes, sir?" and rubbed hands in anticipation.

"This coat," Brinky said. "By any chance did you make it?"

The man looked at it. He called a second man, and this man looked at it and called a third. The three went into a close huddle and jabbered spiritedly, while Brinkhaus remained in the background patiently.

Then the first man turned around. "I believe we made this coat, sir."

"I'm Sergeant Brinkhaus, from police headquarters. Could you sorta check up and see who you made it for?"

The man measured the coat and called a fourth man. He talked rapidly and the fourth man disappeared into an office. In a few minutes the fourth man reappeared carrying some papers. He gave them to the first man and the latter came to Brinkhaus.

"This material was featured three months ago. We made sixteen overcoats of this material. According to measurements, there was only one man who could have had this made. His name is Paul Corson, the address 644 Hill Street."

"I'm much obliged, mister, thanks. And should I ask would you say nothin' about this, is it a promise?"

"Indeed, sergeant."

THE expression on Brinky's face was slightly less downcast than when he had entered. Down below, he considered a taxi parked at the curb, considered his forthcoming insurance instalment, and walked three blocks to a street-car line. He changed twice before reaching Hill Street.

Number 644 was a five-story apartment house in a modest neighborhood. Alongside one of ten buttons in the lobby he saw the name of Paul Corson. He pressed the button, heard the door click open, entered. He climbed a staircase to the third floor and saw a woman standing in an open doorway.

"Good-day," he said. "Are you Mrs. Corson?"

"Yes."

"Is this your husband's overcoat?"

"Why—why—" She stopped and stared at him.

"The tailor says it is."

She laughed jerkily. "Why—why, yes. Yes, of course. Thank you so much."

She was small, dark-haired, pretty. Brinky seemed embarrassed.

He said: "You're husband ain't home, is he?"

"No—no. He doesn't get home until six."

Brinky said: "I'll leave it. Will you ask your husband to meet me tonight at about eight in Herbie Kettner's Coffee Pot, 55 Clove Street?"

"Why, yes—yes, of course."

"The name is Brinkhaus, missus. Thank you."

He went back to headquarters by way of three street cars. Entering Larsen's office, he found Assistant District Attorney Wells Gatlin pacing furiously up and down. Gatlin stopped short and glared at him.

"Where's that overcoat?"

Blinky blinked. "Whuh-what overcoat?"

"You know damned well what overcoat I mean! The one we picked up at the Hot Shot Club!"

"Oh, yeah. Oh, that overcoat. Well, Mr. Gatlin, I'm havin' it cleaned. I fell off a trolley car with it and got it all dirtied up. I'm having it cleaned."

"Having it cleaned! Who ever heard of such a thing!"

"I'll give it to you soon as I git it back."

Gatlin appeared about to be overcome with apoplexy. His lips sputtered wetly. "Damn my stars!" He spun and drilled Larsen with a dark look. "Is this the type of idiot you recommend as your right-hand man?"

Larsen himself looked puzzled, but he said, "I guess Brinky thought it was the best thing to do."

"Best thing! Bah! I said 'Bah'!" He whirled back to Brinkhaus. "You go get that overcoat immediately. Immediately!"

Brinky swallowed. "Well, I can't, Mr. Gatlin. It's being cleaned."

"As a representative of the district attorney's office, I demand—"

Larsen cut in: "Now wait a minute, Gatlin. Just wait a minute. Don't go off the handle. You'll get a look at that coat when it's returned."

Gatlin trembled with anger. "I know! I know! Your whole damned department is working against me! That's what! I'll bet that coat is right in this building! I'll bet!" He drew himself up. "All right! I'll find it!"

He stamped out, banged the door violently.

Brinkhaus said: "There ought to be some kind of medicine for a guy like him."

"Brinky—" Larsen's voice was low— "Brinky, what have you done with that overcoat?"

"I give it back to its owner."

"What!"

"Yeah."

Larsen jumped to his feet. "Then where is he?"

'Well, he wasn't there. I give it to his wife. A pretty little thing, boss. The guy is goin' to meet me at Herbie Kettner's Coffee Pot tonight."

Larsen looked slightly exasperated. "Why in God's name didn't you bring the man back with you? How did you find out who owned the coat?"

"Well, I went around to Ikey Goldfarb, the tailor, and asked him was the coat tailor-made. He said yes. So I went around to all the tailors. So one of them recognized it and I got the name that way. Paul Corson. I didn't want to git the woman all fussed up, so I left it there and told her to tell her husband to meet me."

Larsen dropped back into his chair.

Brinky shrugged. "The lady wasn't the one Corson brung in the night club, so I didn't want to—to— Well, it's the guy we want after all, so what the heck's the use o' gittin' his missus all het up? I hate to have doin's with women and like me pal Ogglecarp useter say—"

"That's quite enough, Brinky," Larsen said distinctly. "See that that coat is not lost. See that Corson meets you."

"Yes, boss." He dipped his head. "Yes, boss."

PAUL CORSON was a tall man of about thirty. He entered Herbie Kettner's Coffee Pot at exactly eight o'clock. Raw night wind had nipped his cheeks. He wore the heather-colored overcoat and stopped beside the cash counter.

"Pardon me. Is there a Mr. Brinkhaus waiting?"

Herbie said: "*Ja.*" Lifted his voice: "Hey, Brinky, dot zhentlemans—" He pointed. "Give a look, please, mister; dot's Mr. Brinkhaus."

Brinky was standing, his broad head tilted to one side, his candid brown eyes watching Corson approach.

"Hello, Mr. Corson. Have a seat right in this here now booth."

"You're the man returned my coat?"

They were sitting down.

Brinkhaus nodded. "Yes. I'm Sergeant Brinkhaus."

"Sergeant—"

"P'lice headquarters."

Corson said: "Oh," softly.

Brinkhaus interlocked his stout fingers and kept looking candidly at Corson. "I didn't want to say anything to your missus first off. I figgered I oughter have a talk with you first. I figgered you'd know why I asked her you should come here. There was a man killed at the Hot Shot Club last night."

"Yes. I read it in the paper— Cigarette?"

"No, thanks. I cut out smokin' account of me missus said I was tossin' all night. You got a very nice missus, Mr. Corson."

"I think so myself."

"I understand you work in a bank. Assistant cashier, ain't it now?"

Corson's eyes were on guard. "Yes."

"I want to be as good as I can about it, Mr. Corson, but law is law, and even if Big Joe Rudnicki was a racketeer, the law is so writ that a dead man's a dead man and we cops have got to do somethin' about it. It was pretty tough when you clean outta that night club leavin' that there now coat behind."

Corson's face was becoming pale. His lips barely moved. "I see. I begin to see. You think that I was at—what's the name?—the Hot Shot Club?"

"Account of your nice missus, I'm sorry I got to say yes."

Corson bowed his head. "I'm sorry your mistaken, Sergeant Brinkhaus."

"You don't look like a bad feller yourself, Mr. Corson. I'm sorry you're actin' like that."

"I can't help it, sergeant. I wasn't there."

Brinkhaus sat back. "You mind comin' to p'lice headquarters?"

"Not at all."

CHAPTER THREE

"I Killed Him"

LARSEN, running a palm back over his yellow mane of hair, said: "Take that chair, Mr. Corson."

Corson sat down beside the desk.

Larsen shifted a powerful desklight so that its hot white beam drove mercilessly into Corson's face. Then he turned out the other lights in the room. Corson shifted uneasily and his lips tightened.

Gatlin blew his nose briskly, jammed the handkerchief into his pocket, smacked his palms together. His eyes were bright bale-fires in his dark, saturnine face. Brinkhaus looked meekly at him and shifted from one foot to the other.

Gatlin rose on his toes, smacked his palms down on the desk. His dark face shot into the glare of the spotlight.

"Mr. Corson, this is murder and Sergeant Brinkhaus claims that this coat you're wearing came from the Hot Shot Club. There's no earthly reason for your denying, or attempting to deny, that you were not there last night. As assistant district attorney of this county, vested with—"

"I was not at the Hot Shot Club, Mr. Assistant District Attorney."

"Oh, ridiculous! Ridiculous! My dear, dear fellow—"

Larsen interrupted quietly with: "Mr. Corson, you admit that it is your coat?"

"Yes, sir."

"And you claim that you were not at the Hot Shot Club last night?"

"I was not at the Hot Shot Club."

"Seems a bit paradoxical, doesn't it?"

"Yes."

Larsen said: "There's only one other answer. Another man wore this coat there."

Corson's face was white and set. He said nothing.

Gatlin snapped: "If you were not there in this coat, then who was?"

Corson's eyes glinted. "The only thing I can say is that I was not there. That can easily be proven by people who were there, I imagine."

"You can't crack wise with me!" Gatlin warned.

"I am not attempting to crack wise."

Gatlin's fist hammered the desk and his voice crackled. "This is murder! You understand? Murder! A man was shot to death last night! Murdered in cold blood! In the city of Portsend, county of Windmore, of which, as assistant district attorney, I am a representative vested with prosecuting powers, I ask—demand—the truth and nothing but the truth. Who wore your coat to the Hot Shot Club last night?"

"I cannot tell!"

"Piffle! Bosh! Do you realize that in secreting evidence—"

"Mr. Corson," broke in Larsen's mellow voice, "whatever sentimental feeling you must have, you must be aware of the fact that in acting the way you are you thwart justice and place yourself in a very undesirable position."

Corson raised a hand against the glare of the light. Gatlin knocked his hand down. Corson stiffened and his lower lip shook, his eyes glittered.

"I refuse to say anything other than I've already said!"

Gatlin snarled: "You listen to me, you damned fool—"

"Gatlin," Larsen cut in, pushing him aside. "This inquest happens to be in my office."

Gatlin whirled on him. "I don't give a damn where it is!"

"You heard me, Gatlin."

"This man is guilty! I demand the right to question him in any manner I see fit to!"

Larsen's voice became edged. "Gatlin,

I repeat that this is my office. I add that you have no right in here if I choose not to have you!"

"Oh, is that so?"

"Try maintaining the dignity of the district attorney's office by taking the air. This man has not yet been booked. When he has been, and when I've finished with him, then you'll be at liberty to question him."

Brinkhaus, sighing, went to the door, opened it and stood looking innocently into space.

Larsen pointed. "The door is open, Gatlin."

Gatlin's face worked and his mouth drew down at one corner. His eyes burned with hatred and words fought for utterance behind his twitching lips.

A man appeared in the doorway. A young man. Tall and lean and with a pale, haggard face.

"Inspector Larsen?"

Larsen pivoted. "Why, yes."

The man walked into the office, drew his hand from his pocket, laid a gun on the desk.

"I killed Rudnicki," he said. "I killed him."

JUNE CORSON was Paul Corson's wife. She sat in an overstuffed armchair, her eyes red-rimmed, a crumpled ball of linen handkerchief moving spasmodically from one hand to the other. Corson stood by the open window staring down into the street.

Brinkhaus sat on a straight-backed chair, his overcoat open, the ends of a woolen scarf trailing haphazardly across the lapels. He looked at once uneasy and sympathetic. It was not warm in the room but none the less he fanned himself with his hat.

"O God. O dear God," the woman sobbed.

"Missus," Brinkhaus said, and then forgot what to say.

She sobbed on. "He s my orother, my brother. Allan is my brother. They'll hang him—hang him. O God!"

Corson turned from the window, grim-faced. He came over and patted her on the shoulder.

Brinkhaus said: "If we can prove it wasn't premeditated, there won't be no death penalty."

Corson said: "He could have got away. I told him to. I intended bucking you so that he would have a chance to get away. But he wouldn't. He gave himself up."

"It was best," Brinkhaus said. "When did he borrow your overcoat?"

"Yesterday morning."

Brinkhaus scratched his chin. "He won't tell us the gal was with him. We've got to find the gal."

"What's the use of dragging in the girl?" Corson asked.

"She'd be his star witness. She'd have to be. He won't tell. You'd best tell me who she was."

Corson said: "We never met her. He'd only talked about her. He never brought her around. We don't know who she is or where she lives. But he loved her. Lottie he called her. But he never brought her around. She'll show up. Maybe she doesn't even know he gave himself up yet."

"You get a lawyer for him yet?"

"Yes. I notified Walton & Arnholt."

"Good," Brinkhaus nodded. "They're the best in town but they cost like heck."

"I don't care. I'll spend every cent I have."

The woman sobbed. "Poor Allan—poor Allan."

Brinkhaus got up and moved closer to the woman. "Missus, I know it's pretty tough. These here things bust out like a rash when folks least expect 'em. Here you got a nice home here and I know it ain't nice havin' all this mess on your shoulders. He's only twenty-five and that's pretty young. You got to buck up, missus, and hope for the best. It's times like this when I wisht I wasn't no cop. If I can do anything for you, let me know."

"You're kind, sergeant—you're so very kind."

"I'm a family man meself, missus." He made an awkward bow. "I got to be goin'. G'night."

Corson went to the door with him. "You're blamed white, sergeant. We'll help all we can—but it seems so futile. You'll take good care of him, won't you?"

"Sure, mister. Sure."

WHEN Brinkhaus walked dejectedly into Larsen's office the inspector was sitting back in his chair. He looked winded.

"Any news, Brinky?"

"Nope."

Larsen mopped his face. "The boy's stubborn as hell. I was after him. Davis and Shumacher were after him. And Gatlin. The boy's all shot—all nerves." He put away his handkerchief. "If we could only find the little guy Flannagan said ran out when it happened. Or the girl."

Brinkhaus went out and up two blocks. He bought two cheese sandwiches and a bucket of coffee. He returned to headquarters and went down to the cell-block. Hennessey let him into cell number 5.

Allan Cable crouched, then relaxed. "Oh, I thought it would be Gatlin again. God, keep that fiend out of here!"

"Um," said Brinkhaus. "I—I brung around some sandwiches and coffee, Allan."

"Thanks. I—I am a bit hungry."

"It'll brace you up."

Brinkhaus sat down and watched the boy eat. He waited until the last drop of coffee had been drunk. He did not smoke cigarettes, but he had brought along a pack for the boy. Cable said: "Thanks,

Gee, you're swell!" He smoked nervously.

Brinky said: "You oughter tell us who the gal is, Al. It'd help a lot."

Cable gave him one look, then went on smoking.

"If she loves you, Al, she'd want to stand by you."

Cable cried: "Why should I drag her in?"

"You got to think, boy, that your life's at stake."

"I know it. I knew it before I gave myself up. I'll take the chance. That dirty rat grabbed her. I told him to let go. When the lights went off I—I just went crazy. I guess I was afraid he'd pull a gun on me. So I shot him. I don't repent it. He deserved it. And now that I know who he was—nothing more than a dirty gunman—I'm doubly glad I gave him what he deserved."

"I know, Al, I know. But a life's a life. We got to look at it that way. You killed a man. Even sayin' he deserved what he got, you should be willin' to help us try givin' you a break."

"Break, eh? Cable laughed scornfully. "That man Gatlin wants to hang me. He wants to! He's worse than any gangster. Give me a break—" He stopped. "I'm sorry, sergeant. You're different."

"You got a nice sister, Al. She's standin' by you. But the one we want is the lady friend you was with."

Cable's jaw stiffened. "If she comes, that's all right. But I got myself into this and I'll take what's coming to me."

Brinkhaus stood up. "Al, should you want anything, just ask for me."

Unexpectedly the boy gripped the old sergeant's hand. "I know you mean well, sir. But try to understand. I don't want to drag her in. I can't. I was drunk a bit and maybe I shouldn't have done what I did. But I've done it. I'll stand trial and hope for the best."

On the way out, after Hennessey had locked the cell, Brinkhaus walked down the cell-block with him.

Hennessey sighed. "Clean lad, Brinky."

"You got a kid, ain't you, Henry?"

"Yeah. 'Bout his age."

Brinky nodded. "Me too."

"Yeah," said Hennessey.

"Yeah," said Brinkhaus.

AN angel-faced girl was sitting in a chair beside Larsen's desk when Brinkhaus walked disconsolately into the office. Larsen stopped talking. Brinkhaus made a hesitant bow with his honest brown eyes hopping from the girl to Larsen.

Larsen said: "This is Miss Blakeney."

Starry eyes, slightly moist, trembled on Brinky; and Brinky bowed and said: "Miss Lottie Blakeney?"

"Yes," Larsen said. "Miss Blakeney, this is Sergeant Brinkhaus whom I've placed in charge of the investigation."

She half rose and made a demure little curtsy. She was beautiful, an ash blonde; slender and of medium height. A lapin coat was open far enough to reveal a flowered chiffon dress.

Larsen said: "Miss Blakeney is Allan Cable's—"

"Good, good," Brinkhaus said, and his tone, his manner, meant it. "I was just down to see Allan."

Larsen said: "Miss Blakeney tells me— You tell the sergeant, Miss Blakeney. Brinky, I'll be back in a few minutes."

Larsen went out and Brinkhaus pulled a chair up to face the girl, sat down and assumed a very fatherly attitude.

The girl said in a trembling voice: "It all happened so fast, sergeant—it's still like a dream, like a nightmare. Allan and I went into that club. A man seated us. Then Allan and I danced. The man—this Joe Rudnicki, so the papers say—came over and said, 'I want to dance with that girl, guy.' Like that. Allan said, 'I beg your pardon, but you are not.' Then the man grabbed me and Allan shoved him away. The man tried again and Allan said, 'You're drunk. If you don't stop I'll hit you.' The man kept trying and Allan hit him. They grappled and then the lights went out. Then the shot. Then—then Allan had me by the arm. 'We've got to get out of here,' he said. I didn't know what to do. I went with him and we ran away fast. In the morning—we saw the papers."

She stopped, stared at the floor, her eyes glazed. Then she said: "Allan had borrowed his brother-in-law's coat. His own was being cleaned. He said. 'Gosh, Paul's coat—we left it there.' We didn't know what to do. He told Paul. Paul told him to run away. Allan didn't know what to do. Then—then he knew he couldn't run away. So—he gave himself up.".

"Do you remember, miss, if this Rudnicki went for a gun?"

Her eyes raised to meet Brinky's. "When the lights went out I tried to do something. I grabbed Rudnicki's arm—his right one. I could feel he was trying to get his hand in his pocket. I said, 'Allan—Allan, look out!' He must have sensed what I meant. He shot him." She took a breath. "He killed him."

Brinky said: "That's good, miss. Remember that about Rudnicki's hand in his pocket."

"And Allan," she said, "when he decided to give himself up, made me swear that I'd stay out of it. But how could I?" Her eyes filled. "How could I?"

"Course you couldn't," he agreed. "There, there, now. Don't cry, miss— You work, miss?"

"Yes."

"Where?"

"The cigar shop in the Hotel Billings. Allan met me there—two months ago. He was saving to buy an engagement ring."

Brinky edged closer. "When you and Allan ran outside, miss, did you see a little guy with spectacles runnin' away too?"

"A little man?"

"Yeah—and with spectacles."

She shook her head slowly. "No."

"And you never before in your life seen this Rudnicki?"

"No—surely not. Why—when he came up to me—I—I didn't know what to say, to think."

Brinky nodded. "Yeah, I heard Rudnicki useter to do that, take a kinda shine to a gal and git fresh with her— I'm glad you turned up, miss. You're gonna be a big help to Allan. Keep in mind kinda that I'm your friend." He patted her hand. "Just remember me should you want something."

"Oh, thank you, thank you, sergeant."

Larsen came in and Brinkhaus rose and said: "I'll be gittin' along downstairs, boss."

He went downstairs to Sergeant Connolly's office. Connolly was the gun expert. Connolly said: "Yup, it is the gun. It is the bullet." He held up a slug. "This, Brinky, was ejected from this gun. It killed Rudnicki. Positively."

It was a 25 Colt automatic, pocket model. Brinky picked it up and examined it.

"If you're looking for the number," Connolly said, "it's been filed off."

"Yeah, I notice."

Brinkhaus picked up a magnifying glass and examined the gun closely. "Mind if I borry this gun?"

"It's the gun, man. It's the gun. Open and shut. It's the gun that killed Rudnicki."

"Mind if I borry it?"

"You mean to stand there and tell me that I'm a liar!"

"No," Brinky said. "Only could I borry it?"

Connolly laughed. "Sure, go ahead."

Brinkhaus said: "Thanks," put the gun in his pocket and went to the door. He turned to say: "How is Mrs. Connolly's varicose veins?"

"Better, thanks, Brinky."

"Good. Should you remember, give her me regards and tell her I ain't forgot what swell liederkrantz she had there that night."

CHAPTER FOUR

Angel Face

THE Swan, pallid, his amber eyes dreamy, regarded his likeness in the Palladian mirror. His skin seemed almost transparent. His eyelashes were long and curved upward. His ebon hair had a precise part down the center. At first glance his face seemed weak, effeminite; after a while you became aware of the rigid jaw, the straight lines of wide narrow lips. His hands moved so gracefully that you were hardly aware they moved at all. By moving his head a bit he could also see the reflected image of Brinkhaus.

Brinky was sitting on a vis-a-vis couch, coat and overcoat open and thumbs hooked in lower vest pockets. Light from a parchment-shaded lamp brought into sharp relief his quaint haircomb of the '90's.

"O' course, Swan, it was a helluva accident. Big Joe had no right a-tall, though, to go crashin' into another guy's party. He musta been pie-eyed."

"Plastered," said The Swan to Brinky's image. "We always had that trouble with Big Joe. Get him on a party and you never knew when he'd go meshuga. Still, he was a swell guy in many ways. He's getting a honey for a funeral."

Brinky wiggled his fingers while still keeping his thumbs in his vest pockets. "Who's takin' Big Joe's place?"

"Where?"

"As the brass hat o' your mob."

The Swan regarded his own image. "I don't know yet. We haven't talked about it. There's Krieger and 'Maxiewaxie' Klein and 'General George' Onkman. We'll see."

"I expect you will, Swan."

"What's that—a crack?"

"Oh, no-o. I just kinda figgered you was some groceries yourself in this mob. I like you, Swan. You don't act like an egg. I figger if you was boss of this scatter we'd have less back-alley jobs."

The Swan's chest expanded. "Thanks, Brinky. There's a swell chance I may handle the reins."

Brinky looked gloomy eyed at the carpet for a long minute. Then he said, without looking up: "You ain't seen 'The Professor' around town lately, have you?"

"The—who?"

"His name's Jehle. He uster be private secretary to 'Long Tim' Coose, what ran things in Philly three years ago till a rival bunch of big shots rubbed him out. I ain't sure, only I heard The Professor was in town."

"Never heard of him."

"It don't matter. I was just thinkin'. I just heard he was in. They say he's some groceries with a gun and I just like to keep checked up on the red-hots. Well . . ." Brinky slapped his knees, rose, yawned. "It's near ten. I'm up past bedtime."

The Swan turned from the mirror. He smiled graciously, bowed and indicated a decanter and glasses. "Have a nightcap."

"Don't mind if I do."

They touched glasses.

Brinky said: "I got a hunch, Swan, you're gonna be the next kingpin o' this mob."

"I'll do right by you, Brinky."

"Yeah, Big Joe was past his prime. The mob needs new blood. Here's to you, big fella."

They drank and Brinky smacked his lips. "Thanks, Swan." He went to the door. The Swan hastened to open it.

Brinky screwed a thumb into The Swan's ribs. "And I expect by and large the mob's takin' orders from you right now."

The Swan chuckled drily, flexed his lips, said nothing.

LEAVING the opulent apartment house, Brinky trudged up the broad avenue until a bus came along. He boarded it and rode as far as Union Circle, got off and walked down South Broad Street. He stopped in front of a pool parlor, opened the door and looked in. He closed the door, walked a block and stopped at the next corner and waited. In a few minutes a man came out of the pool parlor and walked toward him.

"Hello, Brinky."

"Hello, 'Soup.' Anything?"

'Geez, sarge, I been snoopin' all around."

"O. K., O. K. And what now?"

"I ain't heard of him bein' around."

Brinky's voice dropped. "I got a hunch the mug's in town. We ain't got no pictures of him because he was never mugged here. But it sounds like his work. Keep on your toes, Soup, and fall down on me and I'll put a pinch on you."

"On the up-and-up, sarge—"

"O. K., O. K."

Brinkhaus walked on and then cut over into Little Italy. He checked up on two more stoolies, then crossed Cherry Square and entered a speakeasy."

"Gimme a glass o' Cholly Koenigfelt's beer, Tony."

"Hey, sarge, headquarters rang up and said you should ring if you come in."

"Thanks."

He called the lieutenant. "Brinky, Sam. . . . Huh? . . . Yeah, I got it: Southern one-o-four-o. Thanks, Sam." He hung up, then unpronged the receiver again and said: "Southern one-o-four-o." He waited, then said: "Brinkhaus. . . . Oh, hello, 'Big-nose'. . . . What's 'at? . . . I see. Listen, Big-nose, you ain't givin' me a bum steer? . . . O. K., thanks. . . . Yeah, I'll see can I git you a job on the highway commission."

He left the booth, returned to the bar and drained a mug of beer. "How's your little gal's measles, Tony?"

"Swell, Brinky, thanks."

Brinky had an address: 909 Clermont Street. Twenty minutes after leaving Tony's he entered Clermont Street from the north, turning from Hawk. Clermont is level here. Once it was a pretty good neighborhood and in those days the city saw fit to pave it with expensive red bricks. The bricks outlasted the goodness of the neighborhood. The frame houses still stand, but the little front yards no longer sprout flowers and the low iron railings have gone to rust and ruin. An enterprising meat packer started the decadence by buying up a square block at the south end of the street and the winds in Clermont Street are mostly southern.

Number 909 was a gray frame house of three stories. Its front door was flush with the sidewalk. Brinky opened it and entered a musty hall where a gas jet flowered yellowly against a scarred wall.

He climbed to the top hallway. Here another gas jet burned. The wind moaned across the roof and the hall was damp and cold. Brinky counted doors. He pulled his gun from his hip holster, shoved it into his overcoat pocket. He left it there while he drew off the woolen glove from his right hand and held it in his left.

He rapped at a door. He did not put his bare hand back into his pocket. He waited patiently while he heard a chair scrape. He heard a bolt rap open. He saw the door open to a crack. He did not move. There was something shining in the crack the open door made.

"Go ahead, open it," Brinky said. "Nobody's goin' to eat you, mister."

"What do you want?"

"Did you open the door wide, we could talk better."

The door opened, bit by bit, and a small man with matted gray hair and thick-lensed spectacles peered nearsightedly at Brinkhaus.

"Yes, yes, what is it?" he asked in a piping voice.

Brinky walked in, ponderously, and the little man backed up but kept his left hand in the pocket of a faded bathrobe. With the change of light and shadow the thick-lensed spectacles hid his eyes.

Brinkhaus said: "I seen you last about two and a half years ago, mister. You think back and you'll remember what I said. I said, 'Professor, I'm givin' you a break, so take it and lam outta Portsend and give her a wide berth.' That's what I said. Maybe you ain't got the memory for faces that I have. Git your pants on, Professor."

"Why, really—why, really—"

"And take care o' that left-handed rod in your pocket there. Gimme it. There's no tellin' what the hell you might do with it. Come on, gimme that roscoe."

The man piped: "What do you want me for? Why—why do you want me? I haven't done anything."

"Maybe you think goin' around takin' cracks at light switches in night clubs ain't nothin', huh? Like I said now, dammit, gimme that rod before it gits away from you."

"B-b-but—"

Brinky's right hand plunged to his wrist. The gun appeared. Brinky got the wrist. The man tried to leap backward. Brinky's heavy shoe pinned his foot to the floor.

"*E-e-e-e!*" yelped The Professor. "Oh—oh—ouch!" he cried.

The gun fell to the floor and Brinky said, placidly: "That's nice now, that's nice." He flung the man away. "Your pants."

THE Professor limped into Larsen's office yammering: "I—I can hardly walk, sir. He—he bashed me on the foot."

"It was like this," Brinkhaus explained. "A piany fell on it, boss."

Larsen stood up. "Who is this man, Brinky?"

"Oscar Jehle's his real name. He's got others. One o' them's The Professor. Git Flannagan over here from the Hot Shot Club and see wasn't this the guy was sittin' near the light switch. If he ain't, I'm goin' to the tall timbers."

"What reason have you for arresting this man?"

"Well, the first reason was I didn't believe Allan Cable plunked Big Joe in the heart."

"Connolly swears it's the gun and the bullet."

"There's somethin' else I'll be gittin' around to."

Larsen, always just, said. "I still don't see why you arrested this man."

"Boss, ain't you ever had a hunch that you figgered might be good and might be goofy? And ain't you felt like you wanted to keep it to yourself till you found for sure it was good? Git Flannagan, will you?"

Larsen got Flannagan.

The night-club owner took fifteen minutes to get over. "That's the guy," he said. "That's the guy was sitting at the table where you go to the light switch."

Larsen said: "You'll stick by that, Jerry?"

"Ab-so-lute!"

Flannagan left and Brinkhaus looked a little less worried. The Professor looked very worried.

Larsen said: "You threw that switch, Jehle."

Jehle's eyes rolled behind his thick-lensed spectacles. He made fluttering gestures with his hands. "N-n-no, I—"

"Don't be stupid. Flannagan identified you. We can get others—the girls you danced with, for instance. If you didn't throw it, why did you lam out when Rudnicki was killed?"

Jehle blubbered but didn't say anything. Brinkhaus made an apologetic bow to Larsen and Larsen stepped aside. Brinky planted his two hundred and five pounds in front of Jehle.

"You always had a hand in the dope traffic, mister. That's why I told you to lam two and a half years ago. When did you git back here?"

"Four months ago."

"Who come with you?"

Jehle's eyes bulged. He shrank back in the chair.

Brinkhaus turned to Larsen. "Boss, I got a friend, Billy Kiley, on the Philadelphia cops. I called him on long distance tonight and he give me the lowdown on Jehle. Dope's Jehle's long shot, but he always gits the backin' of a mob. And he always has a gal with him. Billy says the gal usually gits a job in a swell hotel drug store or cigar stand—mostly the best in town. The customers go there and they usually ask for a kind of cigarette nobody every heard of. I figger we know who come with him."

"Who? Larsen said.

"Lottie Blakeney."

"Lottie—"

"Yeah," said Brinkhaus. "Allan's lady friend."

Jehle's face became a frozen mask of terror.

Brinkhaus said: "Allan's shieldin' the gal. Al never plunked Big Joe. I took that rod apart and found pink face powder in the works. It's been there a long time. Like it was carried in a gal's pocket-book all the time. The gal's a moll. I described her to Billy Kiley and he said it sounded like the moll they was callin' 'Angel Face' down in Philly. She's a cokey herself."

Larsen said: "Brinky, you amaze me!" He turned to Jehle. "What have you got to say?"

Jehle chirped: "Nothing. I have nothing to say. I won't say anything. You can't make me. Notify my attorney Abe Klotz."

"Ain't it funny," Brinky said, "that Abe Klotz is The Swan's mouth-piece too?"

"I—I won't say anything."

Brinky said: "Boss, I'm goin' to git the Angel Face."

CHAPTER FIVE

The Professor Talks

HE became a spendthrift. He hopped a taxi instead of a proletariat street car. He sat in the back and watched the lights of the city whip past. His woolen muffler rubbed against his chin and one end of it dangled down the front of his overcoat. He got out in front of the Hotel Billings, crossed the broad sidewalk and went in through the revolving door. The lobby was almost empty. His hard heels made a loud noise on the marble floor.

He spotted the cigar counter. The girl was closing up. She saw him coming and a sweet smile overspread her face.

"Hello, Sergeant Brinkhaus."

"Hello, Miss Blakeney. The boss over to headquarters would like to know could you stop by for a few minutes."

"This late?"

Brinky looked apologetic. "He sent me over to ask you."

"I'm so, so tired, sergeant."

He nodded. "Yeah, it must be a hard job, workin' here late like this. I said to the boss, 'Shucks, boss, Miss Blakeney 'll be worn out this late.' But he said I should come. It's for to help out Allan maybe."

She shrugged, smiled her sweet smile. "Of course, then."

He waited placidly while she locked drawers, turned out lights. He waited while she took a cash box over to the desk. She came back and said: "In a few minutes. I'll get my coat."

"Yes, miss."

He roamed abstractedly in front of the desk. Heard the scratching of the night clerk's pen on paper. Heard the voice of the switchboard operator. He stopped roaming and squinted at a fluted Doric column. He went over the desk.

"Please, mister, I'm Sergeant Brinkhaus."

The clerk looked up.

Brinky said: "Would you ask the operator what the call was she just put through?"

The clerk went over to the switchboard, came back. "It was from the ladies' retiring room. The call was made to Westend 999."

"Thanks very much."

Brinkhaus left the desk, drew a notebook from his pocket, turned to the S's. He saw: Swan, Westend 999. He closed the book and put it away and his expression became oddly pious.

The girl appeared, smiling. Brinky bowed politely and they went outside and got into a taxi. It was late. The city

empty it reechoed the more so to sounds.

"Allan—how is Allan?" the girl said.

"Sleepin', poor kid."

"Oh, I hope—I do hope he'll get out of this. I love him so."

Brinkhaus blinked in the darkness. He watched the street ahead, kept his eyes on street corners. The girl's voice came to him as from afar. It was a sweet voice, soft and melodious. Once he saw her eyes as they passed close to a street light. The eyes burned brightly. Brinky returned his watchful stare to the way ahead. He sat on the edge of the seat. He removed the woolen glove from his right hand and held it in his left. For no reason at all he had a vision of Mom waiting up for him by the dining-room table. He wanted her to use the living room, but times were hard and it cost too much to heat the living room. There would be something hot waiting in the oven and a kettle whistling on the back of the kitchen range.

He gave a sigh of relief when they swung into Civic Square and turned down a narrow street where the green lights of police headquarters shone. The girl had stopped talking.

The cab stopped and Brinkhaus got out, helped the girl to the sidewalk. Three men came quietly out of the shadows.

"O. K., sarge, take it easy."

Their hats were yanked down over their eyes, their coat collars were turned up. Steel glinted in their hands. A gun pressed hard against Brinky's back. The girl jumped away and one of the men took her arm and said: "Get in there, sugar." She hopped back into the cab. The man held a gun on the driver. "You be nice, kid."

"Um," said Brinkhaus.

One of the men said: "Keep 'em up, sarge." He joined the other man and told him: "Get in. I'll ride the running board. Tell that driver to get started."

Brinky stood rooted to the pavement, his hands raised. He watched the taxi drive away, saw the man with the gun standing on the running board. Then Brinky turned and barged up to the headquarters garage. He almost fell over a parked motorcycle. He could feel that it was still warm. He hadn't ridden a motorcycle in eight years, but he started it. And blew the siren.

He rode it like a cowboy out of the garage. At the second corner he saw the taxi parked and the driver standing in the road. He stopped.

"Where'd they go?"

The driver pointed. "See that tail-light? A seven-passenger tourin'—dark gray. Plates—F-4066."

"When the squad car comes, stop it. Tell 'em."

He kicked his feet free of the ground and the motorcycle hooted up the dark street. He saw the red light disappear to the left. One end of his muffler trailed behind him like a pennant. His coat tails stood out straight in the wind. He got up nerve enough to take one hand off the bar. He yanked his gun and unlocked the safety.

FLEET Street was a wide thoroughfare, a main drag with street-car rails gleaming coldly in the winter night. The motorcycle's siren wailed. Brinky stuck his jaw out against the bitter wind. He did not take his eyes from the red tail-light ahead. He had a feeling that if he should turn his head to the side the motorcycle would trick him.

But he kept the siren going. Out of the tail of his eye he was sure he saw, now and then, a uniformed cop. His heart was up in his throat. The motorcycle was a demon beneath him and he marveled that he was still sitting on it. He gave it a little more gas. He found that the faster he drove it the smoother it rode.

The street-car rails ended. Brinky was glad of that. Smooth cement lay beyond—a road that went north and east, that would join the Post Road diagonally a few miles beyond. He wondered if other cops had taken up the chase but he was afraid to turn his head. His head seemed locked in one position—with eyes front.

They hit the Post Road. There was a police booth at the intersection and a cop was standing in the doorway. Brinky fired his gun in the air. The touring car pounded on the straightaway. Two miles beyond the intersection, where wide fields began, a spurt of red flame shot from the touring.

Brinky held his breath. Nothing happened. He turned out all the lights on the motorcycle. He took the hand that held his gun and one of the handle-bars and raised it. He fired. The red light went on, winking around a wide bend. Flame spurted ahead. There was a crash. Glass pelted Brinky's face. That was close. They'd smashed the headlight.

He forgot about riding the mtorcycle and consequently began to handle it like an expert. He got more speed out of it. He rode one-handed and raised his gun again. It boomed. The red light went out.

He became aware of a pounding sound close behind him. He looked around and saw a big car. It crept up alongside him because he retarded the throttle. He saw Larsen's face.

"Brinky, you fool—stop!"

"Can't, boss!"

He spurted ahead again. Two jets of flame leaped from the car ahead. Metal rang on the motorcycle and Brinky felt a shock in his left leg. The machine wobbled. He straightened it and kept on. Back of him, and to one side, a machine gun stuttered. Pain suddenly knifed his leg, the reflex of the first shock.

"Um," he said.

A wide bend in the road, and then the lights of a filling station. The car ahead left the highway, skidded up to the pumps. Brinky began braking. Fifty yards from the filling station he stopped and saw the police phaeton pull up beside him.

He got off the machine and started up the side of the road. He could see four men crouched by the station pillars while gas was being run into the tank. Larsen came up beside him with a gun drawn. Butchman came with a Tommy gun. Groves had a sawed-off shotgun and Little carried his revolver.

"What started it?" Larsen said.

"I was bringin' in the gal. She phoned Swan from the hotel. These mugs met us in front of headquarters and she lammed with 'em."

Little fired. A Tommy gun in the hands of one of the men by the touring car cut loose. Lead chipped cement and Groves, getting set, let fly with his Tommy gun. One of the four men wilted and sank to the ground. The filling-station man, in a white suit, ran for cover. Another ran around to the front of the car and started in to the wheel. Little had his gun raised. It belched and the man fell back out of the car and lay flat.

The other two deserted the car and ducked among the pillars of the filling station. Brinkhaus, limping ahead, fired past the red ethyl pump. The two men ran away from the station and made toward the woods on the other side of the crossroad. Brinkhaus fired again. One of the men fell down. The other turned and opened fire with the Tommy gun. Little stopped running and looked oddly at his left arm. He shook it and blood dripped to the road.

Groves started running fast, cursing. He stopped short, braced himself and started his sub-machine gun. The fourth man fell down in a ditch.

A muffled shot sounded in the car. Larsen walked past everybody, his gun leveled, and pulled open the car door. The woman fell out. She was dead—by her own hand.

Brinkhaus limped past the pumps. He stepped over Krieger and went on toward the crossroad. Butchman came running up beside him with the Tommy gun.

"Now you be careful, Brinky!"

They stopped.

A voice said from the ditch: "I'm done for," weakly.

Brinky sat down in the middle of the road—suddenly. He looked around dazedly. Butchman reached the ditch with his gun leveled. Then he lowered it. He went down and dragged out The Swan. The Swan couldn't walk. He was shot in half a dozen places.

Larsen's shoes rasped across the cinders of the station drive and he came rapidly to the center of the room.

"Brinky . . ."

"Huh."

"What's the matter?"

"I just figgered I'd kind of take a rest."

"You want to catch cold sitting on that cold road?"

"That's right." Brinky tried to get up. He sat down again. "Nope, boss, there ain't no use. This here leg o' mine is actin' up like hell."

THE bright white light on Larsen's desk shone mercilessly on the face of Jehle, The Professor. They had taken off Jehle's glasses. His hair was matted and sweat poured down his cheeks. Around him were men—many men. He was hemmed in. He tried to dodge the glare of the light. He couldn't because the men pressed so closely around him.

"She's dead," Larsen said. "She killed

herself. When she saw there was no chance she killed herself. And she killed Big Joe, didn't she?"

Jehle gasped: "Water—water!" and clawed at his collar.

"She killed him, didn't she?"

Jehle's eyes rolled. "Yes—yes. She killed him."

"Get that, Williams," Larsen clipped to the stenographer. "Now, Jehle—go on."

"Water—water."

"Afterwards. Go on."

"The light—take away the light."

"Afterwards."

Jehle moaned. "She killed him. She had the gun in her pocket-book. Cable ran out with her. She told him she did it to save him. He took the gun—and the blame."

"Why did she kill him?"

"The Swan. He got her to do it. The Swan wanted Big Joe out of the way. Said Big Joe was getting soft. Krieger agreed with him. The Swan got on to our dope racket—mine and Lottie's. We had to come through—and he promised us twenty thousand on top of that.

"She met Cable at the cigar counter. He was to be the fall-guy. She made love to him and she knew he was the kind of guy would take the blame. I was to take care of the lights. When Cable and Lottie came in The Swan and Krieger were to dare Big Joe to go out and make a pass at the girl. They knew Big Joe would do it. It never failed. So he did. And Lottie let him have it and made Cable beat it with her.

"When Brinkhaus went for her tonight she must have sensed that the game was up. I was to drop by the hotel at eleven. I didn't because Brinkhaus had me. She must have thought that was wrong too. So she called The Swan. And The Swan and some boys came down, as you said, and sprung her from Brinkhaus. . . . Oh, give me a drink, give me a drink!"

Larsen said: "Somebody get him a drink."

"Well!" exclaimed Gatlin.

"I hope," Larsen said with mellow irony, "that some day you'll get to realize that Brinky is the best right-hand man a chief of detectives ever had."

Gatlin scowled, snorted, disappeared, the door banging shut after him.

A voice in the shadows said: "Who's all right, gang?"

"Gatlin's all right!" they chorused.

"Gatlin?"

"Yeah," they chorused. "In a horse's neck!"

Gripped in his paw was a blood-stained stiletto.

Monkey Murder

by Maxwell Hawkins

Author of "Murder Digs Its Grave," etc.

Angelo was only a chattering native from the jungles of Nicaragua with a taste for peanuts and an ear for hurdy-gurdy tunes. But when murder struck his master down that monk turned out to be the best detective on the force—he could supply missing links even if he couldn't be one.

MURDER was the last thing that would have entered the mind of "Monkey Mike."

He was a little old Italian, whose wizened features and glowing dark eyes were decidedly simian. His hunched body, too, with its long arms and gnarled fingers, looked as if nature had intended it for a life in the tree tops, for swinging from one swaying limb to another.

But the real reason for Mike's nickname was Angelo. Angelo *was* a monkey, a white-faced, flea-hunting native of Nicaragua. He and Mike were in business together. The hurdy-gurdy business. While Mike ground out tinkling tunes, Angelo capered about in a scarlet fez and collected pennies in a dented tin cup.

The kids down around Blanchard Street were crazy about Mike. They like to dance to the tinny melody of his grind organ; they screamed with laughter at Angelo's antics. Even the grown-ups felt a warmth around their hearts when they saw the man who looked like a monkey and the monkey who looked like a man.

Mike had no family, except Angelo. And they lived with monkish severity in one poorly furnished room on the top floor of a grimy tenement building.

But Mike had several pretty good friends. There was Pete Marino, for example. Pete with his thin hooked nose, bushy brows and shrewd eyes. Pete, who owned the peanut cart, and often followed along after Mike, because where a hurdy-gurdy attracts throngs of kids is a good place to peddle peanuts.

Angelo liked Pete, too. But the monkey's affection was mostly mercenary. If he got a chance to dig into Pete's pockets, every once in a while he found a peanut.

Another of Mike's friends was Tony, who ran the basement wine shop. Mike stopped in there every evening regular as the clock for a couple of glasses of dago red. He and Tony would linger over the *vino* and talk about sunny Italy.

Mike liked Tony better than he did Pete. Pete was inclined to be saturnine, almost surly at times. Sicilians were often like that. Tony, however, was open-faced and cheerful.

On the other hand, Angelo didn't care so much for Tony. He never had any peanuts in his pockets.

But the best friend Mike had was Hinkey the cop. He wasn't a cop any more, but a detective. Yet Mike always thought of him as a patrolman, because Hinkey had been pounding a beat when their friendship began. Oddly enough, Hinkey's promotion to detective was due to the same cause as his friendship with Mike.

Hinkey had once saved Monkey Mike's life. Two years back, when a driver had collapsed at the wheel of his heavy truck, and the vehicle was careening wildly down Blanchard Street. Mike was right in its path, but he didn't see it, because his back was turned.

All the kids who had gathered around the hurdy-gurdy scampered to safety. Even Angelo leaped to the sidewalk with a screech of alarm. But Mike just stood there, bowing and grinding away.

Then it was that Hinkey sprang into the street and yanked the old Italian from the wheels which a second later would have crushed the life out of him.

Monkey Mike, still pale beneath his leathery skin and trembling a little, stammered his gratitude. "You sava olda Mike's life, Mista Hink' *Gracia!* He getta even for that!"

And from then on, Monkey Mike would tell everyone who would listen to him: "That Mista Hink' a gooda guy. Olda Mike he getta even!"

That always brought a smile. Everybody knew that he was a little mixed up in his English, and that he meant he was going to repay the big blue-eyed Irish detective.

Whenever Monkey Mike saw Hinkey, he insisted in a torrent of Italian and broken English that they go to Tony's wine cellar for a glass of *vino*. Hinkey usually refused on the grounds that he was busy. He didn't want Mike to spend his hard-earned money on him.

But occasionally he would accept in

order not to offend the old fellow, whose gratitude was almost pathetic. Then he would buy Mike a glass in return, pat him on the back and send him about his music-making.

When, later on, Hinkey was shifted to night duty, he didn't see Mike on the streets. But by then their friendship had grown to such a point that the detective often dropped into Tony's in the evening to see him and sip a glass of red wine. Sometimes Pete was there, too, and on occasion even Angelo would be seated on a table, watching the proceedings with his bright restless eyes.

ONE night late in the summer, Hinkey was standing at the end of the bar in Greek Steve's speakeasy. He hadn't come in there to drink; just to look over Steve's customers. He did that every night. And they were a bad lot. The scum of the Italian neighborhood, and a few who were descendants of other breeds.

He knew most of them by name—Pete Scarpelli, "Little Izzie" Minski, "Wop" Bernadetto, and a dozen others of equally unsavory reputation. As long as they were in there drinking Steve's rotgut, Hinkey didn't have to worry much about them. It was when they were absent that he began to take an interest in their activities.

"What's the idea of poking your face in here all the time?" Steve asked in a low tone, pushing the bar rag down toward the end where Hinkey was standing.

"I like your company, Steve," the detective replied with a hint of a smile.

"Yeah?"

"Yeah. But not the company you keep around this dive."

"Listen," Steve muttered, "I'm paying up regularly, ain't I?"

"Not to me," Hinkey said evenly.

Steve frowned, then he leaned over the bar and dropped his tone. "If a little weekly something would keep you out of here, I ain't saying it couldn't be arranged."

For a second, Hinkey's blue eyes darkened. When he answered, his voice was hard, hard as polished marble. "You couldn't force your dirty money into my pocket!"

"Well, by God! I'm going to put in a kick to the right parties!" Steve snarled. "You're gonna find yourself pounding a beat so far out in the sticks the sidewalks ain't laid yet. See, flatfoot!"

Hinkey straightened up and looked Steve squarely in the eye. "Put in all the kicks you want, but I'll still be around every night. And, if you don't watch your step, I'm going to put you and about half your customers in a seven-foot cage!"

The speakeasy owner was silent for a moment. It was evident that he was holding down his rage with great effort. But he was afraid of this big Irishman with the level eyes, which cut right into him. When he finally had himself under control, he muttered darkly: "O. K., copper, but—you'll get yours some day!"

He moved along the bar, polishing its already shining surface needlessly.

Hinkey pursed his lips, then he laughed softly and turned on his heel.

Outside on Blanchard Street, Hinkey looked at his watch. It was a quarter past twelve. The sidewalks were almost deserted, only a few pedestrians making a belated way along them.

The detective already was dismissing Greek Steve's threat from his mind. He regarded the speakeasy proprietor as loud-mouthed and yellow. To be sure, Hinkey admitted to himself, there was always a chance Steve might hire one of his gunmen customers to turn the heater on him, but he doubted that he would dare even that.

A block down the street, Hinkey descended another flight of steps to a basement. Here there was no peep-hole, no clanking of bolts before a customer was admitted. The door yielded to his touch.

He entered a spacious, beamed room, comfortably filled with tables, which were covered with bright red-and-white-checked table cloths. There were only a few patrons in the place. They were sipping at goblets of red wine.

A plump round-faced man with flashing teeth caught sight of Hinkey and immediately rose from the table where he had been sitting.

"Hello, hello, Mis-ter Hinkey!" he exclaimed effusively, coming forward and rubbing his hands. "I was wanting to see you. Sit down. Have a glass of wine?"

"Thanks, Tony. Just a small one," the detective replied, dropping into a chair at a table near the entrance.

Tony disappeared but returned almost at once bearing a small glass. He set it on the table and then planted his rotund figure in a chair.

"What brings you in so late tonight?" he asked. Tony spoke English pretty well; he'd gone once to night school to learn it.

"Thought I'd drop around to see how you were."

"Glad you did," Tony nodded. He leaned forward confidentially. "I'm kind of worried."

Hinkey shot him a sharp look. "What's worrying you?"

"Monkey Mike!"

"Monkey Mike?" Hinkey repeated in surprise. "What's happened to him?"

Tony gave his thick shoulders a shrug. "Oh, I don't know that nothing's happened to him. Only he ain't been in tonight."

Hickey laughed. "Well, that doesn't mean anything."

"Sure it does," Tony protested soberly. "This is the first time he's missed in six months. When you came in, I was thinking of shutting up early and going over to his place to see if he's sick."

Hinkey stood up and drained his glass. "Well, Tony, if it'll relieve your mind any, I'll run over and find out. If Mike's sick, I want him taken care of, too."

"Thanks, thanks," Tony said. "That'll be fine. We don't want anything to happen to old Mike."

FROM Tony's wine cellar, Hinkey retraced his course to the building that housed Greek Steve's dive in the basement. But instead of descending the steps that led to Steve's place, the detective mounted the stoop and pushed open the door to the hallway of the tenement.

Just before he entered, a dark figure emerged from the shadows of the basement areaway. For a second it stopped, frozen into immobility, and watched the detective. When Hinkey had disappeared, the figure turned and glided back toward the speakeasy entrance.

Hinkey climbed five flights of stairs, dark steep stairs; he walked along hallways filled with stale cooking odors in which garlic predominated. There was no sound except the creaking of the uncarpeted boards. Many of the squalid apartments were vacant, and in those that were occupied everyone seemed to have gone to bed.

Once before the detective had climbed up to see Monkey Mike. He knew the room. A bleak place, where Mike and Angelo slept and ate their meals. Mike did the cooking for himself and his monkey pal on a single-burner gas stove.

As Hinkey made his way gropingly along the top hallway he could see a thin strip of light shining under the door of Mike's room at the rear of the building. He knocked. There was no answer.

Again he rapped his knuckles against the panel, this time more emphatically. He listened tensely. A faint sound came to him. It was a low whimper, such as a child in pain or badly frightened might make.

Hinkey tried the knob. The door failed to open, held by a bolt on the inside.

"Mike! Hey, Mike!" Hinkey called, his lips close to the keyhole. "Let me in, Mike!"

His only answer was that strange whimpering from beyond the portal. Hinkey hesitated no longer. He placed his shoulder against the door and pushed. The wood was old and dry. Almost at once, it yielded to the pressure and splintered, freeing the bolt. The door shot open, and Hinkey, catching his balance, stepped into the room.

A gasp of horror escaped him. He sprang across to the narrow bed on the other side of the room. As he bent over the rigid figure lying there, an angry oath broke from his lips.

Monkey Mike was lying half on his face, his knees drawn up slightly and one arm outstretched. On the side of his neck was a hideous wound, a dark red gash, from which the blood had welled out upon the blanket of the bed.

The pillow, too, was soaked with gore, and the clothing, almost as far down as Mike's waist, had been drenched.

No doubt that the old organ grinder was dead—had been dead for some time. The body was stiff and cold, and when Hinkey turned it gently over, Mike's glassy eyes stared up at him. But the weapon with which the death wound had been inflicted had been withdrawn. Hinkey looked for it on the bed, then hastily around the floor.

At that instant the low, childlike whimper fell again on his ears. Dropping on one knee, he peered under the table, from where the sound had seemed to come. Two bright, beady eyes stared back at him. The detective reached under the table and brought out Angelo, the monkey.

The little animal apparently sensed that a terrible tragedy had taken place; he continued to utter low plaintive sounds. Hinkey saw with a repressed shudder that Angelo's paws were smeared with blood, which had dried, matting the hair around them.

"Probably thought Mike was only asleep and tried to wake him up," Hinkey muttered to himself. "Poor little devil!"

He patted the monkey soothingly and set him down on one of the two chairs in the room. Then he started to look around the place.

Angelo, now reassured by the arrival of someone whom he remembered as a friend, watched him with solemn, curious eyes. The monkey's fright left him. He sat quietly on the chair, his almost human old-man face turning from side to side and once in a while lifting to survey the ceiling.

The room showed no indications of a struggle. Hinkey saw Mike's hurdy-gurdy leaning against the wall; it was resting on its one wooden leg, with the shoulder strap coiled on its top.

The drawers of the cheap pine dresser were partially opened. A coat had fallen from one of a row of hooks containing a few worn articles of clothing and was lying on the floor. But Hinkey realized that these small marks of disorder could probably be laid to the monkey.

The detective's hands worked convulsively. "Why in hell should anyone want to kill that poor old man," he muttered bitterly. "He never harmed a soul—"

A thud behind him caused Hinkey to swing quickly about.

Angelo had leaped from the chair to

the table. He was sitting there with his head cocked wisely to one side, looking at the detective and blinking rapidly.

"Angelo, if you could only talk," Hinkey said regretfully, "we'd soon have the man who killed Mike on his way to the chair."

He walked over to the single window and raised the shade, which had been pulled down to the sill. The lock was securely fastened. Assuming it had been open earlier, the killer might have entered that way. But if he did, he had certainly gone out the door, after locking the window.

Hinkey dropped into the chair the monkey had vacated. The absence of any sign of a struggle indicated that Mike had known his killer and trusted him. Or else he had been taken completely by surprise. He might, conceivably, have been asleep when the knife was driven into his neck.

Angelo leaped to the floor and vanished under the table. Hinkey watched him thoughtfully. Then he got up and, returning to the bed, stared down at the wound in Monkey Mike's neck.

"I sort of wish he'd left the knife behind," the detective murmured. "It would be something to go on."

A sudden peculiar hacking noise made him turn his head quickly.

"Good Lord!" he exclaimed, and sprang toward the table.

Angelo had returned from his hiding place beneath, and now he was sitting on the table top. Gripped in his paw was a blood-stained stiletto. He was swinging it up and down, stabbing the point into the soft wood.

Hinkey pulled the dagger from the monkey's hand; Angelo promptly hopped to the chair.

The weapon was a small white-handled stiletto with a thin blade about five inches ong.

As Hinkey examined it, a sudden appalling thought darted into his mind. He raised his widened eyes and looked at the monkey, then down to the dagger, which he was holding by the blade to preserve fingerprints. Then back to Angelo.

In the horror and excitement of the moment he had forgotten that the door had been locked on the inside when he arrived. The window, too, had been locked. They were the only two possible means of entrance or exit.

And in the room there had been no one but the dead man and the monkey—the monkey that knew how to chop up and down with a dagger!

HINKEY sat on one side of the desk in Jim McHenry's office the next morning. McHenry was the lieutenant in charge of detectives and Hinkey's chief. He was sitting on the other side of the desk. Between the two men lay the white-handled stiletto.

Over in one corner, resting on its peg-leg, was Monkey Mike's grind organ. Perched on top was Angelo, his long chain fastened to a door knob. The blood that had smeared him the night before had been scrubbed off. Now he was busy pursuing a flea in the vicinity of his third rib, unaware that he was the subject of conversation.

"By George, Hinkey!" McHenry exclaimed. "I can't believe he did it! Wouldn't have the strength to jab that knife into a man's neck."

Hinkey looked doubtful. "I'm not so sure about that. He's a strong little cuss —bigger than most of his breed. And facts are facts. The room was locked— both door and window—on the inside. No one there but Mike and Angelo. And the monkey's hacking at the table shows he had picked the trick up somewhere. Probably from Mike himself. I'd like to find out if that's Mike's stiletto."

"It's enough of a case to convict a man," McHenry admitted. "But a monkey—" He broke off with a short laugh. "It's a new one on me!"

Hinkey closed one eye meaningly and nodded. "Now that I've told you the dope, I'll make a confession. I don't think the monkey killed Mike, either."

"Any suspicions?" the lieutenant asked quickly.

"If the room hadn't been locked—yes! As it is, no. But old Mike was a friend of mine. I'm going to break my neck to get the rat that stabbed him."

"Its' your case. Go to it!"

"No fingerprints on the dagger, you said?"

"Not a one. The monkey probably smeared them. And Clives and Mason went over to the room early this morning. Nothing any good in the way of a print there."

Hinkey got out of his chair. "Well, I'm on my way," he said, quietly. "And I'll take the stiletto along, if that's O. K."

He walked over to Angelo, unfastened the chain from the door knob, and lifted the monkey into his arms.

McHenry looked surprised. "Going to take the monk with you?"

"Yes, he saw the murder. Maybe he can identify the murderer for me."

With Angelo tucked securely under his arm, Hinkey made his way along Blanchard Street. In front of the tenement which contained Greek Steve's speakeasy and the room in which Monkey Mike had been stabbed to death he hesitated.

Then, with sudden decision, he climbed up the few steps of the stoop and entered the hallway. A minute later he was in Mike's room. He shut the door and turned Angelo loose.

The body had been removed, also the bloodstained blanket and pillow. Otherwise, everything was as he had left it

early in the morning, when he had carried the monkey and the grind organ to the police station.

Hinkey walked to the window and looked out. He saw that it opened onto a courtyard of good size, entirely surrounded by the back sides of buildings. Most of them were tenements similar to the one he was in. Unlocking and throwing up the window, Hinkey leaned out. He turned his eyes down, and a little thought furrow appeared on his brow. A rusted fire-escape ladder extended from the window ledge toward the littered courtyard. It ended, the detective noticed, about ten feet from the ground. Beneath the bottom rung was an iron-barred door.

A swift calculation convinced him that it must be the rear entrance to Greek Steve's dive.

Hinkey closed the window and walked to the bed. He turned the bloodstained mattress over, and sat on the edge of the bed in deep thought. Finally, he stretched out, assuming the position he pictured Mike had been in when he was stabbed. He glanced toward the dresser.

Angelo was squatting on it and regarding him with pert attention. When he saw Hinkey's head settle on the mattress, he jumped down from his perch and trotted to the door. His long arm reached up and his supple fingers closed about the bolt.

The loop into which it was supposed to slide had been torn off when Hinkey forced the door. But, heedless of that, the monkey shot the bolt across and then hopped back to the dresser.

A slow smile lit up Hinkey's face. He snapped to his feet. So, that was it! The monkey either had been trained to lock the door after Mike got in bed, or else he did it simply because of his instinct for imitation.

And it explained how the door happened to be locked from the inside after the murder!

Hinkey clicked the chain on Angelo's collar and picked him up. As he moved rapidly down the hallway toward the stairs he patted the monkey affectionately on the head.

"Angelo," he murmured, "that lets you out. Your alibi is good with me."

HINKEY retraced his steps to the sidewalk. This time he turned without hesitation down the stairs that led to the basement areaway. He jammed his thumb against the buzzer button at the door of Greek Steve's speakeasy.

He didn't have long to wait. A panel behind a circular opening slid back and one eye and part of a face appeared.

"What do you want? We ain't open for business yet!"

Hinkey recognized the voice. "You're open for my business with you!" he clipped out. "No stalling, Steve!"

There was a grumbled oath. The panel closed and a few seconds later the door was swung wide. Greek Steve stepped aside to permit Hinkey to pass.

Angelo suddenly began to tremble as he caught sight and scent of the Greek. Then he opened his mouth, let out a screech of mingled fright and rage, and tried to wriggle free from the detective's arms.

Hinkey's mouth twitched. "What's the matter with you, old boy?" he asked soothingly as he walked along the short entrance hall and into the barroom. But he smiled with inward satisfaction.

The low room was empty. Hinkey strode across it and fastened Angelo's chain to a table leg. The monkey cowered back against the wall, his head moving nervously, his eyes fixed on Steve, who had followed them and was now behind the bar. But he fell silent, except for an occasional low whimper.

Hinkey walked to the bar. Steve regarded him with a bilious eye. The detective said nothing, just leaned casually against the mahogany and stared icily at the Greek.

"What in hell do you want?" Steve demanded at last.

"Friend of yours was murdered upstairs last night," Hinkey said, ignoring the question.

"No friend of mine. Just another damn grease-ball!"

"Mike was a friend of everybody around here—except the one dirty rat who killed him!"

Steve glared belligerently. "You accusing me?"

"No, no, Steve. I'm not accusing anybody—yet!" Hinkey's voice was steel coated with velvet. "I only dropped in to ask you to do something for me."

"Yeah?" Do something for you, copper?" Steve sneered.

"Yes, do something for me!" Hinkey's voice shed its velvet coating.

The Greek made no reply; he gazed up at the ceiling with feigned indifference and started to whistle.

"You're coming out from behind that bar and go over and pat Mike's monkey," the detective said softly.

"The hell you say!" Steve snarled.

Hinkey's powerful arm slid forward. His fingers closed on the lapel of the Greek's coat, and apparently without effort he yanked him half onto the bar.

"You heard me!"

The other man's manner underwent an abrupt change. His face whitened and his tone became whining, frightened.

"All right! All right! Have it your way."

While Steve reluctantly walked from behind the bar and moved toward the cowering monkey, Hinkey watched with his lids half covering his eyes. Five feet from Angelo, the Greek halted.

The monkey began jerking at his chain, trying to draw away from the man who was standing before him. He curled back his lips from his sharp white teeth. Then he started to screech wildly.

Hinkey's mind was coming to a decision. Should he make a pinch now? Better wait a little while, he decided. There were several other points he wanted settled definitely first.

"That'll do!" the detective suddenly ordered. "I've seen all I want. He knows you—and doesn't think very much of you, either, Steve."

The Greek walked sullenly back to the bar. Hinkey unchained the frightened, excited Angelo and gathered him firmly in his arms. Then he walked to the doorway.

"S'long, Steve, see you later," he said with a faint grin.

"Take your time about coming back," Steve growled.

"I'll take my time—and it won't be long now!"

IN TONY'S wine cellar, Hinkey found the proprietor and Pete Marino, the peddler, sitting at a table. He joined them, placing the monkey on a chair between himself and Pete. They sat around the table—dead Mike's four friends—like a council of war. A war on his killer!

"Not out with the peanut cart today, I see," Hinkey said.

Pete shook his head heavily. "No. No sella da peanut today. Pete seek. Seek because Mike dead."

Hinkey looked at the hook-nosed Sicilian. For a fact, he did look sick. His swarthy face had an unhealthy green tinge; his black eyes glowed feverishly.

"That's tough, Pete," the detective said sympathetically. "Better have a glass of *vino*."

The peanut peddler shook his head, and Hinkey turned to Tony.

"Tony, did you ever see this knife before?"

He pulled from his pocket the white-handled stiletto and laid it on the table. Tony picked it up and examined it critically. Pete, too, leaned forward, his eyes fastened on the weapon that had taken the life of his friend Mike.

Finally, Tony shook his head. "No, Mis-ter Hinkey, I never saw it before. Why?"

"I thought maybe it might have belonged to Mike."

"No! No!" Tony exclaimed. "Mike never carried a knife. He was too old for such foolishness."

"Sure?" Hinkey insisted.

"No, Mike didn't have no stiletto. Ain't that right, Pete?"

Pete nodded agreement.

"When did you last see Mike?" Hinkey asked Pete.

The Sicilian thought a long time. "Oh, about six-seven o'clock. He taka da organ home. I leave him and taka da pushcart home."

"I see. You left him at his door and then went on home yourself," the detective said. He turned back to Tony. "Tony, you know Greek Steve, down the street, don't you?"

Tony's usually smiling face was swept by a black scowl. He turned his head slightly and spat on the floor. "Do I know him? Sure, I know him! He's a—a louse!"

Hinkey's blue eyes twinkled at Tony's vehemence. "Know any reason why Angelo here should dislike Steve? Should be afraid of him?"

Tony looked puzzled, then thoughtful. He rubbed a plump forefinger through his thick black hair as if to refresh his memory by a light massage. Slowly a knowing smile dawned on his round face and he began to nod up and down.

"By golly, I do, Mis-ter Hinkey! Just now, I remember!" he exclaimed, with a sudden excited snap of his fingers. "Hah, that dirty Greek rat!"

Hinkey raised his hand, palm outward, to calm down the impetuous Tony. "We'll take you word for the kind of a guy Steve is," he smiled. "Let's hear about why the monkey doesn't like him."

"Mike told me this himself," Tony said, gesticulating. "He told me about a month ago." He paused to moisten his lips with a sip of wine and then continued.

"One day when it was raining Mike decides to leave the organ at home. Hurdy-gurdy's no good in rainy weather. Mike come over here to drink a little wine. He leaves Angelo in the room and he leaves the window open by accident.

"That damn monkey climbs down the fire-escape and gets into Steve's place, see? First thing you know, he's eating up Steve's free lunch. He thought it was free for monkeys, too, I guess.

"Well, Steve catches him and lams hell out of him with a club. When Mike gets back to his room Angelo is there. But he's all bumps and bloody. Then Steve he comes up and tells Mike what's happened. He says next time he'll kill Angelo. After that, when Steve passes them on the street, the monkey always gets all scared and mad at the same time."

Hinkey's face was a mask as Tony finished. But it was with difficulty that he was hiding his disappointment. The simple explanation of Angelo's fear of Steve had gnawed at the foundations of his theory of the murder.

At last he gave a philosophical shrug, and turned to the monkey on the chair between himself and Pete.

"Angelo," he said with a faint grin, "you're no doggone good when it comes to identifying murderers for me. Well,

what the—" he broke out suddenly. "Why, you little pickpocket!"

The monkey looked up and blinked his round eyes. While the three men had been talking he had been engaged in a surreptitious hunt for peanuts in the pocket of Pete's coat. One at a time, he had dragged forth the contents without the owner knowing it. Now they were heaped on the chair.

Hinkey reached over and picked them up. He placed them on the table in front of Pete—a key, a small piece of twine, and a few toothpicks. Then he stooped down for a letter which had slipped to the floor.

He was about to put it with the other things, when the face of the envelope caught his attention. His arm stopped halfway to the table. For some time he stared at the oblong of paper in his hand; little by little his eyes narrowed. He stole a glance at Pete.

Tony was watching him with a perplexed smile. Pete, however, was busy replacing the articles Angelo had filched back in his pocket and checking up on the contents of the other one. He didn't notice Hinkey.

Hinkey stood up. His eyes were hard, his mouth set in a grim line. He put his hand firmly on Pete's shoulder. The Sicilian jerked his head up in surprise, which quickly turned to fear as he saw the expression on the detective's face. Hinkey's muscular fingers closed. He hoisted Pete from his chair.

"Come along!" he ordered harshly. "You're going to the station with me!"

HINKEY entered McHenry's office. Under his arm he carried Angelo. A foot ahead of him walked Pete, his black eyes shifting from side to side, an almost terrified light making them more glittering than ever.

The lieutenant gazed at the strange group in open amazement.

"Sit down!" Hinkey ordered Pete, pointing to a chair in one corner of the room. "And don't try to run! If you do, I'll pump a ton of lead into you!" He drew his service pistol so Pete could see it, and put it back again.

Next he fastened the monkey's chain to the door knob and set the little animal on the floor. He walked to McHenry's desk. Taking out the envelope Angelo had found in Pete's pocket, he laid it in front of McHenry.

"What does that look like to you, Mac?" he asked, pointing to a reddish brown smudge on the face.

The lieutenant bent over it. "That's easy," he smiled. "A fingerprint. At least, part of one."

"A fingerprint in blood!" Hinkey amended. "Dried blood!"

In quick, concise sentences he explained to McHenry how the envelope had come into his possession. The latter nodded understandingly and looked at Pete, who was slouched in his chair and squinting at them from beneath his bushy eyebrows. His hands toyed with his battered hat.

Hinkey beckoned to him. "Come here! Hurry up!" Then he added to McHenry, "Let me have that ink-pad in your desk, will you, Mac?"

Seizing the Sicilian's wrist, Hinkey pressed his fingers down on the pad. After that he printed them on a sheet of white paper. "Go back and sit down where you were!" he ordered.

He laid the envelope with the bloody half-print beside the ones he had just made on the paper and examined them with eager eyes. Slowly his jaw dropped. He glanced at McHenry with an expression of chagrin.

The lieutenant took the envelope and sheet of paper. He, too, gave them care-ful scrutiny. He shook his head and made a wry face.

"Hinkey, you've pulled a boner! They don't check!"

Hinkey was silent. He simply stared at the two sets of prints. He was a picture of dejection, where only a moment before he had been bubbling with confidence and grim triumph. His blue eyes wandered from the desk to McHenry, then out the window. In them was a faraway, thoughtful expression.

He gave a sudden, quick laugh, and whirled on his heel. Before McHenry was really aware of what he was doing, Hinkey had unsnapped the chain from Angelo's collar and was pressing the surprised monkey's paw on the ink-pad.

Side by side, he placed the envelope with the tell-tale smudge and the marks he had made with the monkey's paws. He gripped the edge of the desk fiercely as he compared them.

A moment later Hinkey tossed the two sets of prints in front of McHenry.

"I made a mistake at first! But not this time!" he exclaimed. "Angelo put the print on the envelope in Pete's pocket with Mike's blood! And that ties our case in a knot!"

He saw the puzzled look on McHenry's face.

"Get it? Only Mike, his murderer and the monkey were in the room. After Mike was stabbed, Angelo got some blood on his paw. He stuck it in Pete's pocket for peanuts, the way he always does at every chance. And when Pete walked out of the room he was carrying his own death warrant in his pocket!"

"By God! You're right!" McHenry exclaimed excitedly. "And no wonder you thought the print was Pete's. For any kind of an ape makes a fingerprint just like that of a human being! Of course Angelo's mark was a good deal smaller than a full human print, but it might easily have been mistaken for an incomplete one."

Pete, who had been following every move, sprang to his feet. His eyes were wild, half-insane, as he lunged toward the door. But Hinkey was too fast for him. He jabbed the muzzle of his pistol into the Sicilian's stomach and pushed him back to his chair.

McHenry pressed a button on his desk. A uniformed policeman appeared.

"Guard that man!" the lieutenant snapped. As Hinkey turned over his job to the patrolman, McHenry cried out: "Hey, what the devil's your monkey up to now?"

Hinkey looked swiftly toward Angelo. The monkey was sitting on the hurdy-gurdy. He had worked the top loose and now was busily occupied in digging inside it. From time to time he extracted a hairy paw. And each time he did so a banknote fluttered to the floor.

Hinkey ran to him and, lifting him from the grind organ, snapped the chain to his collar. While McHenry watched over his shoulder, Hinkey examined the inside of Mike's hurdy-gurdy.

In a space alongside the mechanism a small compartment had been built into the box. It was packed with bills.

"There's almost four thousand dollars there," McHenry said, ten minutes later, as he pointed to the pile of currency on his desk. "But what's the letter that was with it? Looks like it was written in Italian to me."

Hinkey stepped to the door. "We'll soon find out," he said. "The desk sergeant's an Italian. Hey, Paterno! We need you in here a minute!" he called.

Paterno read the single sheet of paper a couple of times.

"Say, Hink, listen to this," he said, and began to translate.

"I have no relatives alive so I am leaving the money I have saved like this. To Pete Marino, the peanut man, two hundred dollars. To Tony Brignole, the wine-shop man, two hundred dollars. To Thomas Hinkey, the policeman, all the rest, because he saved my life."

"Mike Corso."

"It's signed by Pete Marino as witness," Paterno added.

"So that's why Pete killed him!" Hinkey burst forth. "To steal the money he knew Mike had saved, because he witnessed the will!"

"It looks as if Monkey Mike had gotten even with you at last, you lucky stiff!" McHenry said with a grin.

Hinkey became thoughtful. Good old Mike! He'd paid his debt and then some. A lump rose in Hinkey's throat. He looked at Angelo. The monkey was unconcernedly scouting through is fur for a flea.

"Mac," Hinkey said slowly, "I guess all the credit for solving Mike's murder belongs to Angelo. We'll have to make him a first-grade detective!"

It was almost half an hour later that Hinkey paused in the doorway and spoke to McHenry. He had just come from the detention cells, where he had been questioning Pete.

"Thought I'd tell you, Mac, that I'm on my way out to make another arrest."

The lieutenant squinted. "Another?"

"And with pleasure," Hinkey nodded grimly "The guy who put Pete up to killing his best friend! Pete got drunk and spilled about Mike's savings to him. But the other guy didn't have enough guts to pull the job himself, so he talked Pete into going to Mike's room, supposedly on a friendly visit, and killing him. But after he'd done that, Pete couldn't find where the money was hidden."

"Who you going to pinch this time?"

"Greek Steve!"

Master of Mysteries

EDGAR WALLACE, whose splendid story *The Shadow Man* opens this issue of DIME DETECTIVE MAGAZINE, bore a name which had come to be almost synonymous with the very best detective and mystery fiction. Ranking in popularity and appeal alongside such writers as the late Sir Arthur Conan Doyle, and such living stellar exponents of crime fiction as J. S. Fletcher, E. Phillips Oppenheim, Maurice LeBlanc and Mary Roberts Rinehart, he had marshaled a loyal army of readers second to none. The announcement from his publishers that a "new Wallace" was due to appear meant that the 5,000,000 circulation that his works already had would be swelled by several hundred thousand more, and that a play and movie based on the latest effort would in all probability follow suit.

When the news was flashed from Hollywood last February that the prolific pen of Wallace had written its last sentence, been silenced forever by a fatal siege of pneumonia, literally millions of devotees of the detective story all over the world sustained a loss which can never be repaired. DIME DETECTIVE MAGAZINE had just commenced negotiations to procure occasional Wallace stories for its pages and *The Shadow Man* was what we hoped to offer as the first of many—unfortunately it must be both the first and last.

Mr. Wallace was as colorful and interesting a personality as any of the characters which moved in long and lifelike procession through the pages of his stories. Born in 1875, a pauper waif, he was adopted by a Billingsgate Market fishmonger, whose fostering kindness saved the child from a boyhood in charity institutions. His first money came from peddling newspapers in the streets of London and from the age of ten he began to contribute to his own support. From that time on his career reads like that of the typical Alger hero. Various odd jobs succeeded one another in rapid succession until he finally joined the army in time to be sent to South Africa just before the Boer War. During that conflict he served as a war correspondent for The London Daily Mail and after it ended he traveled widely as a journalist. It was not until shortly before the Great War that he turned to fiction, even then continuing to contribute vast quantities of newspaper copy to various journals.

Edgar Wallace

His energy and ability to produce successful material in tremendous quantity became almost legendary. He was the author of more than 140 published novels, and during one period of three years he wrote twenty successful plays, six of which were playing to packed houses in London all at the same time. He was a dramatic critic and reviewer as well as a playwright and producer, and was an official of a British film-producing company. With all his varied interests it is nothing short of amazing that he was able to turn out all the work that he did, but he explained that his working day was twelve or more hours long and without interruption. He used dictaphones and could dictate as many as 1200 words in twenty minutes.

Besides his literary activity he was an ardent sportsman and at one time maintained stables for racing horses which he entered in various meets around the country. He was a great lover of horseflesh and an authority on racing about which he wrote considerable material. At one time he ran for Parliament as a Liberal but was defeated. At the time of his death he had gone to Hollywood to write for the movies. The story runs that he appeared for work on a Friday and the following Monday showed up with a 60,000-word story ready to begin work on. Surely a record for fast composition!

King George of England and the Prince of Wales were both ardent Wallace fans as well as President Wilson of this country. During the War the story was often told of how Wilson sought relaxation and diversion in the detective thrillers of the great English fictioneer.

It is inevitable that Wallace be remembered by millions both as a writer of eminence and as a fabulous and vivid personality.

We mourn his passing deeply.

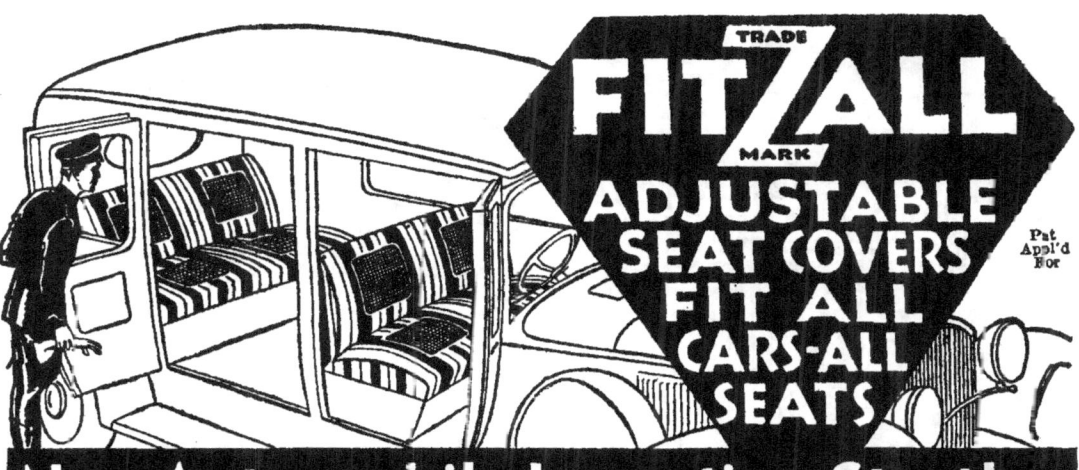

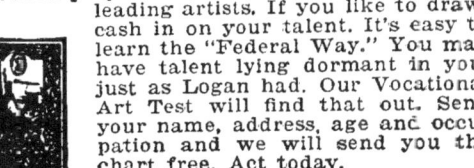

www.ingramcontent.com/pod-product-compliance
Lightning Source LLC
Chambersburg PA
CBHW080912020726
47502CB00008B/2431